Advanced Reviews

"Adrian Koesters writes about childhood like an American Frank McCourt, taking us into a fully realized world of stern-faced nuns and pennies for the Pagan Babies, a world of mothers singing "Chances Are" in the kitchen and adults behaving in unfathomable ways. *Miraculous Medal* is a large-souled study of the space between the mysteries of faith and the perplexities of desire. A thoroughly absorbing read."

—Brent Spencer, author of *Rattlesnake Daddy: A Son's Search for His Father*

"*Miraculous Medal* transports us into 1960s Baltimore, and into a richly complex neighborhood whose inhabitants—from saints to sinners—live out their days in perilous proximity to each other's deepest, most painful secrets. Adrian Koesters' ability to enter so completely into the yearnings and fears of four radically different characters took my breath away. I won't soon forget the verve and pluck of the little girls Marnie and Alice, the other-worldly kindness of Jeb Heath, and the hard-won maturity of Father John. Koesters has created a vision of humanity both heartbreaking and transcendent."

—Marjorie Sandor, author of *The Secret Music at Tordesillas*

"What a miracle this book is! From its perfect understanding of Baltimorese—in dialog its authenticity rivals the work of the late Ernest Gaines--through its mixture of deadpan comedy and equally deadpan horror exposed through the voices of its narrators, this work deserves a Medal indeed."

—Clarinda Harris, author of *Innumerable Moons*

"Like a brilliant miniaturist, Koesters captures the denizens of her native Baltimore in their broken moments and the tragedy of their private pain. The beauty of her work is that in such moments, they also understand the whole of life all at once. To read *Miraculous Medal* is to be pulled into the undertow of her characters' rich and thoroughly expressed inner lives."

—Steven Wingate, author of *Of Fathers and Fire*

"A dream of a book, light-filled and unflinching in its portrayal of four intersecting lives in mid-century Catholic Baltimore. Like specters caught for a moment and held, Adrian Gibbons Koesters' characters are fleeting, luminous, and oh so true. They will haunt you long after you finish the book—and you will be glad for it."

—Sonja Livingston, Author of *Ghostbread*

MIRACULOUS MEDAL

A Novel

MIRACULOUS MEDAL

A Novel

Adrian Koesters

First Edition

Printed in the United States of America

Hardcover ISBN: 978-1-62720-253-4
Paperback ISBN: 978-1-62720-254-1
E-book ISBN: 978-1-62720-255-8

Development & Editing by Lauren Battista
Design by Apprentice House Press
Marketing by Kyra McDonnell
Author Photo by Eugene E. Selk

Published by Apprentice House

Apprentice House
Loyola University Maryland
4501 N. Charles Street
Baltimore, MD 21210
410.617.5265
www.apprenticehouse.com
info@apprenticehouse.com

for Barb and Ruth, and for Ali, in memoriam

Contents

"Vous savez, la foi…" – The Innocents

Amorem tui solum cum gratia tua mihi dones
— St. Ignatius of Loyola

Prologue, Union Square Palm Sunday Evening, April 5, 1952

The priest tossed his cigarette to the curbside. Carmen fell into him and grabbed his hand and dragged him across Lombard Street and down the sidewalk along Union Square. They crossed at Stricker, where she turned up and lurched toward her steps.

"This is my place," she said. He was beginning to think her condition was an act. He had never seen a woman close to this drunk, or high, or whatever it was. He had been in the missions and didn't know such a thing was possible.

"I'm going to tell you a secret," she said, and winked at him.

He laughed, he couldn't help himself.

"What's that?" He smiled and she grabbed at the front of his cassock.

"Mr. Morris was in town," she said.

And she barked hysterically and bent over, holding on to the priest's shirt front, again exactly like a television act. "Mr. Morris is in town!"

And then he heard it: "Mama," a soft voice called out from the third floor window. "Come on in," it called to them.

Then another, "Who's that, Mama? Is he coming up with you?"

He looked up and saw them, one blonde and pretty from what he could tell in the street light, the other brown in nearly every way with a square face and brows that made her look like an old woman in the shadows.

"We aten all the saltines, Mama," she said, and a moment later he was hit softly with something wet. The spit must have fallen from her mouth as she hung out of the window. He didn't think it had been on purpose.

The fair one said, "Stop it, Lucille."

"You stop it, you stupid head."

"Shut *up*!" she screamed. Their heads disappeared into the window and he heard them begin to fight. He looked down at Carmen, who smiled at him as if one happy drunk to another, her eyelids folded half-way down.

"My graces," she said. "And another one on the way. Did I tell you that? I got another one on the way. Mr. Morris was in town. If it's a girl, I'll drown it like a cat. How 'bout that, Reverend? What do you think, should I?" And she laughed again, and said, "Hey, I got something. You want to see it?"

"Wait a minute, you can't— " he began, first in protest that she'd drown her baby like a cat and then that she seemed to be starting to take her blouse off there in the street. The door next door opened and Mrs. Fitzgerald stuck her head out.

"What's all the commotion?" she began, saw him, and said, "Oh, it's you, Father. I'm sorry, I didn't mean to barge in," and she tittered in her open, irritating way. "I never know what is going on with this bunch," she said, nodding in Carmen's direction. Her daughter, Sheila, poked her head under her mother's arm and said, "Hi, Father Mar-tin!" as loud, it seemed to him, as she could.

"Hoy, Faather Mawr-tin!" Carmen shrieked in a terrible falsetto, and Sheila drew back as if she'd been smacked. He turned to Carmen again and said, "You should go on inside. Go on up and get your daughters some supper."

She looked at him as if she could not place who he was talking about, and then said, "No, it's all right. I checked. I checked before I left. They had saltines and peanut butter."

He said, as if he knew her and her family inside and out, "No, they just said, the saltines are all gone. They need a bedtime snack now. You should go on up."

She laughed again. "A bedtime snack. All right, Reverend, I'll get them a bedtime snack. But help me with the front door. I'm not seeing too good in the dark."

He got her in and closed the door behind her with himself on the outside of it, not quite having avoided the embrace he should have known was waiting for him, which he had responded to without knowing he did, returning her kiss and pressing his stomach into hers for an instant but pulling back before either of them could have said it was a response.

Mrs. Fitzgerald closed her door as he came out again. He turned and walked slowly down the steps.

"Hey," he heard one of the voices call again. He looked up. It was the brown one. "Ain't you gonna come up? We could do somethin."

He thought for a moment that he would go, he'd make sure Carmen fed them and that they were put to bed all right.

But he said, "I'm sorry, honey, I can't tonight. Maybe another time."

Part I: Thursday, April 2, 1964
Jezriel Heath

Jeb counted the stairs and the number of swipes with the broom it took to clear each one, three after three after three. The work had been given to him by the priest of the parish, who said it was not unlike, and for its station as completely sanctified, as the labor of raising the chalice over the altar, or the labor of the boy who rang the bells after the consecrating words. Jeb regarded that if the latter were true, sweeping the steps could also be true. He did not know how the priest could bring himself to equate the actual consecration, where his own hands did not even touch the sacred metal of the chalice, and surely this was a disembodied action of which the priest had little if any part, to holding a broom—today, though, Thursday, it was a *damn broom*—but if Father felt this was so, then Jeb allowed himself to agree that it might be so.

Jezriel Maurice Heath was the grand-nephew of the late Miss Maurice Jackson, the only son of Miss Maurice's sister's eldest daughter. He was forty and looked sixty. He smoked. He attended St. Peter Claver Church most Sundays, but his regular job was to sweep the church steps and clear out the school yard at St. Martin's in the mornings before early Mass, which he did not attend, on Mondays through Fridays. On Saturdays he drove a taxi for passengers north and slightly south of Baltimore Street. Otherwise, he walked, not on Saturdays or Sundays, but in the week, for many miles every day. His ostensible object was the sale of newspapers, but he did not hold a real job selling them. He had an agreement with the closest news seller, who had given him a bag with *The Baltimore Sun* printed on it, and he would sell the morning edition to Jeb for a penny for five copies, and Jeb always took ten. Some regular folks would stop him to buy a paper, and if he ever went as far as downtown he'd usually sell out most of them before 10 o'clock or so, but most days he gave most of them away. He was sure to stop by Miss Angela Maurice Summer's front steps every morning, reminding her (she was very elderly) that he was going to come by that Saturday and get her subscription money, which of course he never did and she never remembered he had not gotten from her.

It was something about walking. Often his feet hurt him but it didn't matter all that much. He walked the same route every day, figured the same people saw him every day, figured they thought, *There goes that newsboy again*. He figured most of them called him a newsboy. But what it was, when he had been a boy, thirty years along now, he had thought he wanted either to be a fireman or a newspaper man, but he discovered at that time and still mostly today they didn't let colored go for either of them, and besides that, he had never wound up getting anything past a grade school education. He didn't always follow the stories in the paper, but he was certain that if it was in the paper one would have to be able to discuss it with something more than an eighth-grade education. He had had a great liking for President Roosevelt when he was a boy, he always remembered that. But Mrs. Roosevelt, what did he want setting up with a homely woman like her for? He had heard she was very kind but you don't marry a woman because she is kind.

"They got another homely one in there now," he said to himself. Not like Mrs. Kennedy, *Poor lady,* he thought. Now, she was handsome and then some. Phew. *Poor lady.*

Jeb had started out walking as a boy. When he was ten or eleven or so, he would go around looking for something to do, shine shoes, sell pencils or peanuts, but he didn't often have the pennies you needed to buy the pencils or the peanuts in the first place and he didn't have a shoe shine kit and he didn't know anybody who did who wasn't already using his. But then one day he had stopped at a corner where men were shining shoes, stood and watched and nobody seemed to mind him, and then, not too long after he had gotten to stopping there on most days, one of them had said, "Boy, come here, I have to step out a minute. You go ahead and black them up for me if somebody come along and I'll shine them when I get back, you don't got to shine them. You can do that, boy?"

"Yes sir," he had said, and right then a man came up and said, "Holy, boy, you old enough to shine these shoes."

And Jeb had blacked them up and started in with the brush on them when the shoeshine man came back. He didn't interrupt but let him go on until it was time to use the cloth and then the man said, "Here's how you do this right, real firm and then be sure you get the back without getting any stain on the man's trousers cuff." When he was done, the man said, "I'm paying the boy," and tossed him a nickel. The shoeshine man said, "It's ten cent," but the other man said, "He needs to learn about money," and that seemed to be right to the shoeshine man.

Soon it had got around that there might be a boy who would shine your shoes for half price if you were willing to sit on a box. The man who had taught Jeb told him where to get a tin of black and a brush and how to save up on it, and he had done this. Out of the corner of his eye, though, he watched nearly in hunger every day the man who came up in the wagon and tossed a bundle of papers from the *Baltimore Sun* and the *News-Post* on to the corner, and the store man who came out and paid him for them.

One day Jeb hadn't had a customer and had felt bold, and had asked the delivery man, "Where you get those, sir?"

The man said, "You got to take the street car down the depot and pay for them, penny for 10 papers."

"Oh," said Jeb. After a day went by, he asked out loud, "Anybody know how to use the streetcar?" at which the men had howled at him and laughed and joked the rest of the day.

"Boy, you ain't getting on any street car!" one of them said, "cost you every red cent you got." Jeb had merely thought that this man must not know how to use it.

The day after another man said, "You really need to use the streetcar?" Jeb had said yes, and the man said, "All right. You need this much money and you give it to the driver without touching his hand, you understand me?" Jeb nodded. "Then you go all the way to the back and sit down. If a lady come in, you give her the seat right away. If a man ask you for your seat, you give it to him. If a white lady or white man have to come in the back, you get off the street car and walk the rest of the way you going. You hear me, boy?" Jeb nodded again.

He asked, "How do you find out where you going?" The man said, "Where you want to go?"

"The newspaper depot."

"All right," the man said, "wait here and I'll go inside and see."

He had come back out, told Jeb how to get there, where to wait for the street car, and how to get back on. "But you go after you done shining, you hear me?"

"Yes sir," Jeb had said.

What he had found was that if he wanted to get the early paper, he had to go before the shoe shining. The first time it had not eaten up all his money but near to it, and the papers were heavy, he believed too heavy to climb back up on the street car with them, even if they would let you bring them up, which he also didn't know. He found one corner nearby where he figured he would sell right there to passersby, then after he was chased off by a regular whose place it was, found another corner, dragging those papers by the thin rope until he thought his arms would fall off. It was quiet but he still sold quite a lot of papers because it appeared there was some kind of business across the street, and one of the boys who came out to buy said, "You going to be here all the time now?" Jeb had looked down at the sidewalk and said, "Yes sir I will," and the boy said, "Good, but get here early, we want papers early."

Jeb had stayed doing this for about a week and then decided it was too much. The charm of hearing the papers fall on the sidewalk had been broken with use and custom. He went back to the shoe shining where none of the men asked him about it, and stayed doing that until that priest messed with him.

It wasn't anything like what he had heard happened to other boys with other men, and Monsignor had never before come up to him or anything other than put his arm around Jeb's shoulders and give them a friendly shake.

"Jezriel," he would say, "that was the best serving I've seen from any of the boys. I believe the Lord may be calling you." And Jeb would laugh and blush and shake his head a little, his eyes lit up with happiness. Monsignor, you could trust him, he thought.

He didn't remember too much about serving Mass or going to Mass in those years. What he remembered was the sacristy, the old wood, the marble top of the central long buffet in front of the half-dozen closet doors all in dark wood, one door often standing open to reveal the colored and embroidered chasubles or the long white albs and the shorter white robes of the altar boys. The unconsecrated hosts would sometimes be out in their box and he ached to take one of them and give himself communion, to see if it would taste any different than the transformed Body of Christ.

The smell of wine and beeswax. The quiet.

Then the afternoon he had come in to find Monsignor there, sorting through a drawer of stoles. How beautiful they were! Threaded through with gold. Monsignor had smiled at Jeb, motioned him over with his hand, and without speaking had taken one of the top-most, bright purple it had been with a golden pin to it, and put it over Jeb's head and across his chest, pinning it above his hip as Jeb automatically raised his hands up. Monsignor smiled wonderfully at Jeb, tears in his eyes, and took his hands and held Jeb's face between the palms, and kissed his forehead.

His hands still on Jeb's face, he smiled, and said, "You truly belong to Christ now." Jeb felt elevated and as if he would not touch down again.

Then Monsignor put his hands under Jeb's arms, pulled him to him, and embraced him. Jeb thought nothing of this, Monsignor held him as a relative might, but when he went to pull away, the priest clasped him more tightly and although Jeb did not feel unsafe, what began to happen to both of them frightened him. He did not speak or struggle to get free, but felt as if he might be beginning to be smothered. Then Monsignor pressed his stomach closer into Jeb's chest and one of his legs against Jeb's private parts, and he moved his head back, and looked into Jeb's face, and then leaned in and kissed Jeb on the mouth.

"This will be our sacred secret," he said to him after three times too long at least, but he said it as seriously and kindly as before.

Jeb had had an older cousin who tried to do things like this, only not nice and not sacred and although he had never gotten very far with Jeb, others had told him what it all meant. "You stay away from that man when you're by yourself alone," they said. And he knew at this moment with Monsignor he had to get away from there and he had to not come back.

He disengaged himself without having to wrench away. He had a feeling that if he had had to struggle, something bad would have come of it, he would get a beating or he didn't know what. Whatever it was, he was not going to stay around to get it.

He said, "I thought it was my time to come over for serving, Father, I didn't know it was the wrong time."

Monsignor continued to smile at him as if he wasn't there, saying nothing, the palm of his hand pressed just over the lower part of his stomach. Jeb turned and ran out, the stole still pinned around him. He tore it off, staring at it as if he were on a ship and leaving home port to cross a vast ocean, even as he ran. He pulled out the gold pin and stashed it and the stole in the first ash can he could find, but he could not keep from looking back, the fringe hanging and the glint of gold in the afternoon light, as if his shame were shining for anybody to see.

He had told his mother then that he didn't want to go to St. Peter Claver School anymore, he wanted to go to the public school.

"What for? Why you want to do that when you got that nice school with the priests and sisters?" she said.

"Well, ma'am, the other boys started to treat me a little rough about it. You know, that's for girls and all that thing. I didn't want to make nothing of it but it's getting worse and I don't know."

She thought a moment and then said, "All right. You want to change right away on Monday?"

"Yes, ma'am. I wouldn't ask but it's getting a little rough."

His relief must have shown, for she had said, "Come on, I got to go down to the market anyway and we should see if they have any shoes in the bin would fit you." By this she would have meant, his Catholic school shoes would now be only for Sundays and there wouldn't be a new pair until the fall.

"Yes, ma'am."

And instead of going to Mass at St. Peter's, even after Monsignor had visited them at home and asked why he wasn't there, getting a slightly different but satisfactory explanation from his mother, Jeb had begun to walk an hour on Sundays down to St. Francis Xavier. If he knew Monsignor wasn't going to have Mass, he would go to St. Peter's, but he still wouldn't take communion. He hadn't wanted to think about it. And he never went to confession again until he was a grown man and had started to work on the grounds at St. Martin's.

He had been there working for the past several years now. This past Sunday had been one of those very rare Easters that fell at the end of March, the 29th, his mother's birthday it had also been, but she had not wanted to wait on the Lord after all and had died on Good Friday. They had had to wait until Tuesday to bury her, which had not set well with him, but Father John had said, no, they could not bury anybody on Easter Monday. Somehow Easter Monday was as special as Easter Sunday in those regards, he told Jeb, but he said, "Come on by the rectory and you and me will pray a special Rosary together and then have breakfast."

But, "No," Jeb had said, "Easter Monday or not, that's a working day for me and I better go to work."

Father had looked a little deeply into Jeb's eyes, what he could see of them that were not cast down, and he said, "All right, but listen to me now, Mr. Jeb," he said. Though he was a white priest his godmother had also been Miss Maurice and therefore he and Jeb were related by baptism, and maybe that was why he spoke to him that way. He said, "Mr. Jeb, you ought to come by. Why don't you come by when you get done work, and we can pray it then. We can pray it in the church if you want instead of the rectory."

"Well," Jeb had said. "I'll see."

But then Father had said, "You know you don't have to hold my hand," just as if Jeb had been some kind of little boy asking to cross the street on his own, and Jeb knew he would not stop by after all.

For Jeb had told Father John one day when he was getting over a bad sickness, about the monsignor who when he was ten had always made him hold hands when they prayed together. Now he wished to Heaven he had never told him anything about it. Father had said, no, he thought that was all right. Jeb said, no, that wasn't, because then the one time he had kissed him on the mouth, like if it was bed time at home and you kiss everybody.

"And," he had said, "the only reason I am telling you this is because I snuck away from going to our church for a long time after that, and kept away from the sacraments, until that priest was sent up to the Basilica."

The young man's brows had shot together at that, though, and he said, "That's a bad sin. Did you confess it?"

Jeb had said, Well, he didn't like to talk about that but he knew it was a sin, and then Father had confessed him and absolved him right away. And then he had gone up to Holy Communion at St. Peter's for the first time in almost three decades, though he realized that every adult in that congregation would know he had finally confessed to something and that they would be burning to know what it was.

But ever since then, he had felt Father John was trying too hard to make him feel all right about it. He felt fine in general, but he was never going to feel all the way all right about that, because you shouldn't. Nobody should.

His mother had known something was wrong all along but had never asked him about it until she was on her death bed, and he had told her, and she had said, "Baby, you can't confess the sin of somebody else."

He said, "What do you mean, Mama? I was confessing my sin."

But she had said to him, "You were taking care he didn't mess with you no more. I don't care about that. He took the sin, not you. He's probably burning in you-know-where right now," and she had laughed, wheezing because she was dying of emphysema as he was going to, though neither of them knew that, but still he could not laugh.

He was not sorry that he had stayed away from communion and he would never be, but he ought to have been braver about the whole thing, been more stout. He ought to have found a way. But he was absolved now, and he had been walking all those years in the meantime, and so now all that was all right.

And Jeb had buried his mother on Tuesday of this week, just two days ago, and the whole church had been packed full, with him and all the Maurices praying and responding and kneeling and singing. He had never known an "Alleluia" to sound so sweet as it did in that church at every Easter, but this had to have been the sweetest he had heard yet. He'd felt again as if his feet were a few inches off the floor, and at one point one of the older Maurices had taken the crook of his arm, so maybe they had been, although that kind of business was just Protestant and he knew that quite well.

The last hymn had been, "Let All Mortal Flesh Keep Silence," his and his mother's favorite one. *And in fear and trembling stand, ponder nothing earthly minded*, they had sung as they followed the casket and the bearers out, and in the two days following, until a short while earlier today, Thursday, as he was walking in the weak light of morning, up toward the yard of St. Martin's school, he had felt this so incredibly deeply, that to ponder nothing earthy minded was a greater satisfaction, a holiness, a—he didn't know what to call it, he didn't want to have a word for it. He had been filled with very possibly that same spirit that would soon descend upon the Apostles and disciples in that Upper Room at Pentecost. He had felt that grace, without the stain of sin.

And now, Thursday, Thursday morning again, another Thursday. He opened the back door to the school, a kind of lean-to where he had never gone past but to get the broom. They had someone else mopping the floors and cleaning the windows, some white man, but that suited Jeb fine. He didn't want to waste his days inside cleaning floors and windows. He was a walker, that's how he said it. He had said it to his mother once not too long back, and she had said, "No, I don't need a walker, boy, what's the matter with you?" And so then after that he kept the job description to himself, but still, he liked it. He liked doing it and he liked being it.

Father John came out just then to stand on the rectory steps and smoke his cigarette and have his first (Jeb assumed) cup of coffee of the morning. He knew Father said a private Mass first thing so he could smoke and drink, and that was all right. What was not all right were those purple slippers he had taken to wearing outside during Lent, the fuzzy ones, looked like some kind of awful blanket they made into a pair of shoes. Looked like some woman outside on Saturday with her curlers in and some head rag over them but you could still see the top row of curlers and her kids would be wearing pedal pushers instead of dresses or skirts, right out there in public.

Jeb leaned his head down and touched the brim of his cap with the outside of his right index finger in lieu of greeting, and Father said, "Beautiful morning," as he always did whether it was one or not and Jeb replied, "Praise Him," as he ever did. He did not know that Father John came out there every morning to make sure Jeb was there and all right. He only knew that no matter how early he arrived, Father would come out and shame him by watching him do his work. A man could not have any privacy when it was white folks there, he thought, but you couldn't tell them, you couldn't tell them nothing.

Father John would have been all right if it had not been for this, Jeb felt, but why did he have to go and look at him work every morning? Was he a show? Was he not sweeping right? He gave a swipe to the broom that would have cleaned off the vestibule of Purgatory, and stepped down one and then turned his back on Father and swept the rest of the steps that way, which getting down to the bottom was the right way to sweep them, but he felt Father's eyes burning into the back of him, and something always tightened inside his hands when he felt that. It was only for a moment and Father must have his reasons, but Jeb had become somewhat tired of offering up how it got on his nerves. He swept the bottom step and touched his hat again in Father's direction but did not look at him as he walked to the opening in the school yard fence. By the time he came back, Father had gone inside.

This morning it was heavy with mist and Jeb could still smell where Father had ground out his cigarette on the step. He crossed the street, walked over, and swept it out to the pavement with his hand, and then he took one of his own cigarettes, broke it carefully in half, and lit it with the silver lighter that bore his father's and his own initials. From France, it was, the first time, his father had cooked on one of those warships and though they had never let him on land he travelled back and forth, back and forth taking white soldiers over and bringing them home, on the way home spoon-feeding some of them who couldn't see or lift their hands and pouring slop into the stomach tubes of some of them. He had had some stories to tell about those days. Jeb couldn't exactly remember who had given his father the lighter, but he liked it, old-fashioned, a real conversation piece with "J H" there etched lightly inside the outline of a diamond. The flame was so short he had to lean his head back so as not to burn his nose hairs on it, but he liked half a cigarette and he smoked just as many but then he could smoke a lot more often that way.

Early as it was he could afford to have one right there without it being any trouble.

He inhaled, picked a tobacco bit off of his lip.

The sun was up now, and time to get walking. He took a last drag of smoke, threw the cigarette down into the gutter, and put it out with a pivot of his toe. He looked up and down the street, and turned north up Fulton Avenue to get his newspapers.

What was to happen that day began for Jeb as ordinary as it could be and ended just as commonly. But the rest, what occurred in between times, anyone would tell as exceptional, an exception to the rules, and Jeb would reflect that there were no exceptions to the rules and that he would have to figure out what to do about that. But he would not know these things until many hours away.

He pulled his newspaper bag out from under his coat a half block from the corner where Fulton Moss waited on Fulton Street because they shared the same name, where Jeb's ten papers would be laying flat at the top of the pile because Fulton knew that Jeb enjoyed folding them into thirds and tucking in the open end, filling up his bag with folded papers one slim folded packet at a time, talking with Fulton about this, that, and the other like workmen at the start of the day. They would converse about whatever had happened since they'd last seen each other, who had done what and to whom they had done it, and remark on the chill, or the heat, or the damp, or the dryness of the air.

"While before it's any ice on the pavement," Fulton would say in the winter.

"Yeah, but you know it's coming," Jeb would reply.

Their exchanges were not always this laconic but suited to the weather, which when you came to think about it, he thought, why talk about the weather? It wasn't going anywhere, you couldn't do anything about it. Was that like prayer? Jeb wondered. He didn't know. He thought, *Well, you know, prayer is a duty*. Like they say, the Lord isn't going to come down and shout in your ear, you got to let Him know you're there and willing to enter in, so to speak. How did they say it? *I will enter into the altar of God. I will go up to the house of the Lord.* He liked those sayings very much. *I rejoiced when I heard them say*, he loved to repeat to himself as he walked, *I rejoiced when I heard them say*. It was like singing and yet it was not. And the other part that made him return to it and believe on it despite everything was that when he thought of that priest and the look in his eye and the feel of his mouth, he would say one of these things: *I will enter into the altar of God. I will go up into the house of the Lord.* And then it wasn't Monsignor's house anymore at all. And so whatever Monsignor did, whatever he had done, it didn't matter. Somebody said, he had read once somewhere, *Let stand the justice of God*. Whoever had said that wasn't any fool.

But the weather was not like that, yet you talked about it regularly just the same.

He thought again that, all right, he had confessed not going into the Lord's house, and he made reparation every single day on it, so if it was absolved but not forgiven—well, he also knew better than to be overly scrupulous, because for whatever reason, that was as big a sin as despair, so all those Baptists and AMEs who were about this, that, and the other before the dawn of time, he knew better than to worry about all that mess.

Absolution and penance. That was it. Nothing else but let stand the justice of God, and hope on His mercy.

He did not know where he got this preoccupation with things spiritual but it was a part of what crossed his mind nearly all the time and most of the time, as now, he didn't remark on it. It was just the way he thought about things, the way he was made to think about them.

He looked across and saw that Fulton wore no cap or any kind of hat this morning but that his shirt front was buttoned right up to the throat, and one of his hands was in the pants pocket, seemingly jingling his coins or his lighter in there, Jeb couldn't tell, but he figured the conversation would feature both how chilly it was currently and how warm it was going to get. But as he came up to him, he saw that Fulton's eyes were rimmed red and there was a damp smear on his face, he had stopped but had been crying. Jeb looked down at the man's shoe points and waited to see if he would tell him because it was his business or if he would not, in which case he would leave whatever it was alone. They stood a good long while, how many minutes Jeb would not have been able to say.

At last he looked up, and saw that Fulton was looking over his shoulder far into some distance that exceeded the other side of the street. Jeb cleared his throat as softly as he could but this seemed to make no impression, Fulton seemed to be frozen where he was, out of his own mind even, maybe. But for the shaking of that hand, he would have thought him to be in a trance of some kind, a coma or a fit like would come upon a man who had floated on a ship or had been a grave digger during the war. Jeb saw his papers sitting on the pile and decided to reach out for them, at which Fulton stepped briefly to the side and let him take them.

"You want my ten cent?" he asked him when the papers were all folded. Fulton didn't answer, but the tears began to come out of his eyes and he snuffled and seemed to choke in this throat. Jeb didn't know what to do. He couldn't ask and Fulton seemed unable to speak.

"I'm going to slide a dime in here under this paper so don't nobody come snatch it away," he said. Then he thought some more and said, "You want Miss Ellis or anybody to come get you?" Miss Ellis was a relation of Fulton's a few more blocks up who got a paper from Jeb every morning.

Fulton looked at him, and whispered, "Go on see Miss Ellis. It ain't nothing to do with me."

Jeb stared at him. Bad news didn't take a man that hard, he didn't think. A death in the house didn't take a man that way out on the street, and besides, there wasn't anybody in Miss Ellis's house to die, apart from that baby she cared for during the days and that wasn't even a white child. He could feel himself begin to sweat, the cold of it.

"Somebody gone?" he said.

"No, it ain't nothing like that," Fulton whispered. "I can't say. It's not to do with me. I didn't do it. I didn't have nothing to do with it."

And then he began to hum and rock side to side, singing low but not a song anybody knew whose refrain seemed to be, "I didn't have nothing..."

Jeb was surprised and grieved to see such behavior, and a little afraid for Fulton. He didn't feel he could leave him there on the corner like that, and said, "Listen, Mr. Fulton, let me fetch somebody for you, let me get you something," but even so he couldn't get another word or look out of him. He knocked on a nearby window but nobody came to it, and there was nobody out on the street to call to. He decided to follow his own original advice and go up to Miss Ellis, and see what the matter was, and get somebody down here to help out.

He pressed Fulton by the hand and said something about stay right there, he would not be long, and turned away. But his feet seemed to drag and his paper bag, slung across his body from one shoulder, felt heavier than it ever had. His feet pinched in his shoes, and he thought about either cutting open the toes a little, or seeing about a new pair. He shook his head. He remembered that after his mother passed, his mind was filled with a similarly inconsequent thought, that he had to boil a pot of water, that it was cold and he better boil a pot of water. It was cold now but it was spring and new canvas shoes would be nice for the summer. Not yet, though. But his feet were freezing and pinched and why a man should have to put up with both, he did not think he should. And then he thought, Miss Ellis wouldn't ask him to and she was Baptist, though he didn't know exactly what that had to do with anything.

He walked up to Laurens, and along the way where he was known he was spoken to as he passed, but he did not know the people well enough to ask any of them to walk down and see about Fulton one time. The closer he got to Laurens, though, the fewer people seemed to be outside given the time of the morning that it was. There should be people on the street. He should have sold a couple of papers by now.

He reached the corner store on Miss Ellis's street, where a man who was not well known to him but whom he knew by sight came out of the front door and onto the sidewalk, and seeing him, put his hands in his trousers pocket, and looked him full in the face. Jeb thought of Father John when he did that, always staring you in the eye like he could see inside of there and forgive you for it, but there was not much in the way of forgiveness in this man's face. Jeb made to pass him, but the man stepped over and said, "Where you going?" as if it was his business and furthermore as if he did not know exactly where Jeb was going.

"Going up to Miss Ellis," Jeb said, trying not to stop, but the man took him by the arm and put his leg in front of Jeb's body. He knew better than to react, much, but cold and sweat came all over him again, and he shivered in the man's grasp.

"I'm not here to do you any wrong," the man said. "But you got no business up at Miss Ellis today," he said. "Ain't nobody can do anything for Miss Ellis. Miss Ellis ain't buying no paper today."

He continued to look hard at Jeb but Jeb refused to meet his eyes, and the man didn't give anything more by way of explanation. And this man might well be connected to Miss Ellis, who was not Jeb's family, she was only a lady who bought three papers from him for a penny most mornings and with whom he passed the time of day for a quarter of an hour if the sun was out. In this moment, he couldn't even think of what she looked like. She wasn't tall, she wasn't short, not fat or thin, not full of hair nor with a scalp off which all the hair had been burnt over time. Most of the view he had ever had of her had been from the waist down when she stood in the doorway, and she wore longer house dresses with a short house coat to go over them, and she had nice legs and ankles. That was about all. He liked her, though they didn't flirt, they didn't even joke much. Every now and again someone would say, "You watch out for Miss Ellis, she get you down that aisle for sure one of these days," but he paid no attention to that. The colored baby she cared for always seemed to be at her house when he got there but it was not hers—everyone would say so if it was true—and he had never bothered to find out whose it was, and to be honest, he had never given it a bit of thought.

But he recalled Fulton telling him to get up here, and he said so to the man, who then released his arm.

"Watch yourself," was all he said then.

Jeb walked up Laurens and suddenly it was as if there was some kind of party going on in the street, people coming and going, shouting and laughing, nine o'clock in the morning though it was. They seemed to be concentrated around Miss Ellis's steps, and most of them were young, men he had not often seen and women he didn't think he had ever seen, along with a couple of raggedy looking children who stood close to the house and looked as if they were waiting to get something. He was a little fearful but not much. It was the unique situation and those always made him jumpy at first but he usually could recover himself. He was not now precisely recovering himself, but he was all right.

The people began to part as he came through, and he saw that he was indeed the only man close to his own age in the group. At Miss Ellis's steps, he stopped in front of about a half-dozen young people who were sitting eating food out of dishes, and who were surrounded by small and large articles of household goods. One of them was the statue of the Sacred Heart he had once given Miss Ellis, who although Baptist had been much impressed by it and had always kept it in her front window.

"Good morning," he said, running his eyes over them.

"Morning," most of them replied, one saying, "Morning, sir."

He paused only so briefly, then said, "Miss Ellis standing you to some breakfast this morning?" and then, "Where she at?"

No one answered.

"She coming out? Where that baby, I don't hear no baby crying."

He looked at the girl who held the statue.

"You know something, sugar, I done give that statue to Miss Ellis," he said to her. "She love that statue. Why don't I give it back to her now? She'll be happy to get it back in her window one time."

At that, about every single person in the crowd dispersed themselves as one and nearly without a sound, all but half a dozen of those on the step. The girl—she was not much more than a girl—stuck her arm out with the statue to him, and he took it.

"I'm sorry, sir," she said, "We didn't mean anything. We didn't do anything really," and she jumped up and down off the steps, grabbed the two children who still stood by the wall, and started away. They cried, "We're hungry, we didn't get nothing," at which Jeb called to her, "Listen, girl, wait a minute." She stopped, frightened, and he walked up to her and gave her the dime he had on reserve for tomorrow, and held it out to her.

"Go on down the store and get those children a bite," he said.

"I can't," and she hung her head.

"No, now, you must, they shouldn't go hungry, should they?" he said. "Come on now, I'm giving you this and you must feed these babies with this money, it's nothing to me. I know you ain't going to do anything else with it, are you?"

She shook her head and they cried some more, and he could tell she was trying to keep herself from jerking them or slapping them quiet.

"I'll get them something," she said.

"Get them a nickel apiece," he said.

This time she looked at him and looked at the statue he held in the crook of his left arm, and nodded and he knew she would do it.

When he turned, the steps were empty of the people and all the goods, save one man who seemed to be expecting him.

He walked up to him where, as it seemed, he waited as at a sentry post. This was the one who had sounded the most brash, one of those who had not said, "Sir," to him. Jeb didn't beat about the bush with such.

"Where Miss Ellis?" he demanded.

The boy still held a plate of food, mostly greens it looked like, smelled like a little fish. He put this down on the step and repeated what he or one of the others had already said, "Miss Ellis can't help nobody today."

"What does that mean, she can't help nobody?"

The boy smiled, seemed to deliberate whether to play with this man he could easily beat down if he felt like it, or to tell him and get on with his business. He appeared to compromise.

"She ain't here."

"Well, where is she, then?"

"By now, I don't really know, really."

"What do you mean, 'By now,' then?"

The boy gave in. "They done took her away last night. I don't know if to the police or to the funny farm."

A voice came from one of the windows next door, a woman's voice behind the screen. "That's right. She was screaming fits when they finally got her out of there."

He didn't know her, but Jeb addressed himself to her. "What was the matter, then?"

The woman cleared her throat loud enough to be heard down the whole block.

"I don't know what happened or when it all started up, but I remember you come on Friday last time, that right?" she said.

"Yes, I don't sell papers on Saturday and Sunday. I spoke with her right here on Friday last week."

"Yes, well, she give me one of them papers regular. I give her a penny for them every once and a while."

"Yes, ma'am?" He doubted that was true but didn't particularly care.

"Yes, well, she didn't give me no paper on Friday, after you left she went in and shut the door and nobody heard nothing but that baby crying for two days. It was still crying, though, right up until Sunday evening, late afternoon, I don't know but the sun wasn't quite set yet. It was very chill, that I recall.

"She always went to church, two blocks down, she walked with me sometimes, but she didn't come out on Sunday morning, and that baby was still there, and that baby was never there on Sunday morning or I don't know if she left it but you never heard it but it was still crying off and on all the time, but you know like, weaker and hicuppy."

"Why didn't nobody knock on the door?"

"I don't know. Maybe nobody but me heard it. The folks on the other side ain't lived there for a while now, or at least they ain't been there for a couple of weeks, I don't know if somebody passed and they went down for it or what, but I don't know."

"I'm sorry, ma'am, but you didn't knock or anything?"

"Me? No, I don't leave the house and besides I can't get up them steps. I go out the back."

He would have wondered that she did not knock on the back door or call from the yard but he had taken her measure by this time. He supposed that by "sometimes" they went to church together meant "never" and that she was listening likely because it would have been Miss Ellis who would bring over a hot plate or a box of food for her, and he bet she had not. Otherwise he doubted the woman paid a bit of attention to babies crying or much of anything else.

"Did you see her on Sunday, Miss?"

"Oh! Not until that afternoon! I stuck my head out back and there she was sitting. She had brought out one of her kitchen chairs and she was sitting on the chair right there in the yard, and she had that baby laying down right on the ground, no blanket or layette or nothing to it."

By this time a small handful of people had come out of their places and were standing around. The young man still sat on the steps. He said, "That's right, that's right, they said the baby was just laying there still not making a bit of noise and Miss Ellis nothing either," but he grinned as he said it.

Someone else said, "They said it was cats," and another chimed in, "Yes, that's right, something like half a dozen cats was swirling around and trying to make at the baby and she didn't do nothing, didn't smack them away or nothing."

The woman in the window said, "I seen them cats! They were trying to drag away that baby!"

Someone else said, "I know it! I don't know who said call the law but then somebody finally walked up and found a police and had him come."

The window woman claimed that it had been her, but someone else said, Hush, Arlene, that was somebody else, and she said, Was it? And they said they didn't recall who but they knew it wasn't her because she was asleep in her window until the police got there.

That shut her up, Jeb thought. He didn't know what else would have.

Then another man said, "So up they come and that's when she started screaming. They wasn't no cats in that yard, and the baby had all its clothes on it, but she did have it on the ground, and there was a big soup spoon next to it. I reckon she was figuring out whether she would bury it or what she was going to do next. She was blue as a bruise when they got to her, little Judith I always heard Miss Ellis call her. I don't know if they said what took her, but whatever it was, it couldn't survive her, seems like it just couldn't survive her."

Everyone else made appropriate noises and even the brash young man had the decency to look down at the bottom step.

Whatever made him say it, Jeb never quite knew afterward, but he said then, "Any of you all need a newspaper?"

Only the young man looked up, grinning from ear to ear.

"Yeah, I need one," he said, "sir." And he stood, pulled a penny from his trousers pocket, and held it out to Jeb between his first and middle finger. Suddenly Jeb did not want to give it to him, but then the window woman said, "You get mine, too, you hear me, Daniel?" and he knew he would have to, and handed over two of the folded papers.

"Where's the third one?" the woman called out again.

"That's for Miss Ellis," Jeb answered looking over, trying but unable to see her through the black wire of the window screen. "I'm going to put it inside for her, and I'm going to look around and see what's what in there."

"All right, then," she said, "but don't you make me have to call the police on you." Jeb thought there was little if any danger of her exerting herself to do that.

"She have a key to that door?" he asked of the group in general, and once again the boy, Daniel, stood, reached in his pocket and handed him a skeleton key.

"They didn't think to lock it when they took her out," he said.

"Give me that plate," Jeb only said, "I'll wipe it up."

Daniel downed the last bit of what had been in it and handed it over, and trotted down the two remaining steps and walked away from everyone, tossing the second newspaper on the window woman's step as she yelled, "You don't walk away with my paper I paid for, boy!"

Everybody else looked at Jeb for a minute and then, as if constituting him Miss Ellis's executor for the moment, though they all knew her far better than he ever had or would—and this made sense to him later, as if he had taken it upon himself to act in a kind impersonal capacity as would a solicitor or funeral home director, or something similar—and then one of the men said, "If you need anything, walk over yonder across to my number there, with the rose window above the door, and knock."

Jeb nodded, and went up the stairs and to the door. He tried the skeleton key, which did not work in the lock, and then tried the handle and the door opened.

Miss Ellis did not have anything like a vestibule leading into her front room, but he could tell by marks on the wall next to the door that there had been one at one time. The house smelled of stale feet and underpants, and of fresh rotting things. There was a slight, diaper-y smell underneath everything, the aroma you could not ever get out of a house whenever there was a baby in it, he knew.

Baby things were strewn all over the furniture, which consisted of a rough brown divan, a couple of padded chairs with the seats broken down and flattened almost to the boards, and, he was interested to see, a wing-back chair with the seat high up and a nice, broad seat cushion to it, not new but nearly so, sitting in the place of honor and observation in the front window. Next to it was a small tray table with a pack of cards and a baby's milk bottle with about a quarter of an inch of milk crusted to the bottom. One dingy white leather baby boot lay under the tray on its side. He set Daniel's used plate on the mantel piece, and then himself into the chair, not fully conscious of what he was doing.

I'm late for my walk, he thought, and with the thought gave up something inside of him, permanently or for the moment he did not know. It shocked him. It was something about that chair, possibly, but all at once, after all this time, all these years, he felt he was done walking. He just never wanted to take another walk ever again.

Well, he thought. He slumped in the chair, but he was not sad, he was not given particularly to melancholy, and although his outlook on life was fatalistic, yet it was expectant of hope, as he had been taught to be, and he knew that his walks were a visible sign of that hope. So what did that mean that he no longer wanted to? Perhaps he no longer needed to be the sign, he didn't know. It was perplexing to try to figure it out. He thought again as he had often in reverie before, *Presume not on salvation, but despair not of redemp*tion. *Hmm,* he thought.

And then he thought, *Lord, I'm tired of thinking these things every last minute of every last day.*

He looked out the window, the street below it not wide but navigable, somehow now filled up again as it ought to be with passersby on foot, an occasional automobile or taxi cab, and cart seemingly after cart, selling food and clothes and rags and shoes and even, though not to read, newspapers. He felt his bag still across his shoulders, paining the saddle of his shoulders again as it had when he stood with Fulton.

He lifted and pulled the strap over his head and set the bag on the floor next to him, and at once it was as if the anchor that held him on this earth had been removed. His feet twitched, and they hurt so badly, though he had only walked that half mile or whatever it had been, nothing almost. His chest pained him, deep inside of it.

All at once he was ravenous, and wanted something to drink, and wanted to sit there and have a big cigar or something, and blow the smoke out the window all day long, just looking, just seeing what went by. People did that, he knew. He wanted to do it. He crossed his legs as if to settle himself in, and wished there had been a radio, though he had never regularly listened to the radio in his life. He felt as if he had come home.

He rested his head back against the top of the chair, and after a moment shifted and eased the side of his face into one of the wings. It felt like a lover. It felt in some way like the cool stone of a building, which he had from time to time allowed himself the unworried luxury of stopping and resting his face against in the middle of a walk, down a side street or an alley, never the same building and never for more than a moment.

He wanted that radio. He felt as if he had become only a man's head and that the rest of him had slowly melted away from some mysterious cause.

He wondered then, which was better, to walk, or to rest and think. Which one made a man the better? It was not the same as Mary and Martha, because Jesus never talked to any menfolks who were like Mary and Martha. And their brother had been Lazarus, who had been ordered to come out, but they did not note whether he had done any more walking after that.

So how could he ask that question? Surely it must be better to do.

But no, he thought, with an honesty that was followed by another, terrible idea altogether.

I don't do anything at all. I only pretend to.

He felt stuck to the chair and shook his head a little to clear his mind. This thought itself was unprecedented. He immediately recognized it could be a trap of the devil, but on the other hand, it might be the Lord as well, telling him something he would not have figured out for himself, and immediately he thought again, *Enough of this, enough, I am* tired. However this might be, it appeared he could not do other than think.

And after a few moments, he thought, sitting like this could not be the same as walking and doing, but this must be because it felt new, not because of what it was, he thought, or could it?

Perhaps the Lord had touched him this morning and meant for him to sit there for a minute and figure it all out.

Perhaps he was a sentry of some kind, because Fulton could not get up here. He realized he had forgotten to mention Fulton to everybody.

Perhaps it was extraordinary circumstances, and required the unusual of him. Yes, that made the most sense, and he would keep an eye out for temptations, and keep his wits about him. He sighed. He was not the deepest of men in these respects, in the sense that he was a man who believed in everything, so while his beliefs touched him deeply and constantly, they were not particularly easy to get to or to reflect upon. He did not ever worry about *Are you saved*? and so forth, but if he had had someone to explain what that meant, he would have said he had been born again in his walking. But that was part of the fabric of his being, his skin, his fingernails, all of him. Still, having the thought that he was being called upon to do the exact same thing sitting down in a stranger's chair in her front room was odd in that he realized it was, oddly, also enough.

He settled back into the chair with a sigh of pleasure, and resumed his street-watching.

After who knew how much time had passed, he felt stiff and lifted his head from the wing of the chair and looked around the room briefly. On the surface of things, there did not seem to be anything particularly speaking about the relative abundance of chaos, merely because he had never been let in Miss Ellis's front room before and so did not know if she kept a good house or if she was one of those people who was naturally untidy but you would never guess it to look at her. All those children who had been in here today, maybe the clothes and things had been in nice little piles and they rooted through them to see if they could get something they needed. Or, they might have gone straight to the kitchen and picked things up from there or on the way out. The mantelpiece was just about bare, he had already seen.

"I'll sit here and look out the window a while more," he thought out loud, "since this is where I seem to have been taken first off," and then *I'll look around at the rest of the place and see,* he said to himself, comfortable again, as a man came right up to the window and peered his head in, a middle-aged man wearing a coat and brimmed hat. He saw Jeb sitting there, it seemed, pulled his face away from the screen, smiled and lifted his hand in a gesture of greeting, and walked on up the way. Jeb did not think he had ever seen him before, and the man's greeting was not necessarily of someone who recognized him, but it made him feel good.

He was checking up, he decided, and with this thought he was taken out of whatever this lethargy had been, just as suddenly as it had come upon him, and he was not again tempted to relinquish his bodily energy or will to either of the wings of the chair. He sat upright, hands lightly engaged in his lap, torso against the back but his head stuck slightly out, on quiet alert.

This went on for some time. Nothing much went by in the way of taxis or carts, and again the street seemed to have emptied of passersby. He watched the pattern of sun change as it began to move more directly overhead, and a few clouds above playing with it, now bright and now darker. It looked to be a lot warmer than it was. It was much later than it ever would have been at this place had he been walking.

In the absence of congress or activity, however, and despite the best of intentions, the most disciplined attentiveness is bound to wander and Jeb's was no exception. The initial lassitude that had taken him when he entered the room was never again so strong while he sat there, but he felt his body relax again, his legs part a bit wider, his elbows sink into his sides. He moved his forearms up onto the arms of the chair and rested them there, his fingers cupped over the edges. He leaned his head back again, straight, and closed his eyes, and began to say the Hail Mary.

How long this went on for he was never after sure, but an image finally intruded itself, of an old girlfriend from grade school named Sandra. Jeb turned forty this year, and that made him a lot older than a lot of people he knew, but Sandra had died not many years past her high school graduation, before Pearl Harbor had happened. She had not lived to know about Pearl Harbor, or anything that came because of the war, or anything that came out of the war. He had wanted to speak to her before she passed but they had let very few people know how bad it was, tuberculosis it had been, and those who did know of it had kept their counsel so clearly privacy must have been wanted.

She hadn't been a girl he had thought he would marry one day or anything like that. They had never kissed—the only person other than his mother and relatives he had ever kissed had been that terrible Monsignor—but they had held hands a couple of times, and grinned and giggled in such a way that, not now but in some pleasurable far-off dream, he thought they would have, and that she might have been his sweetheart. She had not minded that he was old enough to be in high school but that he didn't go. He had been duly saddened by her death but had not missed her very much. He had never thought of her again but a couple of times after the funeral.

He ran the tip of his tongue now over his lips and followed this by swiping them with the palm of one hand.

In that moment, the room suffused with light as Jeb had never seen before. Consciousness as it was familiar to him deserted him, and it was only in later days that he could put interpretation to what had happened, and then he said he thought he had been transfixed, like up on the mountain with the Lord, entirely body and yet no body, all awareness but no thought or mindful word, no sound could have come from him in that moment.

It seemed to last many hours and yet not more than a moment. Everything about it was now this thing, now that, now one thing, now another. He would have thought, he felt afterward, that he would have been terrified. But the truth was that he had no feeling at all, as if this was complete experience yet no experience at all. A few years later he would ask one of the teachers at the seminary about it, who would tell him that what he had experienced was known as paradox, and was very characteristic of religious experience, although the look on his face told Jeb clearly that he thought he must have made it up, or looked it up somewhere and then copied it to show off but that Jeb was hardly a likely candidate for paradox.

Now, as he came back to himself, had he been told the words of that teacher, he would have replied that he was himself, nothing different. He did not feel like the opposite of Jeb Heath, that was certain. He did wonder if maybe he had had a seizure or one of those funny eye things that his uncle used to get. He felt light-headed, and hungry, and stood, and went out to the kitchen to see if there was anything to eat.

That room was a solid mess, revolting, piled high with chipped china dishes in the sink, some open cans of things he would not have been able to tell what they were had he not been able to make out the labels, a bottle of milk that had turned into rotten cottage cheese long before this morning. Strange that he didn't feel sick, though. He began to gather things up, setting them inside the top one of a pile of paper grocery sacks that stood in the corner, and when each was full took it out the back down to the end of the yard and set it in the garbage can, putting the lid back on tight each time.

He repeated this for at least the better part of half an hour, at the final trip picking up a couple of bricks off the curb and setting them on the lid to keep it down. He didn't want anybody getting in there by accident and killing themselves. He hadn't noticed anything of what those people had been eating on the steps when he first arrived, and thought perhaps Miss Ellis had been able to make one more meal, or that this was her last meal from yesterday that was still in the icebox and they'd had that, but really, how they had had the stomach to look for it he could not have said.

He started in to wash and rinse the dishes. They were like every set he had ever seen, just about, a thin, cheap set of Chinaware with most of the paint design still on it, a picture in light green and brown of some old Chinese-looking trees and a few boats and peacocks, with great hills and water in the background, the little gold rims mostly flaked off and nearly every piece with a disfiguring chip in the finish, especially on the lips of the coffee cups. On the backs each piece said, "Fine China Made in Japan," but no company name or anything. Miss Ellis never got these at Woolworth's, but that was probably where they had first come from.

The wash water was grey-brown by the time he finished up. He wiped each plate and dish separately after it was rinsed. This, he knew from somewhere, not his mother but somewhere, was how you did if you didn't want them to chip, especially not the lips of the coffee cups. He found the place in the cupboard where they were kept based on there not being much of anything else there, and set them in as nicely as he could. The forks and knives and everything he stood up in a jelly glass and left on the drain board. He shook out the dishrag and dish towel and placed them over the rim of the sink to dry. Looking farther into the cupboards, there wasn't much of anything—a can of Lousianne coffee, several cans of condensed tomato soup, several more of evaporated milk, a nearly empty single box of saltines, cans of tuna fish, a packet of white grits and another of oatmeal. Sugar, a tiny bit of flour, no cornmeal, not much salt. Perpendicular to the cupboard, an old loaf of bread sat in its paper bag on top of the icebox, not hard and dry but green with mold. In the icebox there wasn't much more than a couple of eggs, the ubiquitous block of lard, some old and not yet bad scrapple sitting open on a dinner plate, an end of bacon that had gone bad, and a waxed paper bag of cheese slices. Something remained in a large covered pot that he supposed must have been edible and what the people had given themselves. He couldn't make himself look at it just then. If it turned out to be any good he might have some later.

What was he waiting for, though? He noticed an enamel tin bucket such as many used for a bedroom pot sitting in the corner, behind the table, covered with a solid block of plywood. He walked over to it and lifted it up, and was nearly knocked over by the stench, the first odor he had not been able to bear in this whole minefield of dissipation. It seemed to be full of used diapers and flies, with, he supposed, maggots not far behind. He choked back nausea, put the lid back down, holding it firmly with his hand as if the contents might come to life and beat their way out, and walked it outside and down to the end of the yard. It would not fit in the can, but he would not have left something so horrible unbeknownst to whoever picked up the trash in any event. No animal would be attracted to such a smell, not a rat, he didn't think, so anyone fool enough to lift that up again was welcome to the fruits of his own meddling.

He turned away to the fence and stood for a moment, taking deep breaths. However that smell had not pervaded the entire house he had no idea but he found it waiting for him when he went back inside. It must have been a while since she lifted that lid, but in that case, where were the other diapers? Maybe he would run into someone who could to tell him.

Really, he didn't know why he was staying here, cleaning up, but now he thought about it, that living room was nothing anybody ought to walk into without giving shame and somehow it was important to him that Miss Ellis not be shamed later. He would tidy up and then be on his way. He wouldn't go upstairs, though. That would not be proper for him to likely see something he shouldn't.

He entered the living room to find the impudent young man of this morning standing there, but not taking anything or rooting around at all.

"I thought you might still be here," he said. "I thought I better come by and make sure you were all right. You all right, then?"

"Yes, I'm all right," Jeb said, raising his eyebrows at him. "I'm fine, all right," he repeated. He still found no trace of either shame or discomfort or embarrassment in his face. "What do you need, son?" he asked.

"Don't need anything, man, like I say, wondered if you might need anything."

"What would I need?" This was not so much a question as a quiet challenge. "And I'm not your man." He was beginning to feel that the impudence of this boy, even when he was talking politely, might not have any deep end to it. It might run on forever. The boy proved him right by not answering.

Jeb, then, in a like spirit, walked over to the sofa and silently began to lift up the clothes piled up on it, fold them, and set them in some piles.

"Those belonged to the baby," the man said.

Jeb turned back to him.

"Everybody talking about some baby. I saw some diapers—Lord!—but I never saw any baby bottles or baby food or anything like that. How come Miss Ellis had a baby? It wasn't ever her baby, what, a grandbaby or something like that?"

"No,"—the boy rarely if ever punctuated his statements with "sir"—"that wasn't no relation of hers. I don't know how she came to care for it. I don't know how. She was caring for that baby for some lady who had to work for a bunch of white ladies over on Fayette, but I don't know."

Jeb remembered the woman next door, and the cat story, and her calling him by name. "You Daniel, is that right?"

"No, that lady just calls me that. I don't know why."

He didn't proffer his actual name, though, and Jeb had had enough of that, of this boy acting like he didn't know the right way to do.

"Then what *is* your name, boy?" he asked in a voice that said "sir" better be part of the answer or something would be the matter.

"What would you like my name to be?" The boy was not smiling and most certainly not either deferential or afraid.

And then Jeb knew what the situation was, and it didn't interest him, in fact, it disgusted him. This was one of those boys who had decided they were not going to be anything or anyone other than who they thought they were, and polite and respectful was never what they thought they were. Those boys tired Jeb out. Nobody could be that person on the outside, why didn't young people know this? He thought, *You know,* even the white men he used to shine shoes for didn't try to be who they thought they were on the outside. Most people, he thought, even eccentric ones, knew better than that. He supposed the only person he had ever met, outside his own family and them only when alone together at home, who seemed to be that transparently himself wherever he was had been the Monsignor, and even he had known enough to not be see-through about everything. Even he had known not to show the designs he had or how empty he was.

Something empty. He would not wish this young man to wind up so empty, but it was how such people wound up in the end, he believed, and he had seen so much of it he didn't have the strength or whatever it took to care about such things. Though he probably should, he didn't know the boy well enough to want to fear for him.

"I would like your name to be whatever it is," he answered in a level voice devoid of curiosity.

The boy looked up at him and what he said then changed Jeb's mind, and he was surprised by it.

"It's Stephen, sir," he said, "but I'd prefer it if you didn't call me that to anyone else."

Jeb looked at him for a moment, straight at him.

"All right," he said at last. "Daniel is what I'll call you if I'm ever called on to use your name." And he went back to folding the laundry. He could feel the boy looking at him, and then heard him begin to laugh.

"All right," he said, "God knows none of us are in it for the money."

"Don't you curse at me, boy," Jeb said still without looking up. This was met with silence, and whoever the Daniel part of this boy was, he was back in the room.

"Oh, I forgot, sir," he said, sneering. "I forgot I was among the churched."

Jeb looked up and peered at him. "What do you mean about that?" he said. "You mean, about being Catholic and all that?" He always added "and all that" with people when he didn't know what church they went to.

"You're Catholic?" Stephen said, again at once ingenuous and very much, Jeb thought, the better for it. "No fooling. I am, I mean, I am, too. I don't go, but, I went to church all up until this year." He was charming now.

"Up until this year," Jeb said. "How old are you, then?"

"Twenty-nine."

Hardly a boy. He would have to stop calling him that, but he sure did not look any twenty-nine. Not by height, he was tall, but Jeb didn't know what else. Nothing about life seemed to have aged him. Maybe he didn't smoke or drink.

And then Stephen asked him, "Got a cigarette?" with a smile such that Jeb felt the walls closing in around him. Could he see right into him? And he got mad.

"I bet you knew I was Catholic," he said.

"No, not until you said so."

"So you're making that up because I said I was one."

Stephen sighed, and Jeb thought he must be some kind of a play-actor, except his play-acting was in real life and he could not keep it up the whole time.

He shifted onto his other leg. He needed new shoes.

"You were fooling with me, weren't you?" he said again.

"No, man, I wasn't fooling. I'll be anything you want me to be. What do you want me to be?"

Jeb had never heard anyone ask such a question in the whole of his life.

"You be who you are," he said, "that's all I want."

Stephen laughed. "You sure about that?"

"Of course I'm sure. Why would I want you to be somebody else than what you are?" And then he muttered under his breath, "I couldn't take too much more confusion than I have right now."

And Stephen laughed again. "Life is confusion, man, and that's all it is." He looked around at the remaining disorder in the room. "Look here, what I do know is that I've had as much of this mess in here as I can take. Let's you and me go out and do something else."

"But what about the police? Aren't they coming to see about the baby?"

Stephen looked at Jeb, deliberating, and then said, "I'm sorry. I didn't mean to lie to you before, but there wasn't any baby, and there wasn't any cats."

"But I saw the diaper pail myself, and look at all these things for little babies."

"No, it wasn't that. I used to come up here all the time to help her. After a while I came just about every morning. I think it was that she was running out of her mind—I think, but she was always real polite and well-spoken and made sense when you talked to her. But I think it must have been coming on, anyhow. But nobody ever saw a woman bring a baby or pick one up. They heard the wailing and smelled the smell.

"It was that she couldn't manage the toilet anymore, she couldn't get up the steps to it in time. So she had me go buy diapers every week, and then I'd throw the used ones out right in the bucket, and then the trash man would pick it up. I told her I wasn't emptying any bucket for an old lady in diapers."

"But I come here every morning. I would have seen you, I know I would have seen you before."

"You saw me plenty of times, you just didn't notice me. I passed you on this street plenty of times."

"Did I?" Jeb felt bad about this. "I'm sorry, I didn't mean anything by it. You know, a fellow gets wrapped up in this thoughts and what he's got to do in a day." Then a thought struck him. "But what about the baby crying?"

"She did that herself. She was too ashamed about the diapers so she'd cry like a baby every once in a while. When she had to start using the diapers, I'd come wearing a head rag and hand her up a package with food for her and some more diapers, and she let out talking to that crazy lady next door through their window it was the baby dropping by, and it didn't bother me to do that. But I told her, I wouldn't come and do that in the evening where anybody might recognize it was me."

He stopped and looked around. "I could never get her to straighten up in here after a while. And then I had to go out of town to see my cousins in Delaware for a little while, just this past week, and I think she must have gone out of her mind at last while I was gone."

He stopped again. "I feel real bad about that. They said the crying was something terrible to hear. A couple people banged on the door but she wouldn't answer. I don't know where anybody got that idea about the cats, I bet that old woman next door made that up when Miss Ellis finally went out in the yard and started digging. I don't know what she would have been digging for."

Then he said, "Maybe she was trying to bury the diapers. Man."

He bent over and picked up a clean diaper by one of its points and then dropped it. "Well, at least she won't have to worry about all this anymore. They'll figure her out."

Jeb didn't know what to say to any of that, and they stood silent.

And then Stephen looked at Jeb with a kind of pleading, as if he had gone as far as he could stand to go, and he said, "I can't stand to think about her crying so hard that she couldn't stop. I just can't stand to think I didn't figure out some way she wouldn't be alone."

"I'm sorry, son," Jeb said, "I'm truly sorry about that. You acted so brash and mean and all, I didn't know what to make of you. You know, if I had paid any amount of attention, you might have let me know to help her."

Stephen laughed outright then, his Daniel-self coming back without a pause, and said, "Nah, she wouldn't have let you. It doesn't matter all that much." And then he started to pick up clothes from one pile and toss them unfolded into another.

Jeb didn't take much umbrage at this. He was sorry, though, to think he might not see again that thoughtful version of the man he was coming to like. He thought he would not see Stephen again, or at least not the full man in front of it. He wasn't sure how often a man could go back and forth like that.

"No," Daniel said, and indeed it was all Daniel. "She wouldn't let nobody else come inside. And anyway, wherever they're taking her, they'll figure out she needs help and she'll be a sight better off than she has been in here. I'm wasting my time feeling sorry about it, that's what."

He looked around the room the way a person looks when he knows it will be the last time he sees it, and then said, "Anyhow, this place will be cleared out and somebody new moved in by midnight. You've been holding up the show, tell you the truth—that's why they asked me to come and see what you were doing. Come on, man, let's get out of here."

Jeb was not certain he wanted to leave with Daniel, however, but he felt he ought to go.

"All right, I got my route to do anyhow, and I'd best get on with it," he said, and picked up the newspaper bag.

And then he couldn't tell if it was Daniel or Stephen standing in the door, not moving, but whichever it was said, "I followed you once, all the way down to Lemmon Street," and he looked down at the floor. "You never once saw me and I was behind you the whole time."

And Daniel became wholly Stephen again in that moment, just that moment, worried and comforting.

"No, no," he said, meeting Jeb's eyes, "it was all right. Don't worry about it, it was nothing wrong. I wanted to see where you went, and there was a part of me that wanted to make sure you were all right. I thought maybe a man who could pass me every day and not see I was there might not notice other things. It wasn't anything wrong."

Jeb let out his breath and his body sagged.

"Oh," he said. "You shouldn't do that," he said, "you shouldn't do that, though. What you want to do a thing like that for? You could get hurt that way."

And then he said, "But I appreciate it, I do. It's just that—the thing about it is—" He didn't know how to say what he had to say, but he could see that Stephen wanted him to try, and he did.

"It's just that there's little enough in the world to feel sure about," Jeb said at last. "It's hard enough to know if something is solid or not." His head began to buzz and his feet hurt him. "Don't you know that yet?" he kept on. "Don't you know how it feels when nothing is solid?"

And then the light came on him again. Stephen became nothing more than a thin line in front of him, a reflection of a solid being you would see after closing your eyes when you had looked into a sunny sky, a lamp, a candle flame. It faded at last, after what had felt something like days, glorious days, but Stephen was merely standing there, looking at him, clearly trying to find the words to answer his last question.

How could anybody not have seen that? Jeb thought.

"It's because I do know, sir," Stephen said then, looking him full in the face, his voice making the room cold. "I just didn't know you well enough to know that you knew."

He wiped his hand across his mouth and then the back of it over one eye. "But I wonder if you would let me come with you one day. I wouldn't bother you, I'd just like to take that long of a walk with someone."

Jeb was still reeling from the light. But now he could see that Stephen was all transparency and Daniel all cover, and he was afraid for them both in one way, but happy in another that they both existed. He wouldn't have thought he was somebody a man like Stephen would show himself to. He was struck by that notion, and then he thought, in one of those insights anybody might have from time to time, that something in that light had been following him, and that he and Stephen had shared in some way in the care of Miss Ellis, and that this was what had put them together.

"Yes," he said, and meant it. "You stop me any time and we can go on together. Maybe not today, though, because the day is getting on now."

"Thank you," Stephen said, and then immediately he became Daniel and quipped, "All right, I've got to get out of here, I can't stand around folding somebody's baby diapers all day."

Jeb laughed. Daniel stooped and picked up a china figurine from the end table. "I give it to her," he said to Jeb, and winked, pocketed it, and was out of the door in a flash.

The door stood wide, the light of the sun on its paint, and Jeb felt the newspaper bag heavy in his hands. He didn't particularly want to leave, even now. He wanted to stay, wait for that light again, pray for it, beg for it. At the same time, all he wanted to do was tell someone about it, *Like the four-squares and the Pentecostals, my Lord.*

And then he was back to earth. He didn't bother looking for a key to the door, that key was long taken and maybe Miss Ellis herself hadn't had one. He looked around a last time, remembered he'd already taken that diaper pail down to the garbage can and didn't imagine anything else was likely to be too terrible for anyone to find. Lord knew he didn't have the fortitude any more to take a second look.

He shut the door behind him, slung his bag over his shoulder, and began to walk. He heard the lady in the house next door say again from her window, "You owe me a paper," and without looking up at her or raising his voice, he said, "You got your paper," and to himself, *And it's the last one you going to get,* because he was never going to walk down this street again. He might not know much, but he knew that much.

But this one time, he would walk down it this one last time. Mindful of what Stephen had said, he took a look up and down, noting the few people walking there, glimpsing in their dark frames the ones who sat in their windows and looked out. There was a man down on the step of the corner store also in his shirt-sleeves but a different man from the first one, smoking, humming a little, going up on his toes a little every so often and Jeb watched him for a minute, until he may have sensed being watched and looked up the street. Jeb pulled his hat a little bit lower on his forehead and turned away.

The sun was making itself felt, but good, warm, lively, a little hot on his back, even. He thought of Fulton, of whether they would comment on today's weather tomorrow. He wanted a little something to eat, which was unusual for him, usually he went all day with nothing, maybe a bag of peanuts or a cookie from a bakery, but he was very hungry. There was that place that said, "Fish" on the front and he had never been in there but he understood they sold crabs in season and fishcakes any time and he decided to go on in and see what they wanted for a fish cake or a sandwich. The screen door creaked out, the front door was open and a small iron statue of a pig stood in front of it to hold it ajar, which given how cool the air outside was surprised him, but when he stepped through, he had never felt such a blast of heat, not even coming off a street car onto the pavement downtown.

"Heyo," said a man behind the counter to his left, whom Jeb heard rather than saw as his eyes adjusted to the near dark, apart from a somewhat insane red glow that seemed to be coming from the back of the shop. "What you want I can do for you?"

"Uh, I thought I would get me something for lunch," Jeb replied, blinking and looking around for anything he could make out as something.

Slowly the dark was replaced by a dim light, and then by a kind of twilight and he could see the man and make out his features. He seemed to be sitting high on a stool, though he was incredibly tall, very thin, and very possibly the oldest human being of Jeb's acquaintance to that moment. He looked up, and saw that the man's face was deeply pocked, his hair, although white, entirely covering his head like a cap, and that he had ears that had he stepped off a ledge might safely have glided him to the ground.

"I know you," the man said. "You a Maurice, ain't you? I seen you every day. Every day you done walk by my store and you never come in not one time not once and now here you are and you saying I need me something to eat but did you never need something else to eat before? No sir, you sure didn't seem to need nothing out of my store, and you a Maurice and me just the same."

"Uh, well, sir, I, —," Jeb began, but that was as far as he got.

"Daniel!" the man shouted. "Daniel! Get your ass out here and thow this man out my store says he's hungry and what do I got to give him to eat, and him and me both Maurices and what he do except walk past my store every day for fifty years just about it seem like and do he ever come in no sir he do not and what he want out of my store today? Somebody tell me that. Daniel!"

Jeb had already been hustled out the door about three-fourths of the way into this speech by not his own Daniel but another man who from the looks of him must have been the older man's son, absent the same height and hair only half salted with white but the same ears. Maybe he was a nephew.

"Sorry about that, sir. He keeps the door open to do that to anybody who doesn't know better than to come in. We used to be a fish store, but we were never a diner or restaurant or anything."

"Oh, then I'm sorry, I didn't know. I do walk down this street a fair bit, I didn't mean to be disrespectful or anything."

"Oh, that's all right, he doesn't know. He says the same thing to everyone, except the part about being a Maurice. You a Maurice?"

"Yes, I'm her great-nephew, on my mother's side rest in peace. She's my godmother."

"Rest in peace your dear mother. I wonder how he know that, maybe he seen you in a church or a funeral or some kind of event like that. We all godchildren, my father in there Miss Maurice's godson and I'm Miss Carrie's. You go by Miss Carrie ever? She live a little ways out."

"Oh, I see Miss Carrie from time to time. I give her a paper from time to time. Real nice lady, Miss Carrie, and she got some nice children, too."

"Oh, she's very nice lady, Miss Carrie. So, what, you a Deacon?"

They had settled into a nice visit. The man Daniel's father was still talking to himself but he seemed to have embarked on a story of some kind they could barely hear from the screen door.

Jeb laughed the way you did, self-deprecating but respectful of the question. "No, sir, I ain't a Deacon, but you know, I thought about it from time to time." And saying so, he did think about it. "But I only got to 8th grade so I don't know."

"They can use some, what I heard. They asked me but I ain't been to Mass since I don't remember when. You never know who's going to try to mess with you, you know what I mean?"

"I know that!" Jeb was astonished but grateful to talk to someone who knew about this that he wouldn't ever have to see again. He said in a rush, "I hear what you saying, but you know, you never know. You don't never know but now I'm grown I don't worry about it too much. I go on down to St. Martin's right now in the week and St. Peter Claver on Sunday. They got a young man at St. Martin, white priest, he's not so bad, but still, you know, he still tries to get in your business." Daniel gave a sympathetic cluck. "How they look at you like they want to get at your insides, you know?" Jeb went on. "I mean, what. If you get that way when you're a Deacon, I don't want to do like that."

"Mm-hm," Daniel agreed like a lady, and then, "No," he said, and mused for a minute. "But you say they don't bother you no more?"

"No," Jeb said. "I got shut of that a long time ago, and you know, I make sure of the boys, if any of them hang around after Mass, I shoo them on home."

"That's right, that's smart." The new Daniel looked wistful. "You know, I could help you with that, if you wanted."

"Well, I sweep up before and all that, I could use some help. Carrying cans and all that kind of thing. You could come on in for Mass, I stand in the back, just don't shake Father John's hand too long, he'll get you with that eye of his!" And they both laughed.

"What's your name, man?" the new Daniel asked him.

"Jezriel, Jeb Heath," Jeb said.

"Well, Mr. Jeb, maybe I'll see you next week come Sunday."

"All right," Jeb said, and then he remembered. "Say, what do you all do in there? I seen that red light in the back and it blinded me just a minute."

"Melt down iron pigs," Daniel answered. "We melt down iron pigs."

"Oh. Well," Jeb said, not knowing quite what else to say. "Well, that's something, isn't it? That's something. That has to happen and you all do it."

The man looked at him a little funny then, and said, "I guess," and Jeb knew he had gone a little way too far.

"All right," he said, a bit ashamed but trying not to look foolish. "All right, I'll be seeing you then," but of course he knew he would not be seeing this Daniel again, at least not any time soon. But that was all right. If you couldn't go a little too far with a man, you let him be and no regrets.

And then he realized it was his Stephen who had taught him that, this very day. He liked that notion.

And then he walked. Anyone would have thought a man like Jeb would have walked over every square inch of the Baltimore to which he was entitled, but to date his route had been so circumscribed by habit and desire that it had come to him automatically. He had the number of steps from here to there down in his mind, and when he was tired or aching or bored, he could take up counting them, one hundred steps and then a hundred, and then another hundred and so on. There were people he regularly recognized—many of his paper route customers—and many he didn't know at all, but he knew the houses and colors of the bricks and the kinds of steps, and which ones had something other than glass in the windows and which ones had been kept up properly.

He thought about that now too. What was proper? Was it proper for a white man with chicken skin on his neck to pull a little boy so close to him he could feel him? To kiss that boy on the mouth for too long? To step back with an ecstatic vision in his eyes that the boy could not parse out? Some of that seemed like it was proper, and some of it Jeb knew wasn't ever proper. But a priest had done it, so how could anyone make sense of that?

He recognized that beyond the general confusion and perplexity that he had often put his mind to, that for the first time he was asking another question, one that on the whole he was blinded to the answer of by his own ignorance, and yet that he had to know. There had to be an answer to this, someone with whom you could talk it through. There had to be someone who could teach you, some way to eventually in your life confront such a person and either hear his side of the story or make him quit his ways forever. Nothing else made any sense.

"Hey!" Jeb looked up, found he was standing on a curb where he had never been and that there was a man across the way shouting to him.

"What you want, a paper?" he asked the man.

"No, man, you were about to walk out into the cars. What are you, simple?"

If Jeb was simple, well, he didn't think he was, but he thanked the man anyway and pulled himself together.

No, he was not simple He simply did not have adequate education. These were very big questions to his mind, maybe the most important ones you could ask, and he meant to find the answers to them. He saw a sign in a window, where the Koesters Bread Twins eyed him generously with their brown curls and their apple cheeks and their lovely loaves. Did those girls ever have to ask such questions? No, those girls, they would not be serving Mass, so you knew they did not have to worry. He wasn't sure if this was reassuring or if it made him mad, but then most of what he thought in the context of white people who were not priests or sisters generally made him feel the one thing or the other.

The street was clear, and he crossed it. The man stepped back a step. "Good morning to you," Jeb said to him formally, and "Morning," the man replied. He could feel his eyes in the back of him as he walked on.

He let his mind wander over such matter, and now, having been jolted away, he was as it were fused to the present moment. He didn't like it. He wasn't sure what to do with it. The bag in his arm felt like a bag full of newspapers, heavy, the cloth strap digging into his shoulder and his elbow and making the palm of his hand sweat.

And then it came to him that, all right, if he was going to walk, he would walk. He was a Negro man with a bag of newspapers, and he would walk as if this was something anybody would do or ought to do, that it was honorable work, and he would set his mind aside for now.

He straightened up, saying to himself, "Meet your road, Jezriel, wear those shoes." He passed little churches, big churches. Churches that weren't anything more than the front door of a bakery would be. Fewer and fewer automobiles, fewer and fewer anything. People standing on corners looking at him with envy, sometimes looking like they wanted to say something to him, most passing a comfortable, "Afternoon," or "Hey now," or "All right," and the ladies, when there were ladies, smiling at him wordlessly when he touched the brim of his cap. Small children that didn't interest him, little boys he wanted to swat out of his way like fireflies except that nobody ever would want to swat away a firefly and he guessed not many people would want to swat away such little boys. Good little boys. He thought they were good, probably, but he didn't know.

The day, increasing in itself, was still chilly, the sun become baleful and no longer warming—this morning's sun had been warmer than this one. He thought of the sun changing, in and out of costumes, in and out of identities, one sun after another. *Like Father Christmas, you know,* he thought, a different one for each year, or Father Time fading away to make way for the New Year's Baby, apple-cheeked but blonde and every bit as hopeful and coy as twin girls holding twin loaves of bread in their arms. Smiling at you.

He thought then, how would it be if ladies still wore fancy garments and men still strode abroad in top hats? He entertained the notion with pleasure for a few moments, and to the two ladies who passed him, he took off his cap and bowed a little, but then he realized they both thought he might be crazy a little or drunk, and so he put that thought away as well. It wasn't any use imagining things that might have been once but were no longer.

And then he thought you would take all that for welcome or for the worst kind of mockery, taunting you that you no longer believed a year to come was worth the side-ways stole pinned at the baby's hip it was printed on.

And then he thought, *What a hard lesson.* What a hard lesson for the Lord God Almighty to have set before him on this day of confusion and trying to see into it and not seeing much of anything.

But then he thought, *Well, you know, martyrs.* It was just martyrs in the old days, Lord knew that was so. Perhaps the Lord was leading him into an odd kind of martyrdom? He felt his shoes pinching him. Perhaps this was the meaning of all of this new questioning that brought with it this spiteful confusion? Now, if that were so, and he had a feeling that Father John might well concur with his interpretation at this point, this placed an entire other complexion on the whole of it. If this in fact were the case, he thought, it would certainly not do for him to get raised up in his self-estimation or his arrogance to know, that was for sure, but on the other hand, if you had a calling, there was no doubt that to answer the call was nothing more nor less than your highest duty. And that light, wasn't that something, something like a sign? Weren't the priests and deacons he knew, not arrogant, but self-assured in their knowledge? Was that assurance not also available to him?

In all honesty, he had no idea. But he thought of the light.

He reached the next corner, stopped and looked up and down the absent street, as if searching for something definite. He said a very quick Hail Mary under his breath, in time to hear the door behind him open and to step down and move away, but not fast enough to avoid hearing, "What you want, nigger? Get on out of here, nigger, go on and take your papers and get on out, nigger I swear..." and likely much more to that tune but he moved on too quickly to make it out. It was, he thought, a woman speaking, a colored woman. He realized he had never heard a woman say that word before or even spell it in front of him. But rather than distress him, which in later days he would think had represented an absolute expression of faith in his experience as it was making itself known to him, in this moment he merely thought, "I must go back, it is time to turn East," and this he did.

The houses were unfamiliar and he thought he would not see them again, either, although many were very fine and he would like to have had the chance to memorize them as well. Perhaps he'd become a missionary to this neighborhood, that would be something he would like to see happen, he would pray about that to St. Don Bosco and St. Joseph and so on. He knew he was pretty lost but that soon he would come onto a cross street that would lead him south and he'd find his way back west. This would be the longest walk he had ever taken, he realized. And then the people started to change, too, more white people, more white kids in the street, playing, roller skating and doing all the things that white kids seemed to do all day long and into the night.

He stepped out off the curb and walked down the middle of the street, as if he were a human fruit cart. He was nearly tempted to begin wailing, "Newspaper! This morning! Newspaper!" and where such an idea came from he didn't know except that he worried he had seriously misjudged the space and the time and that his luck, such as it was, might run out.

He walked unmolested in this way, however, for at least half an hour, when finally there were so many people and so much traffic that nobody seemed to know he was there, and this comforted him a little, and enraged him a little as well. And then he saw two white boys standing on a corner who seemed determined to notice him and to make him talk to them. One was pale and round, with tow hair, low earlobes, and Chinese eyes, who seemed kind and gentle, and the other was as skinny and dark as the other was round and fair, with greasy strings of brown hair coming down his forehead, the hair shaved close at the back, as if someone had forgotten to give him a full haircut.

"Gimme piece of candy, boy, gimme piece of candy!" he cried to Jeb. "What's your name and alfress, boy? What's your name and alfress?"

Jeb clenched his hand on the strap of the newspaper bag, and thought, *Call out to me in the middle of the street,* and wanted to school him, and then immediately thought if he were a missionary he could do this. Brother Jezriel, they would call him, he thought for the first time ever. Brother Jezriel, but a real brother, not like Brother Jones and Brother Jackson and Brother Maurice. And so he smiled benignantly at the boys but didn't speak to them, and placed a paper in the hand of the round one. They both pounced upon it as if it were a Christmas present, and he smiled, and walked on. He felt good and a little proud in a way he thought he probably ought to confess on.

But when he reached Baltimore Street he was worn out and his feet were blistered just about all over, it felt like, and he no longer wished to be presented with opportunities to be wise or benign. He limped, unwilling to stop here, knowing that he was nearly close to Miss Carrie's and wanting to get to there as quickly as he could, get a cup of tea and something to eat, ask her to bind up his blisters, which he knew she would do happily and press him to stay for supper.

And then he felt the pain of limping was so usual, the thought of Miss Carrie's high voice and soft arms so regular, the travers-ing of a city on one's own so every-day.

His elation at this beautiful image, despite the pain that he could easily carry for Our Lord for a while longer, was nearly beyond expression. It was comprehensive. He began to pray on each step, "Jesus Christ/have mercy on me, Jesus Christ/have mercy on me," and he continued on this way, now walking on the sidewalk, now in the middle of the street, navigating without thinking, imaging Carrie and Lemmon Street and who-all might be visiting her and how nice and pleasant it would be, until he at last arrived at Pratt Street, and he could walk this last way. Yes, he could walk the last way back up to Lemmon, which, when he reached it, he turned up slowly, being careful not to appear to intend anything, shuffling and limping, though he did not care to shuffle but it seemed to him that there were too many white folks around this place that to look at were of a kind that he did not want to have to speak with or answer to. He tried not to look as angry as he was beginning to feel, the pain in his feet making him feel more with every step.

Miss Carrie was going to give him supper, he thought. She was going to bind up his feet. She would let him relax such that he could return to himself. She would repair him.

On other days he'd come up Lemmon Street, Stricker the last milepost, where he often would stop in the alley, next to the VFW hall yard, and light half a cigarette before he moved on. Reaching it today, he was astonished to realize that after leaving the front of church this morning he had not thought to smoke once, and he said, *I am going to have that cigarette now*. He could not wait for a cup of tea with Miss Carrie to have it, no sir, he could not.

He set down his bag, reached into his shirt pocket for the cigarette and his pants for his lighter. The relief to his feet was beyond expression. He bent his head back to let the tobacco catch the flame, breathed in deeply, and smiling let his head down to exhale the smoke.

And he saw that an old white man he had not encountered before was walking into the alley and right up to him and stopped before him.

He pointed at Jeb's bag. "I used to write them newspapers," he said.

Jeb was so surprised he looked square at him as if he had been Father John. He saw that the man was indeed very old, that the whites of his eyes were red and yellow, and he smelled the reek of spirits on his breath and his clothes, and behind that smell the scent of cat urine and possibly Rapid Shave or Aqua Velva.

"You never," Jeb said, not able to help himself, and smiled at him.

"Oh, I did." The man slightly returned the smile, and then seemed to look far away into the past. "Yes, for a while I delivered them, and then I wrote them, and then I retired and took my pension, and then after that I took to riding on the B&O, they hired me up there to direct the cabooses."

Jeb was not entirely sure what there was to direct about a caboose.

"Yes, sir," he said. "When did you all do that?"

"Oh, about ten-twelve years. I believe I did." He paused for a minute. "You wouldn't happen to have a paper on you, would you? I don't have but a two-bit piece."

"That's all right, sir, I have one I can let you have."

And in the man's face the thing happened that was always seeming to happen, that anybody's good intentions could not keep from happening no matter what anybody did, no matter who they were, what they were speaking of, that seemed to come out of the very being of quarters, and cats, and newspapers, and fish store signs.

"What, do you mean, let me have one?" the man's voice pitched high and very drunk. "Ain't my money good enough for you?"

There had been days when Jeb's mother would say, "You know, if it was one more thing, I don't think I could stand it," and these words from this old, stinking man was a one more thing for sure, and Jeb felt his rage swell again and something like the opposite of light begin to take him, and when he met the man's look full with his own as he prepared to explain that he didn't have the change for a quarter and the thinking that he didn't have that much money in his own pocket fueled his rage even farther, he saw the rage of the man reflected back, and its own drunkenness, and that within both of them there was nothing he or the man could do that would make any difference, not to them and certainly not to the world.

He took a deep breath and let it out, and said, "I mean, sir, if you need it to line something, this one here is the morning edition and it isn't any good, and I'm not supposed to sell it after 3:00."

And then he seemed to lose his air all at once, and he needed a drag of his cigarette, and didn't know if he should smoke, and raised his hand up anyhow, and saw that the end had gone out.

The man's consciousness of what he had said about the money also seemed to have passed away.

"Hey, let me see them newspapers once," he said, "I was a newspaper man myself once although it was the *News-Post*. Hand them up to me once, would you, boy?"

And Jeb did, and while the man muttered, *Well, well, well,* he got out his lighter and re-lit the cigarette, head back, squeezing his eyes shut, pretending that the only thing he could smell was the burnt aroma of the twice-lit tobacco and the moisture of the alley. He turned his back to the man, looking down the cement toward Pratt Street, breathing in the smoke as deeply as he might, inhaling that way twice in succession, not able yet to steel himself to turn around and get away from there.

Carrie, he thought, *Carrie is just a block down, just a block and a half down.*

And then, *Lord Jesus,* he thought, but when he turned back around ready to say something about being sick or feeble-minded or ask the man what time Mass was, he didn't know, he turned to a blank alleyway. The man was gone and so were Jeb's bag and papers.

He took a drag, blew out the smoke, bit the insides of his cheeks, and stepped up to the corner.

The man had turned down on Stricker Street, the paper bag slung over his shoulder, and as he walked the edge of the curb, one step at a time as in a wedding or the army, he took out a paper, opened it up, re-folded it like a paperboy, and tossed it into the gutter.

And then he said, "Go on, get," without looking at Jeb. "Get on out of here, boy," he said to him, and cackled like an old woman.

Jeb stepped back as close to the corner house as he could stand it. He had to catch his breath and he had to not do anything to the man, not even try to get the bag back. He was covered in yet another icy sweat, and he felt something full on his mouth and pressing on the insides of his legs. He told himself he had not had that bag for more than thirty years, that bag was nothing to him, he could get him another bag, he told himself those things until he could breathe again.

And then he heard the air-sucking sound of somebody's screen door and knew he had to leave that alley, and he stepped out to cross Stricker. He stopped at the curb, saw the cigarette was still in his hand, took another drag that burned down to the side of his fingers, and without looking over, tossed the cigarette on to where the first paper lay, and the old man cackled again.

"You see?" he said to Jeb. "You see?"

Jeb put his hand in his pocket, feeling for the lighter and holding it there, and with his other hand, reached up, unbuttoned one button, and clasped the top of his shirt placket as if it were the strap of the bag still slung over his shoulder. He walked that way, not limping, for a block and a half, until he reached Miss Carrie's door, climbed her two steps without hesitation, and knocked, loud.

Part II: Friday, April 3
Marnie Signorelli

Miraculous Medal! Miraculous Medal! Miraculous Medal! Marnie had wakened, and on the clock that used to belong to her father that her mother wound tight for her every night and whose tick-clock sang her to sleep and greeted her in the morning, it said something not quite being the little hand on the seven and the big hand on the twelve. She could not get up out of bed to go bathroom until, but there wasn't very many minutes left and then she would bound out of bed and get her mother and get started on this daggone best day in *forever forever forever*!

Tick-clock, tick-clock, tick-clock. Marnie's bedroom was exactly the one her mother Catherine's had been before she was married, where Marnie woke nearly every morning in a flush of ecstasy but today more so with the thoughts of what was to be hers, today, a little while from now. Everyone thought, and knew, very rightly, that of anybody in the second grade, Marnie had been sure to sell the most door-to-doors, and she would not only win one, but two and even three of the Medals, each one in its own dark-blue-velvet-lined box. Nothing in this life had ever been seen, not Barbie dolls nor paper dolls nor roller skates nor crown jewels, as perfect and beautiful and everlastingly fine as those Medals. That Marnie and Alice had gotten sick with the chicken pox right in the middle of all the door-to-doors didn't matter. Marnie had already filled up three of the forms with names, and you only needed one to get one Medal.

She was going to have *three, three, three*!

And today, *Back-to-school, back-to-school, back-to-school*!

Alice-and-me, Alice-and-me, Alice-and-me!

Miraculous Medal, Miraculous Medal, Miraculous Medal! she thought again, and then, *Daggone it, daggone it, daggone it!*

Marnie did not have to say things in her mind in threes, but had decided to this past Fall when she began to learn the rudiments of Trinitarian theology, after this once when she was waiting in front of church for her mother to step back over from the rectory and noticed that Mr. Jeb, sweeping the front steps, would swipe the steps in a kind of time, one-two-three, one-two-three, and she had asked him about it, and he had paused and turned to answer her, which she did not think he would do because she didn't think he ever noticed children or would talk to them if he did.

"What do you want to know that for?" he asked her, and she was surprised by that, too.

She hadn't been sure. But the skill of temporizing that comes with being in the second grade, where knowledge of the difference between making something up and flat-out lying your head off was becoming more and more nuanced, allowed her to answer, because the truth was she was just being nosy. Still, being nosy was rude, although for the most part rude was a bigger sin than nosy and anybody seemed to be nosy sometimes, she had observed.

"Well, I noticed that I was counting and it turned out to be one-two-three and I thought if you did that on purpose or on accident or what it was that you did."

He looked hard at her until she looked down at her shoes, and then he answered.

"Father, Son, and Holy Ghost," he said, crossing himself with the words.

"Father, Son, and Holy Ghost!" She looked up to him at once, and they crossed themselves in unison, and she laughed along with him out of happiness and not because it was funny.

Her mother came out of the rectory door then and walked over to them, and said something about Don't bother Mr. Jeb while he's working, but Marnie knew better when he looked down at her again, and crossed himself again.

That was when she knew about counting. "Father, Son, and Holy Ghost" you would only ever say one time, because they were already all Three, but everything else that was good, you would say it three times, and that would make it better.

She had asked her mother about cursing a while back, after an unfortunate incident in which she had said "Daggone it!" out loud. After the spanking, Marnie asked were there any words a person of her age could say in exclamation, and her mother had said, *Well, not daggone it.* And not *sugar*, either, but *shoot* was all right but don't let her hear you say it.

She kept *daggone it* to herself after that, and as extra protection she would mark down every time she said it on her little note paper, and then follow it with three "daggones" and that would keep her well until Saturday, and on Saturday she would only confess the single ones. She thought she confessed about between twelve and a million "daggones" a week, but her cousin Father John never said anything about it, that she was becoming redundant or what-have-you, so she figured she better keep on telling them. Though as far as she could see, "daggone" strictly speaking was not any kind of cuss, still it was rude and not anything she should keep on her soul, either, just in case.

The tick of the clock intruded into her thoughts at this moment and she looked over and saw that the big hand was two dots past the seven! *Two-dots-past! Two-dots-past! Two-dots-past!* She grabbed her old baby rabbit, the ratty Dr. Bunny, leaped out of bed, and jumped over the down step landing of the back stairs and into her mother's room.

She was still asleep, facing out toward Marnie, who put the rabbit in the crook of the arm whose thumb she absent-mindedly let penetrate the fastness of her thin lips, lowered that side of her chin to rest on the rabbit's head, and waited, pretending not to notice the white line of dried spit on her mother's cheek.

She hummed, *Back-to-school, back-to-school, back-to-school*! very quietly. She couldn't help it. It had had felt like hours had passed before she had finally been able to close her eyes. She had not wakened, and she had not dreamed. But she had also not imagined that this morning would feel exactly like Christmas morning, or that her mother could, just like on Christmas morning, sleep all the way through it, nearly

Christmas was long past, though, and she had missed her first Easter of being able to take communion at church, Father John had brought it to her at the house as if she was getting Extreme Unction, and she had worn her First Communion veil for the occasion. She had not been to school for May Day practice, or spelling bee, or anything. Alice had gone back to school already and had told her it was nothing interesting but she had not gotten as sick as Marnie. They both got the chicken pox after Alice's father had taken them to the movies to see *The Lilies of the Field*, though he had not gotten them and nor had Alice's Baby Angie or anybody else in Alice's family. And although Alice had not come down with anything on top of the chicken pox, which she said was a gyp, Marnie had taken another illness that she didn't understand, that she called Scarlent Fever though her grandmother kept telling her not to call it that, it wasn't scarlet fever and where had she gotten hold of that idea. But Marnie had been very sick and they were ready to take her to the hospital and finally Dr. Agnew said he thought they had better take her though before he hadn't thought they should. She had stayed two days and Dr. Agnew had come to their house every evening for a week, most of which Marnie did not remember but was told afterwards.

She had a few scars from where she had not been able to not pick or scratch her arm and her legs, but that wasn't anything, more like a badge of courage her grandmother had said. The other badge was that her heart had been affected by all of it, and they all said that from now on, given what kind of a girl she was, she would have to look after her heart especially well for the rest of her life. Alice said that meant she couldn't be so bossy anymore, but Marnie believed probably she was going to be like St. Maria Goretti or the Little Flower and expire when she was twelve and be a martyr with a statue or an altar in a church or something else believably astonishing of that kind. With a Miraculous Medal.

Miraculous Medal, Miraculous Medal, Miraculous Medal!

She took her thumb out of her mouth. She had to go. She tried to wake her mother up by staring at her, but it didn't work. She nudged the bed with one knee, and then the other. Her mother opened her eyes, and looked straight up at her.

Marnie put the skinny thumb back in her mouth, as olive as the skin on her cheek, as olive as her father's skin had been, they said.

"He losing his insides again?" her mother asked.

She nodded, and started to sniff, though she hated sniffing.

"Okay."

She looked at the wind-up clock next to her bed, reading something that seemed to take longer than merely checking the numbers upon it. Her mother's eyes and hers were the same, Marnie knew, because everyone said so, large, brown, and a little sad-looking, the same as Marnie's Catholic great-grandfather whose picture was on her grandmother's bedroom mantelpiece. If you didn't know anything else about Marnie's mother, Marnie bet you would still say, "Look at those eyes. You have your mother's eyes."

Her mother pushed herself up and swung her legs over the side of the bed. "Give him here."

Marnie shook her head.

"How come?" her mother said.

Marnie flinched. She knew that edge to her voice. She shrugged.

"Take your thumb out of your mouth and tell me why not."

She never outright yelled at Marnie, but came so close that it wasn't until Alice moved in next door into what used to be Mr. Petie's house and she heard Alice's mother and sometimes father through the wall that Marnie knew what real yelling was. She did not know that when she did not take her thumb out of her mouth or tell her mother why not, her mother wanted to yank her hand out for her and force her to say something, instead of blowing the breath out of her cheeks and saying, "Go on, then, if you're not going to tell me. Go on back to your room."

Marnie began to feel the whole day getting ruined.

"Bafroom," she said around her thumb like a baby.

But she was not a baby. She had turned seven over an entire year ago, and seven was the age of reason as her Uncle Father John had confirmed was the case, and she had hardly been able to wait for second grade and all that came with it via the institutionalization of the age of reason via the sacraments of Confession and First Communion. He'd said not to worry too much about that, which she ignored because she had not been able to wait until it was the age of reason and she was about as glad as it was possible for anyone to be that this year she'd been able to make First Confession and then maybe in another year enter the

Carmelites and be a martyr and all, and it made her sick and ashamed that she had not been able to keep her thumb out of her mouth since she got sick. She crossed one leg over the other.

"You are eight years old," her mother said at last. "You know how to go to the bathroom by yourself. And you are too old to call it 'bafroom.'" She leaned over and pulled Marnie's thumb out of her mouth, gently, and dried it on one end of the sheet, and gave it a little kiss. "What's the matter with you anymore?"

"I don't want to go by myself," Marnie answered. She tried to think of a good reason why this was. "It's cold in there," she said after a minute. And that was true, it was very cold.

Her mother screwed up one corner of her mouth and said, "All right, already, all right. Let me get my slippers."

She took Marnie by the hand and both of them, one at a time, gave the little jump you had to give to step over the back stairs landing and go through Marnie's room to the bathroom. They went in together, her mother making some business out of straightening things on the one shelf and then walking over to the window, looking out to the porch roof, the garden, the small sidewalk next to it, the back gate, the alley.

Marnie would not have tried to read her mother's more abstract thoughts if she had been aware she possessed them, or known that adults could look out a perfectly beautiful window onto a perfectly beautiful back yard and alley and think, *Everything is dirtier than I remember it, everything smells sour when you go outside, this time of year.*

"Spring, if it ever gets here," her mother said out loud, and, "If it ever gets here."

Marnie breathed heavily, and her mother turned to her, looked down, and smiled, and though she did not look up, Marnie smiled back through her straining damp eyes.

She was used to her mother drifting away like that, saying things out of the blue that didn't make any real sense. Marnie was a no-nonsense kind of a girl, of course, everyone knew that, but her mother, though strict and in many ways severe, didn't always seem to have all the sense you would think that such a magnificent mother would have. She was quite a thinker, though, Marnie knew. She was twenty-five, a lot younger than Alice's mother Miss Agnes. Marnie's mother was a widow and Marnie was an orphan, but not to feel sorry for, Marnie didn't think. Alice was going to be divorced and not come back anymore, but Marnie's father had, she and Alice prayed every day, perpetual light shining upon him and that did not happen to your father when you were divorced.

Paul Signorelli was Marnie's father, and he had died two years ago. Marnie did not remember him very well, she thought because he had died before she had achieved the permanent state of the age of reason. Lots of times her mother had laughed that she was a half-Catholic, half-Jewish wife with a Lutheran Italian husband and they both thought that was funny. And her mother was about the only person Marnie knew who when they asked you, *What are you*? she would shrug her shoulders and it didn't seem to matter to her at all, and this was a great part of her magnificence to Marnie's mind. She was brave or indifferent about things that mattered to other people.

Her father had died of emphysema, and when asked the doctor said she, Marnie, was not going to, but when she got chicken pox and so did Alice, she had gotten that illness on top of it, Scarlent Fever or whatever it actually had been, so she wondered. Her mother also said, no, she was not going to die, which was slightly disappointing, but her mother also warned her every day, don't get too excited and riled up and to save her energy. This was a joke because Marnie lived excited and riled up. The world was too wonderful, too exciting. How could you not get riled up? She guessed if you were Alice, possibly you could not.

But everything riled Marnie up. She was one-half Italian and one-quarter Irish, and one-quarter something else that her mother had never explained because it wasn't a country but Jewish, which was more like Catholic and Lutheran, and yet still she was 100% full Catholic, *You better believe it ma'am* she would say. She wore her lace veil from First Communion to Church on Sundays before she got sick, which you got to do if you felt like it for all the rest of second grade, and she prayed all the prayers she imagined they had every single day except the Rosary because that was too daggone long to pray all by yourself, but she would make her mother pray it with her on Friday nights and some other times if she could manage it. She was going to be a Sister, or possibly the Pope one day. She had heard there were Popes that didn't have to be Fathers first, and she was going to look into that. She would name herself Pope Joan the Twenty-third, and she would be fat and jolly but not bald, and not wear one of those little white beanies, but her First Communion veil whenever she went out onto the Pope's porch and waved at all the shouting and clapping and crying people, or perhaps a cornette.

It was all very wonderful, she thought now, and sighed.

"Are you finished?" her mother asked, and she said yes, and wiped herself and got up and washed her hands. She never forgot anything, but she believed it made her mother feel useful to believe that she had, and so when her mother asked if she had forgotten something, she smiled and flushed the toiled and went out. Then right away she felt that dizziness again that she thought was *finally finally finally* over, but she made it to her small bed and sat down, and then laid down side-ways, with her legs still down towards the floor. She hoped her mother would notice sooner than last time. She had to get to school today, on account of the Miraculous Medal money. But then a miracle happened and the buzzing in her head passed off and she was able to get up after all, before anyone noticed anything. *That was close.*

And then they were on their way to school, across big Lombard Street and through the park, giggling and squealing, "Marnie-and-Alice, Marnie-and-Alice, Marnie-and-Alice!" and "Miraculous Medal, Miraculous Medal, Miraculous Medal!" Alice had not been able to sell enough things to get a Medal and she didn't have three dollars to buy one, but Marnie told her that was all right because her mother had sold enough to get *three* from all the relatives and Alice and Marnie could split the medals! Alice was so happy, Marnie thought, though she didn't quite understand why she had gotten quiet a minute later, but then Alice was always getting quiet about something or other. That was her personality complex, Marnie said.

"All right, you giggle wiggles!" her mother called up to them as they skipped high in the air in front of her, Marnie's skip not quite as high and a bit more labored than it had been before Easter. "Slow down, where's the fire!" And when they did not, she said in her stern voice, "Marnie, you cut out that skipping right this minute."

"Okay, Miss Catherine!" they said back together. Marnie called her mother Miss Catherine on the way to school and back home, because that's what Alice called her and that's what all the Sisters called her when they had to find something out at the rectory where Marnie's mother was in charge of Father John and Mr. Jeb and everything.

The happiness of it all was great, and magnificent, and *sensible*, Marnie thought.

She felt a sudden wave of the buzzing and stumbled a step, but it turned out was nothing that she couldn't say, *Oh I stubbed over my toe*. Alice didn't notice. She seemed to be thinking hard but Marnie couldn't figure out what. "Are you worried about the Miraculous Medals?" she asked. She peered at her face.

"No, it's not that."

The words and her face matched, so that was all right.

"I'll tell you about it on the playground," Alice went on, "it's something that happened while you were sick, when my Daddy came over when I still had the chicken pox."

"Did he get into trouble on the chicken pox from the movies after all?" Marnie was worried about this. Because Alice was the only one with a father between the two of them, though he lived down the shore or some place, but they needed at least one between them, one who could drive a car and sometimes came home early with the newspaper as she and Alice were getting ready to clean the family dog in a vat of Alice's mother's laundry bluing as would occur in their reader, something Marnie was certain to happen at some point or other in real life though at present neither of them had a dog. But they needed a father and Alice's wasn't divorced yet. It made Marnie's mother happy when she said she remembered her daddy, and although she could not bring herself to say "Daddy" three times in a row, she had his clock and looked at his pictures and she loved him but she did not miss him. She and Alice also needed a father who sometimes drank beer and smoked cigarettes and loved to sing at the dinner table with a table full of nuns who said "Ja!" and "Nein!" and wore scapulars and Miraculous Medals just like theirs.

"No, it was something else," Alice said. "I'll tell you later."

And then she turned and said, "Come on, Miss Catherine, slow-pokey-dacky-dokey!" and she and Marnie giggled furiously and sang out "Slow-pokey-dacky-dokey" in time to their steps until they got to Fulton Avenue, at which point they assumed a mantle of sedate severity by which they hoped to impress Father John, whom they intended to be housekeepers for when they were old if Marnie didn't die earlier from being a saint.

And then "Goodbye, Miss Catherine!" they said at the open spot in the fence of the school yard where all the children were gathering before Sister came out with the hand-bell for lining up by grade, class next to class. Marnie felt exceptionally beautiful in her plaid uniform dress and her dark blue sweater, which she had not had on for weeks, and thought only the addition of her communion veil and the still-to-be-awarded medal around her neck would provide perfection to her physical person. She had read the phrase "ecstatic vision" in the little book about St. Catherine Labouré of the Miraculous Medal and thought she might be in the middle of having one, but possibly since she could still see and hear Alice she was not. Alice took her by the hand, which you were supposed to do if you went closer to the fence to talk about anything, and leaned against it while Marnie waited.

"So when I still had the chicken pox all over my daddy came to visit through the back door." She told the entire story, about how her father had been wobbly and yelling, and how it had all ended up with him throwing a peeled onion at her where she sat at the table and ruining everything and her mother and grandmother saying *Get out! Get out of here you no-good*! and how she wasn't sure she would ever get to see him again.

"He might be gone for good. And you know what that means."

Yes, Marnie knew what that would mean. She felt weak and pale, but as she usually did in difficult circumstances, after no more than a moment, seeing Alice leaning against the fence, she pulled herself up, squared her square shoulders, and said, "Never you mind about that. We will get our medals today, and that will gives us extra"—she searched for the word—"indulgingces, and we'll pray to St. Joseph the patron saint of Fathers and Families and he'll get your father back for us."

Alice did not look too hopeful, possibly feeling that her mother had a stronger rein on the temporal occurrences of her family than did St. Joseph, but Marnie, reading these signs, said, "Of course he will. The Blessed Mother will tell him he has to and that will be the end of that right now."

Then Alice did look happy and relieved, a little, and they joined hands again at the sound of the bell and only let go as they got into their places in the two different lines of the second grade classes, girls in alphabetical order, Marnie and Alice nearly shoulder to shoulder because of their names, Alice ahead with only one other girl behind her across from Marnie.

Smelly Billy Agnew, no relation to Dr. Agnew as far as Marnie knew, looked over from Alice's class's line and said very low, "Look at chicken pox heart girl!" She stuck her tongue out at him and looked up to catch a Sister's eye, and instantly looked down at the ground and said something very like "Ahem." They began to move about as one, the girl behind her, whose first name she could never remember no matter how hard she tried and whose last name was Skellar, as usual stepping on one of her heels on the first step. She thought she might be mental or crippled or something. She didn't think it was at all on purpose.

Miraculous Medal, Miraculous Medal, Miraculous Medal she began to say softly over and again, a litany. She knew what a litany was. She knew what everything was, just about, but not always the best way to solve a problem. As she watched Alice walk ahead of her, shoulders slumping, Marnie wished she didn't feel so daggoned sick and frightened. She was scared because now if there was no Mr. Smaling, that Mr. Paddy who seemed to like Alice's mother would be allowed to come into Alice's house. Who could disallow this? Marnie's mother, maybe, but she didn't know. Generally she had noted that grownups did not interfere with other grownups, no matter what it was. But Alice lived right next door. On top of this, apparently the Martians were also coming, though most of the children who said so were only in the first grade and likely they didn't know everything about it. She had not seen any evidence of odd things or events, and her mother had not mentioned it, although very clearly mothers and fathers didn't tell children everything.

Marnie kept thinking. She knew her mother was the best and strongest person next to her grandmother, and her great-grandmother and Miss Maurice who were looking out for everybody from Purgatory or maybe even Heaven by this point, and they could both have scared anybody into not doing anything, and her grandmother lived in the front room on the second floor and nobody would ever think of fooling with her, so Marnie would be all right, but still Alice was not safe and though thinking about what could be done made Marnie feel a little braver for small periods of time, that these things were happening at all was very sickening and she was getting very, very angry over feeling sick and scared all of the time especially after having had Scarlent Fever. And if you added in that she had gone back to holding her rabbit at bed at night and the stuffing was coming out of him because she was biting at him and beating him up in the night when she was asleep. And that most nights she thought she could hear Alice crying next door. That might be imagination, though.

The morning passed nearly to lunch time and the day had already been very, very long. Marnie had not known she could be so tired, but she fell asleep over her arm during listening to Sister read a book, and woke up with a line of drool across her cheek identical to the one her mother had woken up with that morning. Veronica across the aisle whispered to her, "Sister said don't wake you up," but then everybody laughed, and she laughed too, and so did the Sister, sort of, although not really.

It was a new Sister from before, which Alice had forgotten to mention. On the playground at morning recess, she had filled in that Sister Mary Margaret had had to leave for a while. She had to have some kind of operation on her eyeballs, which when she left she was still wearing the beautiful cornette but when she came back she had on the long veil they had all taken to, which Alice said she was very sad over and Marnie had been deflated to hear about. When she came back, Alice said, she was looking behind her glasses through a piece of cardboard paper with a tiny little hole in it, but that was only for one day and then she had a nervous breakdown from tiredness or trying not to yell too much or something. Marnie figured it was too much hardship all at once, getting your eyes sick and losing your most beautiful headdress all at one time.

This Sister today seemed so far to be nice, but she also didn't seem to know much about the standards of St. Martin's School, which were to Marnie of the very highest. She let everybody go to the library, where Marnie sat at a little table and looked absently at a book, one of the All-of-a-Kind-Family ones that the Sister must have been told Marnie was allowed to read, but she had not felt she could read very much, somehow.

Then they were back in class and it was time for Pagan Baby Spelling Bee, which Sister Mary Margaret always said was two good things at once: her class got smarter by practicing, and the pagan babies got everybody's penny for being smart. Marnie was not sure if this would also make the pagan babies smart at some point, but you never knew. She waited, but when Sister stood up and began to speak, it was not to organize the spelling bee lines.

"I am very happy to tell you that the prizes for the door-to-door sales have arrived, and that it is time to give them out. But I'm afraid," she said in a low voice, "that we only have enough prizes from the sales for one order apiece, and children are not allowed to put another child's name on any of their orders. There were not enough prizes sent to the school to go around, so to be fair only one prize each will be given, except for the Eight Grade which has worked the hardest, and they will have a raffle."

Marnie felt something go through her. She had never had a plan interrupted before in her entire life. For a moment she could not believe it. She raised her hand imperatively, but New Sister ignored it. She waved her hand, and grunted, "Oh, oh!" as if she had an answer that New Sister had been looking for and had not been able to find out on her own, but New Sister pretended as if nothing was happening at all. Again for the first time in her life, Marnie let her hand sink down without having been called on. And all at once it felt to her as if she was no longer in the room. Certainly nobody else around her was acting like she was still there. Nobody smiled or snorted. They weren't mad or triumphant or anything, as if they hadn't seen it happen, as if Marnie was not someone anybody paid attention to.

This could not be.

"She is TERRIBLE!" Marnie declared under her breath. "She does not have the manners God gave a GOAT."

"Marnie said G.o.d." one of the nearby boys whispered back, and the relief of it was almost too much, and she snorted.

"I am going to give them out now," New Sister continued without a pause but giving Marnie a look that she had also never gotten from a Sister in her whole life, "and congratulations to all of the students who got their prize. Next year I'm sure the rest of you will do better now that you know how to go around for the sales."

Marnie thought she could feel Alice slumping in her chair in the next classroom over without seeing her do it, as if both Sisters in each room had made the fell declaration at the exact same moment. There was a word, she could not remember it, flubber-something. She was flubber-whatever it was. How would she ever look Alice in the eye? The whole time they had planned they would have the Miraculous Medals and knew that both having them was necessary to their future happiness and friendship. They had said, "No matter where we go, no matter what we do, no matter if we are alive or dead, we will always wear our Miraculous Medals every day, from this day forward," this day of course meaning that beautiful, as they imagined it, ceremony when they would walk up to the front of their rooms and claim their medals, and later put them on around their necks in the back yard or Marnie's bedroom or somewhere at the very same moment.

But all New Sister did now was to ask each person to raise his or her hand when she called the name, and she put the prize down on the desk, murmuring, "Good work," to each one. When Marnie's came, she didn't say that, but placed it down on the desk with a snap, and gave Marnie a look that seemed to say that she would be keeping an eye on her from now on. And for the very first time in her life, Marnie did not care that she seemed to be displeasing an adult. She only wished she could see Alice and what Alice was doing and how she felt about not having any box of her own or anyone saying, "Good work" or all of her dreams shattered.

At last New Sister was finished. She went back to the front of the room and told everyone to get their lunches and their milk money and to line up for the lunch room. When Marnie approached, however, she pressed a palm into her shoulder and said, "Sit there and wait." She left with everyone else and Marnie could not imagine what she had done, but then thought perhaps there were some special instructions related to her illness regarding lunch time, and she began to amuse herself by tracing with her eyes the line of cursive alphabet letters, capitals and smalls, printed on the blocks of brown paper that were taped above the blackboard.

New Sister came back into the room with a flourish, letting the skirt of her habit twirl as she pivoted on the toe of one foot to close the door behind her.

"Now then," she said, "Please come up to the desk and stand."

Marnie did and found that standing next to her as she sat, they were at nearly eye level. And it turned out that New Sister was truly terrible after all, now that Marnie was getting a good look at her close up. She was not pretty, and her breath smelled. She had those little white things on the corners of her mouth like

Dr. Agnew, and hair in her nose also like Dr. Agnew. But she was holding a kind of chart of words in her hand, one that seemed to be covered up in a clear covering like on library books. It was very beautiful, and right away Marnie wished she could have one like it, and right away jealous that New Sister had this one and she did not.

"Well?" New Sister asked.

"Well, what?" Marnie said, meaning it in a way that she would never had meant it to any other Sister. "I mean, what well, Sister?"

But of course it was too late. "You are Marnie Signorelli, are you not?" she said as if it were a fault Marnie had been caught in.

"Yes, Sister."

"Your own father was a non-Catholic, was he not?"

"He was Lutheran and Italian, Sister."

"That is beside the point," she said. Marnie wondered yet again at the white spit in the corners of her mouth that collected it seemed nearly at the drop of a hat.

New Sister went on. "You think very highly of yourself and your abilities, do you not?"

She almost said, "Yes, Sister," as earnestly as she could. She did think very highly of herself and her abilities. She was *supposed* to. It was her whaddayacallit that all the saints have one of.

But, "No, Sister," she said.

And then came the explanation she had not known she ought to have side-stepped.

"When Sister does not call upon you, you must put down your hand immediately, must you not?"

Oh, she thought. But wait a minute, when had she done that? And then she remembered.

"Oh," she said aloud. *You are the stupidest unfairest New Sister I have ever met in my whole life.*

"'Oh' is a rude reply when you are being spoken to by an adult, is it not?" New Sister said with a quiver in her voice. Other than the racket over at Alice's house, Marnie was not sure she had ever seen any adult getting this angry over anything, and she began to be afraid. The buzzing in her head started a little.

"I'm sorry, Sister, I meant, Oh, I won't do that again." *I shall have to confess this, shall I not?* As she thought this she knew in a minute she was going to laugh.

But New Sister seemed not to notice and she seemed right away to calm down. "Very well. I shall depend upon you not to repeat it, shall I not?"

And she said as if she and Marnie had gained an understanding and were suddenly on amicable footing, "Now, then, I wish to gain a sense of your current reading abilities."

Oh, well! If that was all! What a relief if that was all! Marnie said, "Oh, I can read very well, Sister! I'm the best at it in the whole class!" *I am being good now, are I not?*

But New Sister stiffened even more than before, and the blotches of red that rose to her cheeks and nose, would have been visible on her ears and throat as well, had Marnie been able to see them.

"How dare you interrupt me when I am speaking? How dare you commit the sin of pride in my presence?"

New Sister asked her these things softly but in a more ugly way than Marnie had ever heard anyone say anything. She was not afterward certain that Sister had not whispered it. "You are both brash and brazen, are you not?" Sister continued, accusing her of these ugly things but in a more natural voice.

Marnie believed that if her mother was there, she would go ahead and ask the Sister what she thought she was doing. Maybe. But she would still make her be polite, so Marnie tried to be polite. But now she was feeling very strongly that New Sister might be a little bit out of her mind and wondered if Sisters could be out of their minds.

"I'm sorry, Sister, I didn't mean it." *You.*

"You didn't mean it?" And then New Sister was yelling. "You didn't *mean* it! You are telling an untruth, are you not?"

Not a lie, an untruth. Oh. But Marnie flinched and felt sick again and wanted to cry, and her mind seemed to be doing two things at once, feeling afraid and calmly thinking about things at the same time. She did not answer, though New Sister yelled, "Are you not? Are you not?" twice, because although of course Marnie absolutely was telling an untruth she was interested to note was apparently different from a lie, and thought she would have to ask Father John did you confess that as well, she wanted to laugh her head off because she knew that's what he would do when she asked him, and she could not think of anything to say that would not make her laugh and she looked New Sister full in the face the way her mother looked at other adults when they did or said something wrong or rude or foolish.

And then New Sister Areyounot seemed to collect herself. She looked away and smoothed the palms of her hands on the front of her habit, leaving a very light trace of sweat on the white fabric, which even in the circumstances Marnie felt was a real shame.

"You have just committed the sin of Pride, have you not? You have put yourself forward in an unbecoming way, have you not?"

She still appeared to wish for an answer, but Marnie did not know what to say mostly because now she didn't really understand all of the words. Sister Mary Margaret had always praised her for what she had called her "lively exuberance of mind" and had encouraged her to display it as a model of academic fervor to the other children, which Marnie sensed Sister must have found as lacking in them as often as she herself did. How Sister Margaret Mary, who was good and smart, could have encouraged her in Sin, Marnie did not know, and could not believe, but there it was, it seemed.

New Sister did not wait this time for an answer, but remarked in a very tight little voice, "We shall see about this."

She picked up the covered paper, snapped its lovely covered edge on the desk, and pointed to the top two words.

"Read that," she said as if she had said nothing else to her, and Marnie read them. New Sister looked up at her sharply, said, "Go on."

She read the whole first column, waited for something to happen, and when nothing did, read through the second and third columns as well. She did not recognize most of the words but thought she must be saying them right, for it was not until the bottom of the second column that New Sister quietly corrected her pronunciation without stopping her or by producing any other commentary.

Marnie stopped at the end and looked at Sister. Without returning a look or another word, New Sister Areyounot, as Marnie was now calling her in her head, opened the middle drawer to her desk and tossed the list into it as if it burned her fingers, and snapped the drawer shut. But before she could do this, Marnie saw an unbelievable sight: also tossed in, not lined up but as if the person who had put them there did not care about them at all, were four blue-velvet-lined boxes, each holding a perfect oval Miraculous Medal, not given away at all. She gasped and immediately closed her mouth.

"Well, what is it?" New Sister Areyounot snapped at her again but louder. "We are finished. Please gather your things and join your class in the café."

Marnie did not know what a café was, and clearly New Sister Areyounot did not know about the rule that says children must not walk in the hallways alone, but she got her lunch bag and left the room for downstairs.

Lunch also was terrible, because she found out that Alice had suffered as badly as she had feared she would. She heard what had happened from one of the girls in Alice's class, who spread it all down the second grade table with a horrified giggle though the Sister in the lunch room kept saying, "Now, that is ENOUGH!" This girl had craned her neck around in the classroom to look at one of her friends, and had seen Alice put her head down on the desk, and saw her choking down sobs. Then all at once, she said, Alice had sat up straight in the chair, "Her eyes coming out and her eyelbrowls shot up to the top of her bangs." And then, "Ew!" all the children who sat around Alice in the room all had said at once, and then the girl had looked down and saw what they saw. Alice had wet herself.

This was why Alice had not been waiting for Marnie in the lunchroom. She had to go home without Marnie, and Marnie was not sure how she would ever come back to school, without Marnie, without her medal, and with everyone calling her Smelly and saying *Ew* and all the rest of it. After listening to the girl, Marnie got up though this was not approved by the rules of the cafeteria and found a chair to sit miserably by herself and didn't speak to anyone and they didn't talk to her. One boy kept looking at her, though, until she finally said, "What are you looking at?"

He knew better than to answer, "Nothing," which she would have done, and fell back on the truth instead. "They said you had smallpox. Why isn't your face all messed up?"

Sometimes Marnie felt she was allowed to yell in the lunch room or on the playground and hit people or beat them up if they didn't act how she felt they were supposed to in any given moment. Everyone knew this about her and most seemed to accept it. The ones who could hear the boy waited to see if she would feel like it, but Marnie neither flared her nostrils, nor made her hands into fists, nor stood up so fast it knocked over her chair. She got up and went right to the Sister and asked if she could use the lavatory before playground. Something on the Sister's face told her there must have been information about her health not quite yet having been restored to robustness, for the Sister said, Yes, she could, but the one right here on this floor and come right back.

Marnie didn't bother to go into the stall. She examined her face for possible scarring, and then, though later she never found the right time to say it to the boy, said out loud as if he were still there, "They also said there was Martians, you daggone dummy, but Sister said there WASN'T and so there ISN'T. And it was CHICKEN pox. It DON'T LEAVE A SCAR." At least it did not leave a scar on your face when you had been careful not to scratch it there, but she was not going to tell the stupid boy that.

She felt a little bit better. Still, nobody seemed to know she had also had Scarlent Fever, or care about that, except the Sisters who would have known it just by looking at her given that they knew everything just by looking.

She felt dizzy. Possibly in later years she might reflect on this day as one of the few in her life where she had ever given way to physical weakness, but today, all she thought was, *Oh my, I feel so ill.* She put the back of her hand up against her forehead as she had seen ladies often do in the movies and then in the next moment of which she was aware, she was crumpled on the bathroom floor in a heap but did not remember having intended to be. She got to her feet, the room changing into black dots and buzzing around her head for a minute, and she turned to the door as the Sister opened it and came in and asked her what she thought she was doing taking so long to use the lavatory.

But then the Sister looked strongly at her and said, "Do you feel all right, Catherine Marie?" which is what they always called her at school.

"Yes, Sister," she said, the buzzing in her ears getting worse. It was an untruth.

"I think you had better go back to the recess room and stay for today. You don't look as well as you should."

"I don't feel as well as I should, do I not?" she said.

"What?" the Sister said, and then, "Come along now and don't be smart."

In the recess room were all the children who had forgotten their lunches or pennies for the Pagan Babies, or who were too stupid to be allowed outside on their own. She could read everybody a story, or tell them about her Chicken Pox that had devolved into Scarlent Fever. If Alice wasn't around, the playground was never very much fun anyway. But apparently all the children had been told not to tire Marnie out and she sat down by herself and the Sister told to put her head down. She was not tired. She was bored. It was nearly silent in there and the atmosphere of stupidity, her own included, got in under her arms and felt as though she was breathing it in. For the thousandth time since she got back to school, she did not feel like herself. She began to think that nothing was going to resume being the way it had been and was supposed to be.

And then, her head down on the desk, she thought of Alice, and how miserable she must be and how little she was able, like Marnie, to pull herself together and look on the bright side. And now, when the Miraculous Medal was supposed to be going to fix all that forever, Alice was not going to get one.

And then Marnie thought of her next plan. It came to her all at once, and, yes, this was a plan that New Sister Areyounot would never see coming! It meant breaking one of the Ten Commandments, but she was prepared to do that. And she would, too. Because it was fair, and sometimes fair was more important than hell, and to be brave, and she would do it if she got half the chance. And she would get back at New Sister for ruining everything, everything, *everything*.

Back in the classroom the afternoon dragged on and everyone's head was again down on the desk where Marnie felt that her head might have to remain until the end of time. Apparently there wasn't going to be a second reading time, or listening to reading out loud time, or come up to the front of the room and say something interesting about yourself time. New Sister Areyounot was the most boring Sister that had ever been, more boring than Marnie would have believed they even would allow to have in the Sisters. She seemed to like adding better than subtracting, and printing better than cursive, and heads down on the desk for a moment better than anything. She didn't appear to understand that standing up and getting a good stretch in silence was necessary to have earned one's head down on one's desk, nor that sticking in a little subtraction and cursive writing and story time was a solid educational technique that ensured the betterment of the smart children in the room, who then would donate their superior understanding to the dumb ones. She didn't seem to give a care about anything important whatsoever.

But Marnie didn't care either, so there. Her plan was taking hold in her mind, and all she had to do to succeed was hide in the cloak room for a minute right after school was over, after everyone else had filed up and walked out. Sister would never notice that she, Marnie, was not among them, she was sure of it. She worked it over and over in her mind, adding little details to circumvent the requirements posed by the physical world and satisfying herself that, somehow, though her seat was in the back of the room where everyone had to file into the cloakroom first, she would ultimately discover how to stay there while everybody else entered and left without anybody giving her away. She pictured herself whispering, "Shh!" to each one of them with her finger against her lips, looking portentous, and each of them acquiescing with a solemn nod. She was the smartest person in the world.

She allowed a drop of spit to settle under her mouth on the desk, letting a little light come in by separating her fingers to ensure the amount of spit was not more than she could wipe away unnoticed with her hand.

"Heads up everyone," New Sister Areyounot said at last. What was her real name again? Marnie could not remember. Naturally, Roger, which whoever heard of anybody being called Roger, had fallen fast asleep and did not waken at the Sister's call. Sister remedied this by picking up her pointer stick from the ledge of the blackboard, walking softly up to him, and poking him in the side. This produced nothing except him sighing in his sleep and turning his head to the other side. Sister then took a step back so that her backside was nearly overflowing onto Cathy Flathmann's desk, raised the stick high above her head to the sound of a collective gasp from the children, and smacked it sharply down onto Roger's desk right in front of his head.

He jerked up in his seat, wide awake, his eyes bugging out straight ahead of him.

"What is the answer to the question, young man?" New Sister asked him.

He didn't answer. Marnie didn't know how he could have since she had not asked a question, not even, "Who is that boy who still has his head on the desk?" which no Sister in creation would have asked in the first place.

"Why don't you know the answer?" she said to him. He was going to cry in a second, Marnie could tell.

"I didn't hear the question, Sister," he said.

"And why didn't you hear the question?" she said, and Marnie thought, *You are telling an untruth, areyounot*?

She was getting sick to her stomach and her ears were buzzing yet again. She almost thought she could hear the ears of everyone in the room buzzing, thinking the same thing as she, that a Sister was flat-out lying her head off in front of them.

"I don't know, Sister," he persisted. Marnie doubted he knew that he had still been asleep by this time.

"Now, I am going to ask you again," she said, "what is the answer to my question, and then I am going to count—"

Marnie couldn't believe it. She was a counter-up-to-three. Or, worse, ten.

But before New Sister could begin to count, another Sister, not the Principal but a Sister almost like her, put her head in the door, and said, "Is everything going well, Sister Immaculata Mary?"

Sister Immaculata Mary. No, Marnie had not forgotten it, she had missed it altogether.

The children stood as one, including Roger, and said, "Good afternoon, Sister." Nobody else remembered her name, either, though a couple of children mumbled "Sister Wah-wah-wah" as if they did.

Sister Apparently Immaculata Mary smiled and said, "Everything is going very well, Sister." So she didn't know the other one's name, either. "We were about to begin doing some addition problems this afternoon."

"That is very good, Sister. Please go ahead and I'll listen to the answers for a minute. Children, you may all sit down." Marnie noticed that although she smiled at them, the Sister did not otherwise take her eyes off New Sister.

By some Divine intervention, Roger knew he ought to keep standing and did, and New Sister turned to him as if they were recommencing a real lesson, and said, "Now, I was asking you, what is 3 plus 1?"

He exhaled in abject relief, and Marnie saw his left hand working. "Uh, 3 plus 1 is 4, Sister," he said, and collapsed back down into his seat.

"That is correct. Next time, don't sit down again until I say you may."

He stood up in confusion, and she laughed, and everyone laughed. "You may be seated."

Before he could, however, the other Sister stood up, and called him by name. "You did very well, Roger. We can all be proud of you. Try not to count on your fingers next time, but do the sum in your head."

Roger stuck his teeth out in what for him was smiling and said, "Yes, Sister," and sat down again. Marnie knew that he had been spared from this persecution for some reason she could not figure out, but she also knew a bully when she saw one and now she knew where she was. She was not going to let New Sister Immaculate Mary Areyounot bully anybody. She wouldn't let her bully Alice, though Alice was not in her room—this Sister would have Alice for breakfast, she knew, but Marnie would never let her—

She lost this train of thought somehow, and the last thing she remembered was singing she hoped not out loud, "Immaculate Mary Thy Praises We Sing," over the buzzing, and everything got very blurry again and then next thing she knew she was outside in the back yard around the swimming pool they did not have and a little fuzzy ugly dog was running around it and it was Marnie's job to make sure it didn't go to the bathroom in the pool. But Marnie was the only one there, so she was not quite sure how this had become her job. The pool was enormous, though, sunk into the ground and shaped all curvy. But they didn't have a swimming pool or a dog, or she and Alice would have washed it in bluing that they would have put in the swimming pool, but it seemed that this was going to be her dog. And she didn't like it whatsoever. It had straight hair in its eyes, and when Marnie tried to look into them so she could tell what the dog was thinking and feeling, the eyes were very small and very covered up, so she could not see. But the dog did seem very sad, and Marnie did not know why, but she did not want to make it happy, she just wanted it to go away.

And then it seemed that Marnie had been to sleep, and all that about the dog was some kind of dream which she only knew because she was waking up and nobody mentioned it. And right away she knew where she was, at Bon Secours, like those worst two days when they thought she might not get better, she knew the windows and the light and the doors and the metal frames of the beds in the room. A nurse was there, and her mother was there, and her grandmother, and the nurse was saying, "No, she's just fine. The doctor will be in in a minute."

And Marnie said apparently first before anyone noticed she was awake, "That dog was one complete, full, entire gadget."

Her mother turned around to her and said, "What on earth!"

Marnie laughed loud. "I don't know!"

Then she felt woozy again, and said something like "Did the Scarlent Fever come back?" and her grandmother immediately said, "Scarlet Fever," but looked up sharply at the nurse.

The nurse said, "No, honey, it didn't come back, you had something else and there was a leftover side effect from after over-exertion."

Marnie didn't answer but looked at her mother who said, "You got too tired at school today, honey."

Marnie wanted to say, *I did not do any such thing, did I not?* but with three pairs of eyes upon her settled for folding her arms across her chest over the hospital bed sheet.

"Marnie," her mother said, and her voice said *Watch yourself*.

But Marnie was daggoned tired of watching herself and Alice and Roger and New Sister Immaculate Stupid Bully Never Explains Anything Areyounot, and before she knew what she was up to, she burst out crying. At that, the nurse hustled her mother and grandmother out of the room, saying, "She's still a little too weak and has had too much excitement today. Let's give her a minute," and then came back in and said something rational like, "Now, that's enough of that, you don't want everyone to think you're still a baby," and straightened the sheet and pulled the screen back next to Marnie's bed. Marnie was not at all surprised that under the sway of this crisp treatment she ceased crying immediately and felt very much better.

"Everybody just—"she began. "They just all get on my nervous system, don't they, Sister?"

The nurse didn't seem to notice she called her that. "Yes, young lady, that is exactly what happened."

She took a damp cloth and wiped Marnie's face with it and gave another tug to the sheet and another smoothing sweep with her arm down the length of the blanket. "Now, you quit laying there and feeling sorry for yourself and rest up like you need to so that you can go home tomorrow."

Tomorrow. "Can my Mommy come back?"

"Yes, and Grandma, too, but you have to rest a while first. Can you tell time?"

"Yes," Marnie lied.

"Well, when the big hand is on this and the little hand is on this, then I'll send your mother back in."

So Marnie did know how to tell time after all. That was nice to find out.

"If the doctor comes first he'll look at you and then talk to her. Then we'll see."

It was the magnificent self-satisfied competence and complacency of such a woman that in that moment decided Marnie to become a nurse. Probably a Sister Nurse, if she and Alice did wind up going into the Sisters. She had thought, Teacher or Sister, but now that she had seen this nurse up close, Nurse was obviously just as good or even better. Besides this, she suddenly realized, the Nurse wore a habit, too, and the hat of her nursing habit was second best to a Sister's cornette, and even better come to think of it since Sisters didn't get to wear cornettes anymore.

Marnie nearly swooned at this thought, quick and jumbled as it was. She would have to tell Alice and then save up for a Nurse's kit from Woolworth's from her Tooth Fairy money. She knew her grandmother would sew her a nurse's habit and cap, and then she could be a nurse on Hallowe'en forever too. And then instead of playing babies, she could be the nurse and Alice could be the patient or the nervous relative waiting out wherever they made you wait. Alice could switch back and forth. Or Alice could be the baby patient and the mother who had the baby, while Marnie was the nurse for everybody.

The bliss of it all was already in her head, unfolding in a single vision, and soon she was asleep again, with no dreams to disturb her.

The doctor came in some time later, the sun already all the way down and the lamp light from the table next to her bed hurting her eyes though they were closed. She whimpered a little and opened them, feeling the doctor's hands against the sides of her neck. He smiled at her but didn't say anything, and proceeded with the exam, feeling her shoulders and wrists, pulling up her undershirt to listen to her chest with the cold stethoscope bell and the connected funny rubber hoses that went up to his ears, pressing into her stomach, quickly opening the band of her underpants and looking down before she had time to shut her eyes closed, and squeezing her knees and her ankles.

"Let's take another listen up here," he said, mostly to himself she thought.

"Let's have you sit up," he said, and put one arm under her shoulders and lifted her up, and the next thing Marnie knew, she was waking up again with her head on the pillow, and the doctor was looking down at her with one hand under his chin and his arms against his chest. Her mother was there, too, looking very worried or very something. Marnie was afraid for the first time all day.

"It's called orthostatic hypotension and it should not happen to a little girl going from lying down to sitting up in bed," he said, exactly if Marnie were not there or was there but could not understand English. Now she was too frightened to speak or cry or imagine herself in the role of the nurse who would take care of Alice and comfort her about the north-oh-poh tensions that were being caused by not having a Miraculous Medal and very possibly by Mr. Paddy Dolan trying to be Alice's mother's boyfriend and being at her house all the time. She wondered if she should mention these things to the doctor but decided better not or at least wait.

He continued, "It's very common to happen going from sitting or lying down to standing up. Probably she is very tired out—" and here again Marnie had to press her lips together to keep from protesting she was no such daggone thing—"but we have to take her heart condition into account. I heard in my examination a very small heart murmur. Again, this is common, nothing to be overly worried about, but she needs to rest up and not run around too much. She will probably need to stay home for the rest of the school year, but we'll see."

The day before Marnie's heart would have broken from the words but now she was elated and almost gasped out loud. She tried to school her face into a picture of indifference, but it was very hard when everything went from one jubilant moment to the next when you were in a hospital bed. She felt a moment's qualm that she would not be present to champion Roger and the other children who had been born with less gumption than herself against the wiles of Sister Areyounot, but comforted herself with the thought that likely she could work out a plan for this later.

"Well, young lady?" the doctor was asking her in that way doctors always used when they wanted you to agree with what they were about to tell you that you have to do. "Can you promise to be a good girl and stay in bed for a few more days while you get a little more rest?"

"Yes, Dr. Agnew," she said, trying not to sound too relieved or happy. "But—" She remembered the Miraculous Medal and how she had been going to steal it. "Um, did they get my book bag and all?"

Her mother said, "What do you want to know that for, Marnie? Yes, we got it. All your things are in it."

"Did they give me both Miraculous Medals?" She knew asking that way was a flat-out lie, but, well, she could confess that one later, too.

"I don't know," her mother said in that way that meant Marnie had asked something that embarrassed her in front of another adult. "We'll look later. Don't worry about it."

Marnie folded her hands over her chest and tried to follow the ensuing conversation. Her mother said, "No, my cousin can come and help us. He'll get us a taxi and carry her in and all."

"That should be just fine. Keep her downstairs and use a pot for now. She can't go up and down for a good while yet and I don't trust such a spirited girl to stay put upstairs. She can watch the television or listen to the radio for half-hour at a time. Turn off the lights at 7:00."

"Yes, doctor," her mother said, darting another annoyed look at Marnie.

"Draw and crayons?" Marnie asked. "Paper dolls? Read?"

The doctor smiled. "For little bits at a time. When Mother says stop, you stop, now, do you hear me? Otherwise we'll have to keep you shut up over here and you won't like that."

Marnie would like that very much as it would allow her plenty of time to learn about Nurses and nursing, but then she thought, No, better stick closer to Alice at the moment.

"And friends come over?"

"She has her best friend right next door," her mother said. "She's been over a couple times since they both got sick."

"Not today. Maybe tomorrow for a little while, before dinner or so."

"Yes, doctor," Marnie said in imitation of her mother, and in the best Nurse Sister voice she could imagine, and everyone laughed and she did, too. She was happy again, she was herself.

It turned out Father John had already been at the hospital doing some parishioner visits and was been happy to help get them home.

"He's my first cousin once removed," Marnie had explained proudly, "and he used to be Jewish," at which everybody laughed, but she didn't. Her grandmother had explained all about it. It wasn't funny.

"Your great-grandmother, God rest her soul, went ahead with Miss Maurice and had him baptized when nobody was looking. That's why Miss Maurice is his godmother," she had told her. Marnie was a little confused but saw nothing incongruous in the information. She knew there was a whole side of the family, her Cousin John's mother included, that was all Jewish, not just a quarter, and part of her life vision was also somehow joining with Father John to convert them all as Catholics, though she had never discussed this with him directly. She remained worried that her own father had been a Lutheran, which she believed was another kind of Jewish, and her mother confirmed he had been Lutheran when he died but that she was fairly sure they'd all be in Heaven together. She had been a little indirect on the point, though, and Marnie had not asked about it again.

"Sweetheart, once Jewish, always Jewish," Father John said now, with a look at her grandmother. Marnie didn't know what the look meant, but all of a sudden nobody was saying anything. Then the doctor, who walked down the hall with them as the nurse wheeled Marnie up in front of everybody, surprised everybody by saying, "Yes, for my part I believe that is quite right," and he looked down and smiled at Marnie, and she laughed up at him, and everybody seemed to relax. There were a few parting instructions and admonitions, and they were allowed to go home.

Everybody fit inside the taxi and the ride back was quiet, mostly with people looking out the windows like they do when they have had a long day. Marnie sat comfortably on her mother's lap and laid the back of her head on her shoulder, and began humming the Stabat Mater, kicking her foot up a little at "lac-ri-MO-sa" and giggling as she always did at "dum pen-DE-bat."

Father John began to hum it along with her, and soon they were all singing in a low voice until the cab driver said loud, "What's that now? Pig-Latin?" Nobody laughed, but nobody got mad at him either. Marnie wondered as she always did why pigs had to talk in Latin, but she had never seen a pig in real life so there was no way to know at the moment.

They had a new fold-out couch in the middle room where Marnie had slept during the day when she was recovering before, but when they got home, Father John laid her on the sofa in the living room and her grandmother went and got a pillow and blankets.

"Can I watch TV?"

"There's nothing but news."

"Afternoon at the Movies."

"No, that's over, it's past supper."

"Can we look?"

"Oh, for Heaven's sake," her mother began, but Father John said, "Let's see what there is."

The television warmed up to the sound of the fingers snapping out the theme song of "77 Sunset Strip," and her mother said, "No, you are not watching that!"

"Why not?" John asked, turning, surprised.

"It is not for children," Marnie answered back in a repressive manner that made John laugh out loud, but she was serious. "Isn't it?"

"Turn to something else," her mother said in a rush.

Marnie's grandmother came in with a bowl of tomato soup and some crackers and Jello.

"Just like hospital food!" she said with a smile and Marnie smiled back.

"Grandma, you know what I decided?" She pushed herself up on her elbows. "I decided I'm going to be a nurse. I bet they have to eat hospital food, so I want to practice."

"Well, you can't get better food than what you get in the hospital if you're sick. Here, let me help you with the bowl."

"Do they have kosher food in the hospital?" Marnie had always been fascinated by the idea of having two whole sets of dishes in everybody's kitchen and was sad that they didn't have that at her house.

"I don't know, honey, I guess not. Here, let me put the napkin on your shirt."

"Maybe if they had Jewish hospitals."

"Yes, maybe then." Her grandmother was never sad that Marnie could tell, but when she sighed this time, it sounded a little sad. "Here, take a spoonful."

Marnie sipped the soup and popped half a saltine in her mouth. She looked over and something else was on the television. "What's this?"

"Don't talk with your mouth full," her grandmother said.

"The Great Adventure," her mother said in the absent voice everybody uses when they try to watch t.v. and talk at the same time.

"Oh. What else is there?"

"Nothing. Destry isn't on anymore."

"Oh, that's good, I hate that one. What's this about?"

"Daniel Boone."

"Who's he?"

"Um, he was in history. He was a trapper, he trapped out in the country like Daddy used to."

"He was a fighter in the war," John added.

"You mean like the war they have now?"

"No, honey, the Civil War."

"Oh! That's the good one about the Free State," she said and began to hum "Away! A-way! Away down South in Dix-ie!" through the tomato soup cracker mush in her mouth. She bounced in her hips and pedaled her feet, and her grandmother laughed and said, "Somebody's feeling better!"

"Mm-hm!" Marnie answered with her mouth closed.

The screen door wheezed then, and then the sound of a rap they all knew.

"That's Agnes," her grandmother said.

"I'll get it," her mother said, and went out to the door. Marnie could hear her mother plainly, but not Miss Agnes, not after the first cry of "Hello! I just came over to see how everybody is! How is everybody?"

Marnie immediately said, "Can Alice come over?" and her grandmother said, "Hush up," and Marnie sank back into the pillow and said, "Huh."

"No, she'll be fine," her mother was saying, and her grandmother muttered, "Might as well tell the town crier," and then they could hear Miss Ann, Alice's grandmother, saying something down by the steps.

"No, Mom, I'll be in in a minute." Miss Ann said something else, and Miss Agnes said, "For Heaven's sake, Mom, he's just sitting there!" and Marnie felt a kind of cold feeling she had not had to feel all day. She looked over at John, who was still absorbed in the story of Daniel Boone but who did not seem to be worried about the conversation at the door.

"All right, okay, uh-huh, okay," her mother was saying. "Maybe Alice can come over tomorrow afternoon a while. Okay, thanks, goodnight, thanks," she said and came back in.

"I swear to the Lord both those women can talk the hind end off a donkey."

"Catherine," her grandmother said.

"Well, really, Mother. I don't think Petie's mother or Sheila's had to gab like that once they got going, even at the wedding. And nosy. I swear."

"Everybody's nosy around here," her grandmother said.

"Well, that's the truth, Lord knows."

"Except John." She looked over at him and laughed, and Marnie looked up at her.

"Who isn't nosy, Grandma?"

"Oh, your first cousin once removed."

John looked up then. "I did, I heard everything you said. I only pretended I wasn't listening."

Marnie's mother cried, "Oh, really! Well, I will believe that when I see it!" Marnie and her grandmother laughed and Father John looked embarrassed.

"Well, all right. Didn't the doctor say something about half an hour and lights out at seven?"

Marnie said, "Nuh-uuhhh! Please! I want to watch some more about Daniel Boone!"

"You were not even looking at it," her grandmother said.

"Yuh-huh, yes, I was, really, please?"

"Tell you what," Father John said, "If Mommy says all right, we'll turn off Daniel Boone and play Monopoly a little while. How about it?"

"If you settle down and don't raise any more ruckus," her mother said.

"Yippee!" Marnie cried and, "I'll go fix the kitchen," her grandmother said.

"Oh, Mom, leave it for once. I'll do it after while," her mother said, but "No, no, you all go on. I can never land on the good properties anyway."

Marnie laughed, "I know, Grandma, I always have to share my money with you!"

"All right, now, that's enough," her mother said, and put a hand to her forehead. "All right. One or two times around the board and then bedtime."

And in a second, Marnie felt so tired out she didn't even answer yes or no. She felt cold again and asked for her robe.

"Let me get it," Father John said.

"Get her pajamas, too. They're both on the bed upstairs."

Three turns later, John was still languishing in jail after Marnie's mother had sent him there practically on her second move. She could collect up all the properties and money and houses like anything, but they had an agreement that Marnie was rent-free on her mother's properties but had to pay everyone else, except Father John now who was in jail, though she had landed on his Baltic Avenue three times in a row. She had begun to close her eyes in between turns, but nobody had said she ought to go to sleep. Her mother and John were speaking low.

"John, I don't know if you can do anything about it, but I don't like to see him going over to their house all the time now. It wasn't even a month ago the last time Jimmy was there."

"I don't know what you want me to do, Cathy. They hardly come to church at all. I've barely spoken to him since his father's funeral. I doubt he goes, but if he does it's to Fourteen's."

"I don't like it. Alice and even the baby. And that one girl of Carmen's going over to babysit. I swear, if she's over there, I have Alice come on over here. He's always there when she's there."

"Well, people have to work, Cathy." His voice sounded hard.

"Does her mother have to work? I swear."

"It's not the same."

"Marnie, your turn."

Marnie was not sure who she was talking about. Of course Alice's mother had to work. Her mother had to work—all the mothers worked. Her mother knew that. She opened her eyes and found her boot where she had left it on the Reading Railroad, which she had neglected to purchase. "Do I have enough for that?" she asked, and her mother said, no, she'd have to wait for the next time.

"A dollar is one, a five is five, and how many do you need?" Marnie asked the established question for purchasing. She put her arm out for the boot, but her arm felt so heavy she didn't want to move it, and she said, "I'm sleepy. Can I go to sleep here?"

"For a minute," somebody said, but then the next thing Marnie knew, she was back in John's arms and being lifted down to the mattress of the fold-out couch in the middle room. Sheets and a pillow were already on it, and another blanket was being pulled up to her chin. She felt someone sit on the edge of the bed, and it was John.

"Can you stay a little?" she asked.

"Sure, honey, I can stay. Open up and stick out your tongue, though," he said, and when she answered, "Extreme Unction?" he laughed loud, throwing back his head, and said, "No, funny girl, baby aspirin. Look what you made me do, I dropped one on the floor. Take this one," and she did, and he looked around on the floor and when he couldn't find it, opened up the bottle next to her and gave her the other one.

"They're good," she said.

"I know." He smiled at her. The world was solid as it could be. She chewed the second aspirin softly, her mind wandered a bit, and then she thought of Alice.

"Father John, why do there got to be bullies?"

"Have to be, Marnie, not got to be."

"Oh, for goodness sake," she said without being able to help it. "Can't anybody say something around here without somebody correcting you?"

Her voice began to rise and she didn't seem to be able to stop it. Father John put his hand to her head. "Take a drink of lemonade, sweetheart. You're right. And I don't know why some people have to bully others. But it has always been the way. It's a bad way to do, but people do it for some reason. Thankfully it's not everybody, nor even most people."

"But there's always somebody, isn't there?"

"It does seem like it, Miss Marnie."

She paused. "Can I tell you about something?"

"Sure," he said. "You can tell me about anything you want."

"Could it be like confession, though, where you can't tattle on me?"

He bit his lip and his nostrils flared. She knew he was trying not to laugh.

"Wait a minute, I'm serious, though, can it be?"

"Yes, it can be, but wait, I have to get my stole out of my bag." He reached over and took the bag from a table by the wall, opened it, and took out the thin white stole, kissed the embroidered cross on it, and put it over his head.

"All right, we may begin," he said. He turned his knees all the way out and looked away from her.

"Is that how they do on Extreme Unction?" she asked.

He turned back to her. "What do you mean?"

"Well, I don't know—when they come to the person's house they don't have the confessional door and all."

"Oh," he said, "yes, that's usually how we do it. Sometimes if the person is very ill or very close to dying, I will lean down to them so I can hear them, but usually I close my eyes unless they want me not to. And usually I don't sit down on the bed."

"Oh," she said. She was quiet for a moment. "Well, you can keep your eyes open if you feel like it. Bless me, Father, for I have sinned, it has been I think six days since my last confession—no wait a minute, do we count today? I only ever said one week since my last one up until now."

He put his chin down to his chest and then turned his head even farther away. "Just a minute, let me think," he said in a kind of covered-up voice. He turned back and "Yes," he said more regularly, "that would be six days."

"Okay, it has been six days since my last confession."

"And what are your sins?" he asked.

"Well, of regular sins, I have talked back to the New Sister twice, and once to the Sister in the lunch room, and I decided to steal a Miraculous Medal for Alice because I was going to give her one of my extras which I was supposed to earn for filling out three contest forms but then New Sister said, no, that's not going to be given out after all, and Alice was miserable and wet her pants right there in the desk but that's not the worst thing I wanted to tell you about Alice."

"Wait a minute—did you steal the medal?"

"No, Father, but I saw she had four extras in her desk. I fainted from Scarlent Fever before I could go back tomorrow and get one."

"I see. Why were you at her desk then?"

"Oh, she gave me some kind of word test or reading or something. The top of it said Reading Proficiency." Marnie spelled it.

He turned to look at her again.

"What does that mean?"

"I don't know. I didn't know what most of the words meant. Something about how many words can you read I guess. But I could read them and I could say most of them, she only corrected my pronounciation two times. "

"I see. Why were you going to steal it?"

"Because I don't have three dollars to buy one, and Alice's mother probably does but she can't ask her because Alice's mother doesn't give a care about them. But Alice and I, we do.

We want to wear them every day the same for the rest of our lives, no matter what. So I thought, I could steal one, and give mine to her as a present, and then save all my money and buy one for me, and then confess and give back the one I stolen."

"That's quite a plan."

"Yes, sir. I mean Father."

"Tell you what, I have a better idea. I happen to have a spare three dollars, and I could buy one, and then you could give yours to Alice, and I could give you the one I buy as a kind of cousin present to commemorate that you got over your fever. How would that work?"

Marnie paused and thought about it. "I don't know, Father. I think I would rather suffer since I had the intention anyway and that's already a sin."

He thought this over for a minute. "Okay, here's what we'll do. Is that all the sins?"

"Yes, that's all of them for now."

"Okay, so go ahead and say the heartily sorry prayer."

Marnie said it.

And Father John said, "I absolve you from all of your sins in the name of the Father, and of the Son, and of the Holy Ghost. Go thou and sin no more. For your penance, you will not talk back to anyone for one week, you will say three Hail Marys, and you will give any one of your cousins that you choose all of your saved money—"

"Including tooth fairy money?"

"Including tooth fairy money, for as long as it takes until you have given three dollars. In return, that cousin will donate the given money to the poor box—"

"Could it go to the Pagan Babies?"

"The money could be assigned to the Pagan Babies, yes. In the meantime, you will give your Miraculous Medal to any friend that you choose, and you will accept the gift of another

Miraculous Medal if anyone should so offer you one for any reason before you have managed to give over the full three dollars to your cousin."

Under these terms, Marnie thought she could easily keep from talking back to any number of Sisters for possibly the rest of her life. "Yes, Father!" she said. "Do you want me to say the Hail Marys right now?"

"Yes, go ahead, but I have to stay here so you can tell me the rest."

She immediately felt quiet, and said, "Just a minute," and said the three prayers under her breath. "So, Father, you know Alice, right?"

"Sure."

"Well, what I have to tell you is that Alice is telling me some things."

"Go ahead."

"I think it is about Mr. Paddy. He is going over to Alice's house all the time, and Alice says he is acting like Miss Agnes's boyfriend and Alice's grandmother Mrs. Coppins doesn't like it and Alice doesn't either, because for one thing Alice's mother and father are married and Alice already has a father which is Mr. Smaling. So she doesn't like that."

"No, I can see where she would not like that, I don't know that I like it."

"No, sir, I mean, Father. But that's not the bad part."

"Really?"

"No."

He didn't say anything. She screwed up her eyes for a moment and then felt suddenly exhausted. She let the breath out of her mouth.

"I don't think I can tell you," she said.

He stirred a little on the edge of the mattress. "Sweetheart, if it's a sin, then you have to tell me. Are you nervous? You don't have to be nervous with me, you know that, don't you?"

She nodded. "I'm scared."

"You're scared? What of? About being sick or the hospital? Alice can come over here tomorrow. We can give her the Medal then. She couldn't come to the hospital because the rule is no children."

"No, I don't mean that. I mean, I'm scared of when she is at her house."

He was quiet and looked down at her.

"What are you talking about, Marnie?"

Had he gotten mad at her all of a sudden? She couldn't tell. If he was mad, she couldn't tell him.

"Oh, nothing. Father, I don't want to talk anymore. I just want to go to sleep now."

There was a look on his face that she could not make out.

"Are you scared of me, Marnie?" he asked her.

Why would he think that? She didn't think she ever sounded scared of him.

"No, no, I'm not."

"Are you mad at me for any reason?"

"No!" She knew what he was doing now. Her eyes started to water and she would cry in a minute. "No, I'm not mad at anybody."

"I'm sorry, honey," he said right away, and she could hear that he wasn't mad at all. "You must be so tired," he said. "Let me turn the lamp off and you can get some sleep."

She clutched at his arm. "But stay here for a while until I fall asleep?"

"Sure, honey, I can do that." He leaned over and turned off the lamp. The lamplight from the living room shone comfortably in, and Marnie's mother called, "John?"

"We're okay, Cathy, I'm going to stay with Marnie for a little while."

The soft darkness broken by the light of the living room and the one window returned the feeling of comfort and solid earth that Marnie felt had been lost. She was wide awake now.

She whispered, "Father John?"

He whispered back, not quite so softly, "Yes, Marnie?"

"It's Mr. Paddy. I don't know him, though, really."

"Oh, yes?"

"Mommy said if he comes over to Alice's, I have to come right home. And he won't let Alice come back with me."

"Oh, I see. So you don't get to play as much if he comes over."

"Yeah."

John didn't say anything else, so she started again. "Mommy said don't stay there if he's there. She said come right home if he comes over."

"Well, that's probably a good idea. You don't know him very well."

"Yes, but Alice knows him. And Alice's mother lets him come over when she's not there."

"Oh, I see. Isn't anybody there?"

"I don't know. Sometimes her grandpa. Sometimes Lucille babysits or Miss Carrie."

Father John seemed to get very still where he sat. "Do you go over there when Lucille is there?"

"No, just Miss Carrie."

"Well, can't you stay if Miss Carrie is there?"

He didn't seem to understand anything she was trying to say. "No, Miss Carrie takes Baby Angie in the kitchen, and then Mr. Paddy goes upstairs. And then he calls for Alice to come up."

"He does *what*?"

"I'm sorry!" Marnie began to cry. "I'm sorry!"

Marnie's mother came to the doorway and said, "What's the matter? What's going on?"

John turned to her. "I think tomorrow I'd better talk to Alice's mother after all."

"What'd she say?"

"I'm sorry," Marnie said again, still crying.

"All right, now, that's enough of that," her mother said. Unlike with the nurse at the hospital, when her mother spoke that way it always only made Marnie want to cry harder, which right now she couldn't help doing. "Go on, John, let me settle her down."

After a few minutes of more brusque talk, several kisses and wiping away tears, Marnie was able to stop crying. Her mother said, "Don't worry. Whatever is the matter, we'll take care of it. You don't have to worry."

"I'm sorry," Marnie said again.

"Well, that's all right. It'll be all right. Now let me hear your prayers, laying down," she said as Marnie began to sit up.

"O My God, I adore Thee," she began. Her mother prayed with her and she heard John's low voice from the living room. "*... Pardon me for the evil I have done this day... Watch over me while I take my rest...Amen.*"

She sighed and turned over to the wall. "Can Father John sit with me some more until I fall to sleep?"

"Sure, honey."

She felt the rise of her mother from the edge of the bed, and in a moment, the heavier but more comfortable weight of her cousin, whose hand she felt smooth her hair and tuck up her blanket. Marnie shut her eyes, ready for sleep, but lying there, they intruded, those things Alice had begun telling her before they got the chicken pox and after. She had not seen anything different but she knew Alice would only tell her the truth. Her mother had not mentioned anything about it, though maybe she wouldn't. And she remembered that her mother was the best person plus the strongest and the most wicked who could scare anybody into not doing anything, even the Martians, which she would have to mention to Roger. And nobody would fool around with her grandmother. But still Alice was not safe and though Father John would speak to someone about something that could be done, that these things were happening was very sickening and she was getting very, very angry over feeling sick and scared about them all of the time.

Then she remembered that there would be an extra Miraculous Medal after all and that she had said a good confession in case she should die before she waked, and that because this was so, things might soon go back like how they had been. If only she could get well. She was going to get well, and be a nurse, and take care of Alice's babies.

As she dropped off to sleep, she thought she could hear Alice crying next door. That might be imagination, though.

Part III: Saturday, April 4th
Alice Smaling

Sometimes Alice wished that Marnie would shut up, but not too often. She loved Marnie. She wanted it to be March again, Easter again, before anybody had to go to Carroll Park for picnics again. She missed her father. And yesterday, in school, about the worst that could happen, had. She was glad that in the morning she had been able to tell Marnie about her father, about Mr. Paddy.

No, really, Marnie was the best girl Alice had ever met or could imagine. She had all the best ideas, and she never seemed to be sad or worried about anything. She was happy and peaceful all the time, "Maybe like an angel," Alice thought, but that wasn't right. Maybe like a saint. They had lots of jokes with words that if you said them one way they were fine and the other way they were bad, and she had told Alice already about how one time she had picked up a penny off of the living room floor and not told anybody but had hidden it in a little box underneath her bed, and she was going to spend it on a bunch of candy some day when she could put a plan of escape from her house into action, perhaps when she turned nine and could cross the street alone.

Where Marnie was loud and brave, Alice was quiet and a scaredy-cat, she thought, but until recently not frightened all the time and of just about everything. She was accomplished in her classroom even more so than Marnie in hers, drawing cursive, subtracting with two rows, having the swiftest—she had learned that word, swiftest—aisle-racing ability during relays of any other girl, telling time on a clock with quarter tills and pasts, and singing anything that anyone asked her to sing. But those things were slipping away from her and they had been for a while now.

Alice had been back at school for a week in some ways, but in most ways she felt she wasn't anywhere. All she could think about was why her daddy had to get drunk all the time and how it made him throw onions at people, and where was he and why didn't he come back. And why did Mr. Paddy have to be there instead.

The Sisters kept looking at her in a curious way. One of them asked her if she had forgotten how to read. She didn't think she could have, but when she looked at the pages of her reader, there were times that she couldn't make the words on the page mean anything. Sometimes they seemed to not stay still. She cried a lot, and yesterday she had gone and wet her pants and everybody was already calling her Smelly before she left, except not Marnie, of course, because Marnie was in the other room and she hadn't been able to tell Marnie about it, and then she realized that even after telling her all the other things, she would not be able to tell Marnie about that. She might even have to run away it was so terrible.

A week ago it had been Holy Saturday and she was nearly done being sick. And just a week before that she had still been enjoying, when she wasn't itching, being polka-dotted in calamine lotion, the only other ornament to her person besides a pair of rhinestone-studded cat's eye glasses. Her mother had said when she first got her glasses in kindergarten that if Alice had to be stone blind at the age of six, at least she could have some fashionable glasses, and Alice very much, even at age six, preferred to be fashionable. She remembered how when she had gotten her glasses and all the children called her Four Eyes, Marnie had assured her she would belt the next person who said it and then Alice had hoped someone would say it, but somehow they knew and nobody did. But Marnie couldn't belt anybody for calling her Smelly. Marnie didn't know it had happened.

Her mother always had the radio on during breakfast on Saturdays. Alice was sitting at the kitchen table and the radio was on and people were praying out of it, in Latin, *Ave Maria* and so on, Hail Mary in the language she believed her mother and grandmother could speak just as she could talk regular, that she was determined to understand the words of, even as now she could read most of them even if she did not pronounce them correctly. She did not know why her mother kept the radio on to the Rosary, nobody had died that she was aware of. She wanted her to turn it off, the heavy sound coming out of it hurting her in some way she could not describe, hurting her deeply inside her head.

It was April now. March was over. If she could make things change, she would have it stay March until Christmas. April was warm and pretty, not hot like swimming pool weather, which Alice hated, but still she wanted it to be March, any month but April.

"Can I go out on the back porch?"

"You may not."

"How about upstairs?"

"You sit right there, young lady."

Her mother was mad and disappointed, or worse than disappointed, but Alice had no idea over what, and she didn't think she could stay there for too much longer. She could not remember needing to get out of a place because of how it sounded, and then she realized that, yes, she had needed to once or twice before she'd gotten the chicken pox, but now the chicken pox was over but it seemed to be worse. She wondered if everything was going to sound like she had to get out of there from now on, like someone in charge was dying. The sounds yesterday of the children laughing and the Sister scolding and the very quiet of the corridor as she waited in somebody else's uniform for her grandmother to come and take her home had had a different quality to them, much stronger, and it had remained to the point where even Baby Angie's gurgling made Alice want to run upstairs once she got home, and shove her head into a pillow, and bite it.

Alice could no longer remember exactly what had happened in the few days before her mother had packed them up and brought them here to live in her grandmother's house. The Pope had died, and the President had died, and adults were never, ever, supposed to get a divorce, but her parents were going to get one. She thought it must be her fault; her mother never did much about it when her father started in on her, and that was the only reason she could think of that she'd let him. And she looked too much like him, with the big split between her front teeth and her dark eyes, "That means you're full of shit up to here," he told her every time with a laugh. Her mother always said, "Jimmy!" after that to make him stop cussing, but he would say it again and again and Alice would try very hard not to laugh about it so her mother wouldn't smack her and the two of them wouldn't start up about her getting smacked and who got to do it.

She liked her father a lot then, though. She didn't mind when he took her to a bar instead of to church on Sundays. She loved the smell of the icy cokes he got her while he had a beer and loved the tinted glass above the bar that glowed ruby and emerald in the darkness, "National Bohemian" and "Pabst" floating backward in their stained glass window signs. This was the kind of thing she'd lie in bed and think about all the time right before they moved, because Alice had been sick again then, not with chicken pox, she wasn't sure what it had been. She could hear Angie downstairs messing around in her playpen and her mother singing "Chances Are" loud in the kitchen, but everybody had stopped coming up to check on Alice and see how she was. Sometimes she'd look out her bedroom window and see her father's car parked on the street. It scared her and though she tried hard, she couldn't make herself feel safe and happy at the sight of it, like it might tuck her in or take her temperature to be sure. A couple of times she noticed a Tip-Top Bread truck where her father's car should have been. She could hear her mother laughing then and the radio playing loud, but still nobody hardly came up for her.

One afternoon her father's car had pulled up when the truck was still there. She didn't know exactly what the matter was about it, but after she heard the sound of the front door close and there was a lot of other noise, things falling down and breaking, and then the door shut again and the bread truck drove away. She heard her father screaming that Alice was his only real daughter and he was going to kill them all, but he didn't do it, though she had been sure he was going to. She heard the front door again, a terrific slam this time, and from her window she could see him get into his car and drive off. Then she heard her mother crying, Alice thought she must be sitting on the bottom step below her bedroom from the sound of it. She cried for a long time but Alice knew better than to go down to her. The sun went down in her room, she was hungry, she needed to go to the bathroom. She pulled the sticky flowered sheet up over her head and hummed to herself for what seemed forever, until she finally fell asleep.

The next day Alice's mother had packed them up and taken them on the bus into town. At the bus station they all piled into a cab coated with the man-and-cigarette smell that was in all the city cabs, but as soon as they pulled in front of her grandmother's house the comfort of the cab changed to a sick feeling she understood well but didn't have the words for.

Her grandmother had come running out into the street yelling at her mother to tell her what-all was the matter, and as she pulled the baby out of the car her mother said something in that shorthand she spoke through closed teeth when she didn't want Alice to understand, so Alice never did figure out if it was because of the man in the bread truck or because of her. They went inside and sat down to dinner as if they had been coming home to that house every night all of their lives. Her mother never said another word about it, not then or after. Alice changed schools and churches and got new friends and everybody acted like that was all right, the way things should have worked out. And Alice had gotten Marnie.

Mostly it all had been all right, but she missed her father so much sometimes it made her stomach hurt. It was funny that at first he still got to come and see them. Every week or couple of weeks or so he'd pick her up and take her someplace, but then he'd get drunk and by the time he got her back home her mother would be waiting in the doorway and there would be another big fight. It had been a long time, though, since they had gone to the movies with Marnie, and since then Alice had started having nightmares. Bluto from the Popeye cartoons would scream at her, or "The Tingler" from "Monday Afternoon at the Movies" on TV would chase her and catch her, or her grandfather would turn into a big monster running behind her through prehistoric-sized lilies at the funeral parlor. She always cried in her sleep and her mother would have to come and wake her up. Sometimes she held Alice close, crooning, "It's ok, my pumpkinette," and sometimes she yelled, "Oh, for God's sake, will you shut up and go to sleep!" Once during one of the dreams Alice threw up all over herself. Her mother came into her room in the dark and changed the sheets and never said a word. Alice walked around on her tiptoes for about three days after that, until last week Sister at school told her to use her whole foot, she'd get flat arches.

Now she knew she had to get out of the kitchen, away from that radio, and knew just as surely that she could not do it. She looked hopelessly at her mother, put her head in her hands, and began to kick her legs away from the seat of the chair.

"Pray some," her mother suggested. That sounded like a good idea, but after the first couple of words she got lost. She went for the way it sounded.

"Mrrrowww, mrrrowww, mrrowww," she intoned, her eyes closed as they were always when she was communing with G.o.d. She could not bring herself to say *God* even when she was talking about him or to him, in the exact same way that everybody she knew could not say *hell*, even when they were not cussing. Her mother made a noise and Alice opened her eyes again.

"Go on out a while," her mother said, and her eyes filled with water and her nose went a deep red.

Alice jumped up and hurtled herself out the door. Marnie wasn't outside, but when she looked down the yard, there was Mr. Paddy, his hand on the gate.

At first she did not recognize him and thought it was her father who had come back, and she called out, "Hi, Daddy!" and rushed to the screen door, but stopped hard when she realized who it was.

She thought immediately of the skin of an onion, not the crispy brown outer skin but that thin, sticky one on the inside, and at that moment something happened to her that had happened a few times now since Easter. She was no longer at the back door on Saturday morning, but she was back in last week, last Saturday, Holy Saturday, and it was not morning but late afternoon, and she was not standing at the back door but sitting at the kitchen table, and not, she felt, in her mind, but there as she had been and yet framed in a kind of circle, the edges comprised of darkness and she was not remembering last Saturday, Holy Saturday, but living in it again:

She was just about healed-up from the chicken pox that had covered her from the crest of her brown hair to the soles of her dirty feet, though she could not go out and not go to Church until every last scab was gone. The Saturday before, she had been so ill the doctor had come and said, Stay in bed and don't be around anyone for at least a week. But on Holy Saturday, she sat in her underpants at the kitchen table, eating supper alone in the late afternoon. She hadn't been allowed to sit at the big table all week, but Mommy said if she hurried up and got better, then she wouldn't have to keep sitting at the little table with Baby Angie, and now she was at the big table, so she knew she was almost done.

At the big table you got to serve yourself from the serving dishes if you were very careful not to spill and drink a cup of hot tea with lots of sugar and Pet Evaporated Milk in it, and watch Grandpa dip his green onions into his jar of horseradish and maybe or maybe not fork out one of the pickled pig's feet from the jar, and try not to snort when he fell asleep into his mashed potatoes or when Grandma set her teeth in her napkin, and all of that was fine and regular. But it was nice to be by herself, too, to have the whole table to herself, because she still felt a little weak and a little stupid and was still too sick to mind either very much. Her mind was only half on the Easter Bunny and whether or not she would get a basket, and half that Baby Angie would be taken to church and give her a break for a change.

The last light of dusk was beginning to settle in. She could see out the back door of her grandmother's house that the shadow that showed up at some time at the end or the beginning of the end of every day had made its way down the cement walk, up over the gate, across the narrow alley, and up the rusty corrugated steel wall of the garage opposite Marnie's yard, with some sun bright at the top. The movement of that light on all that she could see from where she sat was constant and good as the stars. Better, since from their house you could never see hardly any stars, not like they could down in Glen Burnie when they had practically lived in the country and there were whole yards full of corn in the summer, right over beyond the dirt alley. Here there were always street lamps, neon signs, and the headlights of cars and things always pulling out, never stopping where they were it seemed to her. The parked cars seemed to sit there and never go anywhere.

She was feeling pretty full, kicking her feet to the sound of Grandpa snoring up in the back bedroom, letting the heel of her foot bounce against the chair leg in time with the sound. She was almost ready to ask to leave the table and join her grandmother in the living room, where she could hear the television but didn't know what it was. Maybe Jackie Gleason. Jackie Gleason made her feel sick. She didn't know. Maybe that lady who made recipes with all the ingredients in the little glass dishes. No, that was the daytime.

Her mother puttered across the kitchen in housecoat and slippers, clearing away the food, fixing the iced tea for everybody else's supper later, putting away dishes, humming "Chances Are." She stopped every once in a while and smiled blankly at her, but Alice didn't mind that too much.

She did want to get done and out of the kitchen before her father might come by. You never knew when he would, but for some reason Saturdays he did, although right before Easter, she didn't know. He wasn't Catholic and so she didn't know if Holy Saturday was anything as far as he was concerned. That last Saturday he had come over, he had taken her and Marnie to see *The Lilies of the Field,* after which he had gotten drunk and they had gotten chicken pox. Alice had loved that day and hoped something like that could happen again. But after the chicken pox and how mad her mother had gotten, probably not.

"Mommy, is Daddy coming over tonight a while?"

"I don't know, honey. He damned well better not be."

Her mother had shrugged as if something itched her and Alice wondered if she might get the chicken pox as well, or even scarlet fever like Marnie. That would be interesting, she thought, and, as if reading her mind, her mother snapped her fingers twice and said, "Finish up, now," in that singsong way she had. "I've got to give you another bath and put on calamine lotion before you go back to bed and I don't want to be doing it at midnight."

"It's only a quarter past four," Alice muttered.

"What was that, Miss?"

"Nothing," she answered, trying to make it loud enough but not sound flip.

"It'd better be nothing," her mother said, and went back to cleaning up.

Alice continued with her plate of tuna casserole, ending by eating the top crust of potato chips and pushing the canned green beans to the outer edges where she hoped they would look less numerous. She wrapped the front of her ankles around the chrome legs of her chair, flinching a little at the cold and feeling the sticky pull of her thighs on the vinyl seat. She leaned against the metal edge of the red Formica tabletop and picked up the orange she had saved especially and that rested now on the table above her dinner plate. She slid her short thumbnail near the belly button of the orange, but her fingers were still so covered with sores she couldn't get the nail in. She scratched her chin once, turned the orange upside down, and picked off the little green bud from the stem end. Poking her thumb deep in the small white depression, she pulled as hard as she could, but even with such a good opening she didn't have the strength to pull off more than a small section of skin. Some juice that seeped from the indentation slid into one of the sores on her index finger and stung a little. She tried one more time, but it was no good, she couldn't pull it off.

"Mommy, I can't get it," she called out.

"Can't get what?" Her mother looked around. "Well, just pull on it some more."

"I can't, I tried, it's too stiff."

"Too stiff?" Her mother laughed in that way that always made Alice feel good and bad at the same time. "Here, let me see."

She came over and took the orange. "I see all those green beans, Miss."

Alice said nothing, but watched as she slid her long, painted thumbnail under one of the grooves Alice had already made. She pushed her thumb around in a circle, slowly creating a curl of orange skin, covering the length of her thumb with tiny white flakes of pith. Alice held her breath, listening to the skin cracking apart and hoping her mother would make it, one solid curl of orange peel. She reached the bottom of the orange and without a pause yanked off the last little bit.

"There you go," she winked, handing the fruit back.

"Can I keep the peel, too?" Alice blurted. She hadn't meant to ask, but now that the question was out of her mouth, she held her breath again and waited.

"What do you want with that? It'll just get orange juice all over everything."

Alice knew that sound. If she answered right, not too sneaky and not too innocent, she could keep it. "No, it won't, I promise, I'll be really careful."

"Well, what do you want it for?"

Alice knew it had to be something that would sound reasonable. It would not sound reasonable if she said that the curl of orange skin made her want to grow up to be exactly like her mother, looking beautiful even in a housecoat, looking smart enough to split open an orange with pointy red nails and then wink at you like she was the only person in the world who could do it. It had to be something plain and practical.

She had it. "It's from this project book where you take and keep some orange peel until it's really hard and then make candy out of it. Sister said we could do it at school and she'd help us, but we have to get the peels from home first. Everybody's gonna bring some." She waited as her mother considered, the bumpy orange skin aloft in the balance.

"Well, ok, I guess. Just don't let me catch you keeping it under your pillow or something, hear me? I'll wrap it up in some wax paper after while."

"Yes, ma'am." Alice let out her breath and smiled as her mother dropped the peel into her open hand. She pushed the edges back together until it made a whole empty orange, and placed it carefully next to her plate in the middle of a thin rod of sun slanting in from the side window. As she separated each section of fruit and sucked the rippled meat from the paper of its inner wrap, she kept an eye on the orange peel shell, as if it might disappear somehow, and thought of all the hiding places she could put the skin where nobody would find it.

She started to hum very quietly, the way she used to when she ate something especially delicious, before her mother had decided she was old enough to have the manners not to sing while she was eating.

She saw but didn't immediately register the shadow of someone blocking the remaining light coming in the back door. The next moment she made out her father's form and heard him rattle the wooden screen, trying to skip the metal latch. She jumped at the same time her mother flinched. They both waited, but not, Alice knew, for the same thing.

"Let me in!" he finally screamed through the screen. "Let me in there, goddamn it to hell!"

Alice thought she better escape to the front room, but the training that kept her seated until she had permission to get up made her wait too long. He had already spotted her through the screen by the time she had made up her mind to run, and screamed even louder, "Look it there! Look at her staring at me like she don't have good sense! You'd goddamned better get out here and let me in, Agnes!"

Alice passed these words through her mind again in the time it took him to force the frame of the screen door up and off the metal latch. She wondered if she should mention to her mother later that a metal latch probably wasn't enough to keep out a drunken man. On the other hand, Alice had already noted more than once that it seemed there was something about all the yelling and hitting her mother liked a little. It could be exciting, she thought so too, for a while. As he charged two steps through the back porch and into the open door of the kitchen, though, she felt only the far-away numbness that was unexpected and yet quite familiar, a kind she had often bitten through the skin on her fingers from and not even felt and always forgot she had done until the next time she did it.

Her mother moved away from the sink and stood next to her, not saying anything and not telling her what to do. Everything was starting to look dark to Alice and though her father kept screaming she could no longer make him out very clearly. She could hear Angie upstairs crying in her new booster bed, and then her mother shouted, "Now look what you've done! The baby's awake!" as if that were the worst thing that could happen. Her grandfather moaned in his sleep and then his snoring commenced to fall again down the back stairs.

Her grandmother hustled in from the front room.

"What do you think you're doing here, you lousy no-good!" she squeaked in her pruney voice. "This is my house! You can't come in here like Judas Priest and order people around!"

She picked up the phone that sat atop the yellow metal stand behind the table. "I'm calling the patrol car!" She spun a bulbous index finger around the zero on the telephone dial.

Alice's mother turned her back on this production and her guns on Alice's father. "What do you want, you drunken son-of-a-bitch?" as calmly as if she were asking him to hand her the Yellow Pages.

He shut up then for a moment, wiping his mouth with the back of his left hand, looking a little like he didn't know. His chest lifted and he lurched against the chair at the end of the kitchen table opposite Alice.

"I want my goddamned daughters!" he heaved finally, as if it had come to him in a flash what he was doing there. "I want them, goddamn it! I want this one!" he screamed, lurching at Alice.

He toppled over the back of the chair at the end of the table, righted himself, and gaped around the room. He spotted the pile of onions sitting on the counter and picked up one whose outer brown skin had already been peeled off. He stared down at it, weaving a little harder, and belched. Alice giggled loud, she couldn't help it, and then she immediately clapped one horrified hand over her mouth and stared at him with her eyes wide and good so that he'd know she thought it was a joke he meant to do, that she wasn't laughing at him, that she remembered the days when he'd have laughed and then belched some more. But he couldn't see into all that, she could tell he was too drunk for it. He glared at her, seemed to try to focus and say something else, but contented himself with staring at the onion again. Then he drew it back over his shoulder like a baseball—she wondered for a moment if you could use an onion for a baseball if you didn't have one—and then brought his arm back forward, leading with his index finger, accusing her, the onion cupped in the palm of his hand.

"She's mine!" he screamed. "She's always been mine! I don't even know about the other one! You filthy whore, you whore, you whore...."

He cried then. He didn't wail in the embarrassing drunken way she was used to, but sobbed down his extended arm the way she always used to do when she was five and fell down on the cement. Watching him like that made her happy for a minute. Then she felt frightened and suddenly itched terribly but didn't dare to scratch.

"You'll never get your hands on my daughter," her mother spat through her teeth, but in a way that made it sound to Alice like she didn't mean it, she said it the way they say it on television when the ending turns out right. But when she peeked over to see, there was such ferocity in her mother's eyes that for a moment she did believe that it was for her, Alice, and not to kick her father out again and to win.

At once he stopped sobbing and wiped the back of his left hand, the one holding the onion, across his snotty nose. "No," he said, looking hard at Alice. "I'll go, but I won't leave until I know she doesn't want to come with me. She has to say it." The pleading in his eyes seemed to reach across to her, crushing her chest and making the sores on her body itch more desperately.

Her mother didn't answer him. She turned to Alice and asked, "Well? Who do you want to go with? Him or me?"

They all waited for her answer, her father with his red cheeks crusted in stubble, her mother's lips pinched together and daring Alice to open her mouth to answer the question, her grandmother interested, like a parrot.

She couldn't do it. She burst into tears. Her mother's voice came through them, then, kinder this time. "Who do you want to go with, Alice?"

She had to say something, and there was nothing else she could say. "I want to go with both of you!"

They were all quiet then, and Alice felt stupid and clumsy, ugly, like Baby Angie still crying upstairs. Still, somehow this had been the right answer.

"Well?" her mother demanded. "Well, Mr. Loudmouth, are you happy now? Jesus, Mary, and Joseph!" she said mostly under her breath, and turned her head to the side and licked one corner of her mouth with the tip of her tongue.

Crumpled halfway now over the rim of the red vinyl chair, her father looked like the air inside him was being let out from somewhere in his body and his crimson skin seemed to be wrinkling in time with the escaping breath. After a moment, though, he straightened up, looked squarely at Alice, and then drew the peeled onion back again and hurled it at her with all his strength. He was still drunk enough, though, that instead of taking out her eye, the onion slammed into the middle of the table and slid down its length, collapsed into the edge of her plate, and splashed her hand and face with onion juice. The impact toppled the orange peel over on to the red Formica in a slanted curl.

Afterwards there seemed to be a moment when her mother or somebody would do something to make sure she was all right, but again nothing happened. For that small, slow time, all of them stared at the onion, lying in a mess on the table, as if it and not the terrible rendering of her family had caused what her grandmother was sure in a minute to classify as all the commotion. Alice had stopped crying, but her eyes were tearing up again from where some of the onion juice had hit them, and there were drops of onion juice on the lenses of her glasses. She could see the translucent, filmy inner skin of the top layer of the onion separated from the layer underneath and clinging to the skin of her orange.

Her mother was the first to say something. "Are you satisfied now? Get out," she commanded him in a voice flat but one that Alice thought neither Joseph, nor Mary, nor Jesus would have defied. Her father looked a last time at Alice, his eyes clear, red, and full of a promise she wanted to snatch before it was taken away. He turned then and walked out, through the kitchen door, off the back porch, and down the walk. She could see the top of his head as he paused to let himself out the back gate. Then he was gone.

Her grandmother only muttered, "I never in my life," as the back door slammed after Alice's father. The patrol squad was hammering at the front door, but Alice knew her grandmother would make something up and they'd go. Her mother stood motionless next to her for another fifteen seconds, then sighed robustly and said in the same singsong voice she had used before, "Honest to truth! Time to get that bath started, Miss." She leaned over the table without looking at Alice, picked up her dinner plate, and swept the orange peel and smashed onion across the table's surface onto the plate. Alice didn't move. Her mother didn't repeat her command. She dumped the contents of the plate into the full garbage pail, where the orange peel and onion sank into a heap of coffee grounds and green beans.

Alice's whole body had felt so tight she thought she might not ever feel loose again in her life. Her thoughts came up from that faraway place, as if they'd been pushed upstairs and inside the socks and pillowcases stuffed into one of the bedroom drawers. Her orange peel was lost, she knew that. As she squinted to make out the splotches of orange in the mess of garbage, she decided that she couldn't have kept it any more anyway, not after the skin of the onion had touched it. She tried for a second to want another one, but knew in the way she knew that she would never see her father again that another one would be no good.

I'll hold it in my eyes, she had said to herself. That had sounded good. It'll be like a movie, she said, like *Lilies of the Field,* except Daddy came and threw an onion at my eye and I almost went blind while I had the chicken pox. This was a decision, the way she would tell it to herself and Marnie and anyone else forever after.

And she began to come back to herself, and her father was gone and so were the chicken pox, her hand was on the screen door, she had already wet herself at school the day before, and her body was every bit as tight as it had felt when she sat in the kitchen with her mother and her father a week ago, but for a moment, she was not sure when it was, which Saturday it was. There were coffee grounds and eggshells in the garbage pail this morning, too, but it seemed there were always coffee grounds and eggshells there. Alice didn't know why they always were at the top. She had considered this for a happy, unentailed moment this morning as well, before the rush and flood of shame returned, as it would, she imagined, always return for the rest of her life. She had disgraced herself, she had not been able to help it, and her mother knew it, and there was nothing to be done. She didn't seem to want to be around Alice at all, and Alice had to get out, just get out, and she had jumped up to the door, and called for her daddy, and flung herself out, and she looked down the walk and it was Mr. Paddy, his hand on the gate, there he still was.

And she knew then that remembering anything else whether she wanted to or not was not going to make him go away. So, maybe she would try to do it on purpose next time.

I'm going to tell Daddy about him, was all she thought as she watched Mr. Paddy beckon with his bad hand, the one that looked like an animal. She went out the door, letting it slam, and walked slowly down the pavement toward him, her eyes on the sidewalk. He had never come by their house this early in the day before. Maybe because it was Saturday.

"Hello, Alice," he said. "How are you this morning?"

"Fine," she said, feeling sick and cold, and then, realizing she was being rude, she said, "Thank you very much." He didn't say anything else, but kept looking at her in that way that made her feel very bad all over, and to counteract this, she said, inanely, "The Pope died."

He smiled, a very nice smile, and she felt better. "Yes, I had heard that," he said. "That's been a while now. That was bad, that was."

And then Marnie's mother, Miss Catherine, came out back and threw an area rug up on to the clothes line. She looked over at Alice in the yard with a look that seemed very mad to Alice, and then she said, "Good morning, Alice. I think you had better go back inside now."

Alice hung her head. Miss Catherine didn't seem to want to have anything to do with her, either.

Then her mother came out on to their back porch and waved to Paddy Dolan.

"How are you?" she called out in her gayest voice. "Why don't you come on in and have a cup of coffee for a minute?" She looked over and saw Marnie's mother then, and turned red. "Oh!" she said, "I didn't know you were there—I'm sorry, I didn't mean to interrupt."

"No, I was just asking Alice if she'd like to come over and play with Marnie this afternoon. She was going to come in and ask you, weren't you, hon?" Alice didn't think she had heard Miss Catherine say anything of the kind, but she didn't know. She must not have heard right.

"And I was just coming by to say we'll have that picnic this afternoon, shall we? What a coincidence," Mr. Paddy said, with the strangest smile at Miss Catherine Alice had ever seen.

Miss Catherine returned the smile with a look that made Alice think, *I'm going to learn how to do that,* and she said, "Thank you, but no thank you." Alice was going to learn how to say that, too.

Miss Catherine turned to Alice and her mother. "The doctor said Marnie can play this afternoon. But maybe she can come over now for a little while, too."

Alice looked up at her mother, who looked a little helpless, and down at Mr. Paddy, who was still staring at Miss Catherine with his mouth slightly open.

"Go on in and come around the front," Miss Catherine said, taking Alice's mother's silence for yes. "That way you can bring a doll or what you want."

But it seemed to Alice that Miss Catherine didn't actually look at anybody, that she wasn't talking to her, Alice, and that it might be that none of them were really there after all, that maybe this was happening just like last Saturday had just happened all over again except that Alice did not remember this part. But then it was also true that Marnie's mother was a very big person to Alice's mind. She was skinny except for her backside and she had kind of flappy elbows which Alice's mother always said in private made her look like the stuck-up widow she was, but Alice thought of her as very big, almost as big as Mr. Paddy, and she knew that her own mother's harshness was no match against her, and that felt real, so this all was probably not imagination after all. She wondered for just a moment if then that meant that maybe all the part about her daddy had in that case been imagination. She felt sick.

But she ran into the house without another word or look down the yard, taking her mother's silence at Miss Catherine's request also as permission, and stopped only to pick up her jacks set and her paddle ball before slamming out of the front door and flying into Marnie's house.

Miss Catherine met her there and took her by the elbow, but it didn't hurt. "What were you talking with Mr. Paddy about?" she asked.

Alice thought she must be in trouble but could not understand how Miss Catherine could know why. She said, "Nothing. He had just told me hello, and I had told him about the Pope being dead."

Miss Catherine relaxed her hand and said, "Oh, all right. But you listen to me, now, you hear me? You come on over here if he comes over the house, it doesn't matter when. Just come on over."

This made Alice feel good, but also sick, because she knew she was not in trouble but also that as much as she might want to, she would never be able to do it. Then Marnie came, as Alice thought, jumping into the living room, and shouting, "What did you bring? I have a new baby from Father John! Come on, let's play house!"

Alice never minded playing house with Marnie because she fairly divided up who had to be the mother and who the father and always remembered which one of them had been the mother last. Sadly, today it was Alice's turn to be the father, but they had given themselves very respectable and satisfying names, one of which was Mr. John Martin, which she didn't mind at all because Father John was Marnie's cousin and Alice was always very impressed by that because she did not know you could have a cousin that old. He was a very, very nice man. They had both agreed that they were going to marry him when they grew up and would take turns being his wife, and then, when they found out he could not have a wife, his housekeeper.

"My goodness! What a nice, big, fat baby I have here, Mrs. Martin!" Alice said, and the girls spent an hour taking the doll's clothes off and on and inspecting the dresses and diapers that had come with it in its case.

"I got it for Easter," Marnie explained, and when Alice suggested that Easter was way back last week she said, "I know. They forgot to give it to me and Mommy found it up in the cupboard this morning. She laughed and laughed! I cried at first, because you know what?"

"What?"

"Don't you think it was so lonely all that whole time, sitting in the cupboard? Because Father John brought it for a trick a long time ago and it had to sit in there longer than the Easter clothes." They had decided between them that although it was very definitely true about Santa, the Easter bunny had to be a fake. "Because all the chocolate will melt in April," Marnie said, and Alice had nodded in agreement, but she added, "Except not this year because it's March." And then she added, "But still, if he's a fake, he would be a fake this year too."

Marnie said, "Yes. He would."

Marnie's new baby had lovely shoes. Alice began to tie up the laces of one of them. She wanted to ask Marnie if she knew about yesterday and what she thought about it, but couldn't do it. Marnie didn't seem like she knew, so maybe they would never have to talk about it.

"How come your Mommy don't like Mr. Paddy?" she asked at last.

"Mmm-mm. She never told me nothing about him, except don't go to his store when I said once, Let's go up Dolan's because we had forgot to get some cans and she said No, I don't never go up there anyways. I said Why and she said Mind your own business."

Alice thought about that a while, couldn't make anything of it, and then forgot all about it, as if they had not been speaking of Mr. Paddy ever at all.

"Let's play Sisters and sing *Amen*!" she said, and they dropped the doll, and went hunting for the big white napkins they used to turn themselves into small, serious German-speaking nuns who lived in the desert and let a beautiful black man eat white bread and milk at their table.

They heard the knock on the door without registering it. Miss Catherine walked through from the kitchen, saying, "I wonder who that is on a Saturday?" In another moment, Alice's mother was standing in the doorway of the middle room.

"Come on, Alice. It's time to go now."

Alice barely looked up, and began, "Please can I stay a little more while?"

"Alice, come on, we're going."

"Please? Just two more minutes."

"Alice."

She lifted her head, as if to forestall something. Miss Catherine came to the kitchen doorway and crossed her arms in front of her but this did not seem to deter Alice's mother.

"It's time to go, right now. Mr. Paddy is waiting for us and we're going for a picnic in Carroll Park for lunch. You don't want to make Mr. Paddy wait, do you? That would not be nice."

Alice didn't like the staccato production of all of these words. *That-would-not-be-nice* sounded like somebody was going to get hit, or somewhere someone was already getting hit. She looked at Marnie, the tip of whose nose was somewhere deep between her bent knees, her arms folded around them.

She pulled herself to her feet, mumbled, "Yes, ma'am," and went toward the door.

Marnie didn't follow but her mother walked through with them. "So I'll come around then, ten minutes to two, and get Alice," she said.

Alice's mother said nothing but moved her through the vestibule with the flat of one hand. Paddy Dolan was waiting by their steps, smoking.

"Look who it is, the little lass, the little beauty," and he produced a wolf-whistle that made Alice sick. She heard Miss Catherine say, "Tuh!" behind them.

"Hello, Mr. Paddy," she said.

He guffawed and slapped the hand with the cigarette over one knee. "Hello, there, my angel Alice," he said, but stopped at the sound of a window sash being raised.

"Get on inside," Alice's mother snapped to her, and then to Mr. Dolan, "We'll be just a minute!" and steered Alice up the steps and through the door.

"But it's not even lunch—" Alice said when they reached the living room.

"I know it's not. The picnic is going to be lunch."

"But what are we going to do until then? I'm not hungry."

"We'll, I don't know, we'll relax on a blanket. You can swing on the swings and all."

They were upstairs. "But it's cold outside."

"Then put on a sweater."

"But you don't wear a sweater to a picnic."

"Then don't wear one!" Her mother pulled some clothes out of the bottom drawer where her shorts and everything were. "Wear these! And stop back-talking me!" Baby Angie began to cry in the crib. "Oh, for God's sake, now look—" She hauled the baby up over the bars and put her down on the bed, giving Alice a look. "What are you waiting on?"

"Nothing."

"Nothing what?" She did not wait for an answer.

In the time it took for Alice to change clothes, Angie had a new diaper and had been put in a long sweater set and shoes and a hat. Her face was red and she looked warm. Alice stood shivering in her sleeveless shirt and shorts and said maybe she would have a sweater after all.

"Too late. Get downstairs."

"But—"

"But me no buts, Miss, or you'll get what's coming to you."

Alice saw that her eyes were nearly boiling over. She hung her head and followed her down the back stairs and ever closer to the door where the stroller and Mr. Paddy waited by the steps, the slow tears and gulping crying beginning to leak out of her, in her head the voice her own but not her own saying, "*Idontwantto Idontwantto Idontwantto.*"

No, she would never, she would never. When she got big enough—but here, imagination failed her. Something would happen, even if she could not stop the waiting for it to happen, not stop thinking of how to stop it, not crying over anything that nobody would ever cry about all the time. And then she did cry out loud, one short wail that her mother pretended not to notice.

When they got to the bottom, Mr. Paddy was in the kitchen with her grandmother, and she followed her mother in, still half-crying and still trying to stop.

"There she goes again," he said in her direction, with his harsh, humorless laugh.

"For heaven's sake, Paddy," her grandmother said. "She's just a child. Children cry." She stood up. "I'm going to get lunch together, thanks for coming by," addressing this straight at him.

"Oh, but," her mother began, but her grandmother interrupted. "We'd love to have you some other time, but this noon isn't the best. Thanks again for coming."

He said nothing but looked at Alice in a way that she believed meant there was something else she would not escape coming, and her mother looked at her like the trouble-maker she obviously thought her to be.

"Let's go," her mother said.

"Agnes, just a minute," her grandmother answered, and said to Mr. Paddy, "Thanks for coming by now, have a nice time at the park. Agnes and the girls will be out in a minute."

She stood in the middle of the floor until they heard the front screen door wheeze itself shut behind him and then she went in briskly to the living room and shut and locked the inside vestibule door. They followed her.

"Mother—"her mother began.

"Agnes, I don't want to hear it. You can spend time with who you want to spend time with, but that man does not come into my house again, and he does not speak to my granddaughter again. If I find you left him alone with her for five seconds, you'll have me to deal with and I don't mean maybe. I never in my life."

She gave Alice's mother a look as near to sensible as Alice had ever seen her give, and realized suddenly that her parrot-stance was some kind of—she didn't know what to call it, maybe like a costume made out of looks rather than clothes. She didn't know why her grandmother wore it, but there was something else under there, something Alice believed would put up with certain things and not stand for others. She wanted to know why it was that her own mother would put up with certain things and never not stand for others. Alice did not love her grandmother very much, but she felt a little safer, and that felt better than the nothing had before.

"Come on, Alice," her grandmother said. "You can help me in the kitchen."

"No," her mother said. "We were invited on a picnic and we are going on a picnic."

"What did I just say?" Her grandmother's voice raised to the squeaky pitch it held when she meant to be loud.

"These are my children and I am not a child. I will do what I like and I will see who I like even if it's not here, and they will come with me. We are going."

Her grandmother clearly had not given in, but shrugged her shoulders and said, "All right. All right. Just don't come crying to me," she said. "Don't come crying to me when he's the last man on earth who will take a decent look at you."

"Come on, Alice," her mother said. "Mr. Paddy is waiting."

The sun was shining down on them in the park, bright and hot as if it were summer. She could see the heat of noon shimmering in the air almost as if it were July, and in July she would recognize the sight of that shimmering and how it always meant she would not remember anything for a good long while afterward. She played on the swings and fell off them, and ran around by herself and fell down, and watched her mother and Mr. Paddy kiss in public laying down on the blanket while she moved the stroller with Angie back and forth and did her best to make sure Angie did not fall out of it, though she had run over her own foot to keep that from happening, keeping her back turned on them most of the time but needing to look some of the time. She had seen Mr. Paddy's hand slip up the back of her mother's blouse and move around to the front and her mother pull away and laugh, and say, "Oh, you!" and thought she would die from seeing it.

Her mother got up to a sitting position and straightened her hair and Mr. Paddy leaned next to her on one elbow. It was like a movie Alice had seen on Monday Afternoon at the Movies, except the two people were a whole lot younger. Mr. Paddy was looking straight at Alice.

"Come on, then, lass," he said. "You better get on them swings again."

"Oh, Paddy, what a nice idea. Why don't you push her this time, Pat? At least then she might have a chance at staying on them!"

They both laughed. Mr. Paddy walked behind her, as he always did, and gave the low whistle audible only to herself, as he always did, and said, "Up with you, neeve-lass" as he always did. Unlike after school, however, because she was not wearing a dress, he could not pull her skirt out from under her seat as he otherwise always did and let his hand rest too long between her bottom and the seat.

The words he said every time she swung back in front of him were unknown to her, though she had memorized them to repeat to Marnie, who would also not know what they meant when she heard them. He said them over and over until at last she began to drag her legs on the ground to stop the swing.

"What's the matter, lass, are you done?"

She didn't answer him, but ran back over to her mother, who was still sitting on the blanket, gazing at Angie in the stroller, and absently said Wasn't that nice and all.

"I'm hungry. Aren't we going to go home to eat with Grandma?"

"We'll stop for something on the way home."

She said they had better get ready and Alice better go to the restroom before the walk.

And Alice thought she heard herself crying out, all at once as if a dam had burst but the dam were very far away, as if it were someone else *I don't want to, I don't want to, I don't want to* but found that her mother was merely looking at her and realized she had not made a sound.

"I don't want to go to that one."

"Well, for heaven's sake! It's just a bathroom! For pity's sake, can't you just be a good girl? Are you scared to go by yourself?" She turned her head towards him and said, "Paddy, go on and take her over. She doesn't like the outdoors bathrooms, somebody might be in there, you know."

She turned back to Alice, "See? Mr. Paddy is going to walk you over there. It's right there!"

Mr. Paddy answered, "Agnes, you take her," but he looked down at Alice as if he were saying silently between them, "You see? I am giving you a chance." And he added aloud, "I'll stay with the baby."

"You'll stay with the baby!" Her mother laughed like a hyena. "What you don't know about babies! She'll wind up spitting up all over your nice shirt. Besides, I don't want to get up, my legs are asleep." She blinked her eyes.

He chuckled and looked at Alice, saying to some place inside her, *See there*? Aloud he said, "Well, I guess it's you and me, little girl, isn't it?"

"But I don't have to." Alice could only whisper it.

"Alice," her mother interrupted, "we are going to a nice restaurant and you need to use the bathroom before we go. Do not make me say it again. Paddy, hand me down the baby."

So Alice turned and walked the impossible stretch of lawn toward the park restroom building, in front of the nets and the people playing and the dogs running around and the baseball game far off in the distance. She passed a lamppost that she was not to know Paddy was well acquainted with, and she did not see him toss his cigarette over to the base of it. The thing she was most aware of was the blinding light of the sun, and how it seemed to make everything look like it was made of Tupperware. And beyond that, the weight of him walking behind her, whistling though a circle in his mouth. "SSSsss, sss-sss-sss-sss."

From this point she would never be sure what the matter had been, what she had thought was the matter, or what the matter had turned out to be. She began to hear the song in her head, "*Amen! Sing it over*!" but it did not cheer her up, it was that she simply could not turn it off. Mr. Paddy stayed right behind her, seemingly not at all bothered at how slowly she was going, even when she heard her mother call, "Get along, you two!" He was saying something else, something very low as they walked, but she could not understand it, something that sounded like it had the word *neeveneeve* in it.

They got to the door, and she turned to look back. He was right behind her, her face nearly in his stomach, blocking her view of the door and the lawn beyond it. She stepped to the side of him and saw her mother, still sitting, bending over Baby Angie where she lay on the blanket. She could hear her saying, "Where's the baby? Where's Baby Angie? Where's my girl?" and then saw her bend down and blow into Angie's belly.

And then, "Come on, girl, I don't have all day to wait," Mr. Paddy was saying in a voice she had not heard him use before.

She did not look up at him, but said, "Okay," and turned around and moved farther inside.

And then the next thing she was aware of was that Miss Catherine was there, shaking her and saying, "Are you all right? Are you all right?" and she did not know why but she was not all right but she could not say so. She could not say anything. All she could feel was the cold air on the skin of her bottom, and then Miss Catherine saying, *Wait a minute,* and taking some toilet paper and wiping her as if she had gone. She pulled Alice's underpants up from way down around her ankles and then pulled on her shorts.

"Come on," she said to Alice, and that was all she said.

Mr. Paddy and her mother were standing over the blanket, Angie back in the stroller and Alice's mother yelling something like, "But you weren't supposed to go in with her!"

"Well how was I supposed to know that? You don't think I spend my days taking little wee lasses into the public toilet, do you?"

"You were the one who said you wanted to do it!" Alice's mother sounded nearly hysterical.

"I don't know what the woman thinks she saw, but she's crazy! I never touched the girl, I was nowhere near her! I was looking at meself in the mirror, smoothing over my hair, if you have to know the truth!"

And he laughed, Alice heard him, but she herself was still very far away. She was not sure she knew what they were talking about.

She and Miss Catherine reached the blanket and her mother bent down to her. "Are you all right?"

Alice nodded. She didn't know what the matter was supposed to be.

Her mother looked at Miss Catherine. "What are you doing here anyway?"

Miss Catherine looked straight down at her with that same look Alice was going to remember and keep on her face some day. She didn't say anything except, "Alice and Marnie are going to play all day today. I'll take her up church for confession after lunch."

Alice's mother seemed to try to meet Miss Catherine in the face, but wound up looking at Alice instead.

"Oh, all right. They can have a nice time, then, can't you, sweetheart?"

Her smile was as fake as it could be, but her voice was all right enough and Alice felt better, though standing there her legs were beginning to hurt her, and she shifted on them.

"All right, get your sweater, Alice," Miss Catherine said, and then with a rush Alice's mother said, "Oh, can you believe it, she said it was too hot out to wear a sweater and I didn't make her, you know how they get..." and she laughed a strange chirruping laugh Alice had never heard before.

"Yes," said Miss Catherine, "I know how they get."

"You can tap on the door and Mother will get one for you."

"Never mind," Miss Catherine said, "she can wear one of Marnie's."

"Oh, sure!" said Alice's mother. But then as if she thought the better of it, she said, "If you're sure about germs and all."

Miss Catherine looked at her again, and for some reason Alice suddenly found this so funny she began to laugh and laugh, and she couldn't stop until Miss Catherine gave her a little shake and asked her what she thought the matter was with her.

At Marnie's house Miss Catherine pulled out some clothes from Marnie's own dresser, some corduroy pants and a long-sleeved shirt with a Peter Pan collar. She took her into the bathroom to change though Alice said she did not need any help.

"Don't worry about that," Miss Catherine said, "You don't have anything I haven't seen before," and rather than embarrass Alice, this made both her and Marnie go "Oooo!" and laugh hard. Everything was right, everything was back to regular. Nothing had happened except Mr. Paddy had finally gotten yelled at, somebody had finally given him a talking-to, that was what Alice thought.

In the bathroom, Miss Catherine put a washrag to the faucet and wet it through. "Give me those shorts and that top and I'll wash them for your mother," she said, and then, "Here, let me get these once, too," and she bent down swiftly, pulled off Alice's underpants, and without looking at her, wiped her between the legs with the rag.

"Is that better?" she said, pulling up the clean pair of underpants.

"Mm-hm," Alice said, but then again from in some very far-off place she thought, *Liar, liar, liar*! and she did not know if she meant herself, or Miss Catherine, or both of them.

She seemed to be going back and forth from regular to funny ("Not funny ha-ha, funny odd" as somebody or other usually said at least once a day) and finished dressing and followed Miss Catherine back to Marnie's room, where it seemed she could only feel regular, and they far from silently played a new game that Marnie told her about, Nurse and Patient in which Alice categorically refused to be Nurse Baby all the way through until lunch time.

After, when Marnie found out they were going to go up to Confession, she pleaded with her mother until she cried to go with them.

"Please, Mommy! Plee-hee-hee-hee-heeze!" she cried. "What if I die? What if I go to aitch ee double toothpicks? Don't you even *care*?"

"Now, that's enough—"

"But don't you even care I'll never get to see you in Heaven, or grandma, or Cousin John or Alice or Miss Maurice or *anybody*?"

"Now, Marnie. If you go to hell, you'll know plenty of people down there." She meant it for a joke and Alice laughed, but Marnie only cried harder.

"But they will be all *bad*!"

Then the front door opened and Marnie's grandmother, Miss Lida, could be heard coming in with her grocery bags.

"Anybody home?" she called out and Marnie cried louder still.

She walked through the doorway and said, "What's all this?" in the way that she liked to do, and Marnie flung herself at her legs and cried, "Oh-oh-oh-oh-ooooh, Grandma!" Alice was embarrassed that she was acting like such a baby.

But Miss Lida looked over at Miss Catherine as if she had done something wrong, and said, "Take these, Catherine," which she did, and then Miss Lida disentangled Marnie and kneeled down and said, "Now that's enough. Not another word until you stop crying. Hello, Alice."

"Hi, Miss Lida," Alice said. "She wants to go to confession," she added, thinking an explanation might help. Her bottom was really starting to hurt her, though, and she wanted to sit down. She thought she must have fallen down off the swings, but couldn't remember when she would have.

"Ah!" Miss Lida said. "Well, you're going to go to confession, that's what I was about to tell you."

Marnie hiccupped and wiped her face and did all the things a person does when she is trying to quit crying, and said, "I am?"

"Yes. John is coming over this afternoon after confessions to make sure that you go." She and Miss Catherine always only called him John.

Marnie was transfigured. She turned to Alice. "Did you hear that Alice? Did you hear it?"

Miss Lida said, "Oh, for heaven's sake. Stop acting. John has been coming to hear your confession every Saturday since you got sick."

"Yes," Marnie said, still in ecstasy, "but he came yesterday and I did not think he would come today!"

"Oh, for pity's sake," Miss Lida said. "Child, you are going to wear me out. Alice, come on out and see about helping me with the groceries. Marnie, you sit here until you can act like a normal human being. Confession two days in a row, who does she think she is, Sarah Bernhardt?"

On the way up to church, Miss Catherine was silent but this was not unusual for her. Alice did wonder for a moment if she might be mad, but when she looked up, Miss Catherine smiled down at her and squeezed her hand and Alice knew she was not.

"Do we get to go to the library afterwards?" she asked.

"Not this time, honey, John is going to walk us home."

"Oh, I forgot!" She loved Father John so much and she thought he loved her probably almost as much as he loved Marnie. "But maybe he would like to go for a minute?"

"Oh, sure, maybe. We can ask him." They would not have asked her father if he had a minute. What she liked about Miss Catherine was that she always said they could ask about anything, even if the answer was no. She did not know where Miss Catherine had come by this extraordinary quality, and somehow it did not make Alice sad or jealous.

As they turned down Fulton Avenue, though, and she could see the spire of the church, she began to feel bad again. But just at that moment, out of nowhere that Alice could see, a woman around Miss Catherine's age walked straight up to them, and they stopped.

"Oh, please, don't stop," she said. "I just wondered if I could walk with you a little way?"

Alice did not recognize the woman, but Miss Catherine answered right away, "Oh, sure. We're just going up the block though, into church for confession."

"That's all right. But let's just keep walking," and then she began to talk to Miss Catherine, in a normal tone of voice, about something Alice did not bother to follow as they walked along. Her eyes were fixed alternately on the sidewalk in front of her and on the great expanse of steps in front of the church to which they were getting closer with each step. Alice felt her stomach grow cold and her face get hot and she wondered if there were some way she could get out of going to Confession today, though she did not know why she didn't want to go. She seemed to float up the steps when they reached them, through the heavy door held open for her by Miss Catherine, and down the aisle until she felt a hand on her shoulder. Miss Catherine pointed to the pew behind her. She genuflected and went in and Miss Catherine followed her.

"Can I sit on the inside?" the woman whispered in that loud church whisper everybody can hear.

"Oh, sure," Miss Catherine said, and changed places with her.

The woman smelled lovely, of soap and makeup and hair-spray, and something else that Alice had not smelled before, and she almost wanted to ask. Miss Catherine leaned over and said, "You can get in line, Alice," but in the time that Alice took to try to say why she didn't have anything to confess after all, inside the near-absolute silence of the church there was a commotion like a door banging or something falling over in the vestibule.

Alice and Miss Catherine turned around, but the woman between them did not, as if she had not heard anything. Alice heard her whisper, a very soft whisper, "Don't leave me, please," and saw a man who was not but who looked very much like her father walking up the aisle.

He seemed neither to look to the left nor the right, but stopped at the middle, where the pews divided to make a path to the side aisles. He stood, seeming to look up to the ceiling above the altar, where Alice had allowed herself to be lost in thought many a time in the presence of the Blessed Mother, and the Ascending Lord, and the Holy Ghost Dove and The Triangle Eye of God the Father littered with gold stars and clouds and bodiless baby angels.

The man began to shout.

"I have come here seeking REPENTENCE!" he cried, and although one or two people turned in the pew to look at him, they immediately turned back around to face the front. Most of the people in the way front were very old. There was no one on the altar, and although Alice was waiting for him, Father John did not appear to see what was the matter. She worried he might have forgotten to come.

The man kept yelling. Alice did not understand him but she did feel the same as at the park that things were getting very far away except that this time instead of getting brighter they were getting darker. She wanted to lean over and look at Miss Catherine but could not. The other lady remained still, smiling even, and did not move an inch. She was breathing hard through her nose, though, Alice saw.

"FORGIVE ME, FATHER," the man yelled. "FORGIVE ME, FOR I KNOW NOT WHAT I DO!" at which the lady stiffened and closed her eyes.

The man moved to the front of the church. He did not genuflect, in fact, he seemed to not know where he was or how he had gotten there. He turned around to face them, and still Father John did not come out.

"Now, I'm no preacher," he said, not yelling or screaming but scanning the crowd, "but I do know one thing! And that is that the Lord is my Savior!"

He looked from side to side, but the people did not look back at him, and they most certainly did not answer him, which he did not seem to expect.

He looked around. "Now, I'm no preacher," he began again, "but the preacher knows the sins of woman are manifold! Yes, they are manifold, and they are manifest!"

He continued to scan the people until his eyes stopped on their pew. Alice felt he was looking right at her. "Manifest," he said, in a very low tone. "Made manifest to me this day," and he began talking again about something else that Alice could not understand, his voice rising higher and higher.

And then he screamed, "And that bitch right there did it! She did it to me!!" and he pointed right at Alice.

Miss Catherine stood up then, genuflected, and walked toward the man. Alice could not breathe and the woman whom she did not know grasped her wrist. As she approached, Miss Catherine tapped the shoulder of a man sitting at the end of an aisle, and he rose and walked with her, and they went up to the man who had stopped screaming and cursing but stood and looked at them though he did not seem to have calmed down, and Alice was very cold and very scared. The woman reached for her hand and held it tightly.

The older man began to speak quietly and the man appeared to pay attention, and then the older man called out, "Father?" at which Father John finally came out, holding a censer that already had smoke coming out of its top.

The man saw Father John before anyone else, and screamed, and threw himself down to the floor. "Aaaahhhh!" seemed to be all he could say, and Father John put down the censer and quickly went up between the altar railings and down the steps toward them.

Miss Catherine left the man with Father John and turned and rushed back to the lady and Alice, and said, "Come on!" They got up, and Alice did not know whether to genuflect or not. When she got into the aisle the sight of the two men beginning to help the one who had called her a bitch froze her to the spot until she heard Miss Catherine hiss, "Alice!" and felt her tug her around by the arm. They hurried up to the lady and walked as fast as they could without running out of the church.

They went up Fulton Avenue the opposite way from home and kept walking until Miss Catherine saw a taxi, and hailed it. The woman was shaking and had not spoken, but Miss Catherine had kept up a quiet flow of reassurances that, if they were not helping the lady, the sound of them was helping Alice. Miss Catherine rooted in her purse for some money, gave it to the driver and told him to take her where she wanted to go.

"Take her to the police station or the hospital," she added, and Alice saw she was shaking.

"The hospital," the woman said, and then laughed, and then made her mouth say the words, "Thank you," but did not say them out loud.

"Are you all right?" Miss Catherine turned back to Alice as the cab drove away. She wiped her hand across Alice's forehead and smoothed her hair and wiped her own eyes.

"I'm all right. Why was that man mad at me? I never saw him before."

"He wasn't, honey. He was mad at something else, I don't know."

"You?"

"No, I don't know him." She seemed to be letting Alice figure out the subtraction by herself.

"Oh," she said after a minute. "He was mad at the lady."

"Yes, I think he was mad at her. Oh, shoot, I didn't even ask her name once. Well. Let's go back to church. I'm sure he is long gone by now."

"Are you sure?"

"Oh, sure, honey. That man needed the paddy wagon." Miss Catherine laughed. "Well, I'm all shook up! We sure had an adventure, didn't we?"

And Alice laughed and everything was nearly all right again.

When they got back, sure enough, all the people were coming out and Father John with them and he said the man had gone after all.

"Just let me put on my hat," he said, and went inside for the berretta with the big black fuzzy ball on top. Alice smiled but saw that Miss Catherine was mad.

"Why didn't you come out before?" she said to him when he returned, standing in the middle of the sidewalk with her hands on her hips.

He was unperturbed as he always seemed to be.

"What did you want me to do, Catherine? He hadn't done anything, and it was sanctuary. Grandmother always said sanctuary was one of the most sacred duties of a pastor next door to confession."

"It was sanctuary! Grandmother! Is that what they told you in seminary school too? And what do you mean, he hadn't done anything? He scared everybody out of their wits! He was screaming his head off in church! Alice thought he was mad at her and we never saw him before!"

"Well, there wasn't any way for me to know all that, was there?"

"He was cussing a blue streak, John!" Alice giggled and she looked down. "That's enough out of you, Miss. John, that man was dangerous. He followed this poor woman inside and she told me he was going to go at her. I don't even know if he was her husband or not."

"Well, I didn't know about that. What happened to her?"

"I put her in a taxi, and she's either gone to the hospital or to the police. Either one—I hope she goes to the hospital, at least."

"Well, all's well that ends well," he said. "Just let it be. You got her away and she'll be fine."

"Oh, you! For a grown man you make me so mad sometimes I could spit!"

Alice couldn't keep from laughing again, but though Miss Catherine looked down she winked and smiled a little.

"And anyway, that's a fine attitude for a man in your position," she said, turning back to Father John. "What did you do finally?"

"We led him out and he walked away."

"What!"

"Well, Catherine, what did you want me to do? Like I say, he didn't do anything. I couldn't call the police."

Miss Catherine stopped and let go Alice's hand, and she looked up to see her give that one look to Father John, and her mouth fell open, and she froze where she stood at the way Miss Catherine's voice sounded.

"No, of course you couldn't do anything," Miss Catherine said. "Nobody ever does anything."

"Catherine..."

"Yes, well, all right. I hope so."

In later years Alice would know what this had meant in particular but in that moment she believed what Miss Catherine was saying was true always, because in her experience nothing had ever happened to prove it untrue, and for the first time in her life she did not believe Father John when he said, "Now, Catherine, you know that's nonsense."

And all Miss Catherine would say was, "Is it?" in that same voice, and besides the look that Alice had never seen her give to

Father John before, Alice believed she would memorize those words and use them in as many situations as she could from here on out. It was like an excuse to talk back if someone was being unbelievably stupid or blind or mean or if she knew they just didn't give a care. She just liked the sound of it, the don't-take-anything-off-anybody sound of it.

She bet you didn't even have to count it and thinking that, remembered she had been spared having to go to confession, and before Father John could say something else asked, "Can we stop at the library?"

"Oh, yes, honey, I forgot in all the commotion," Miss Catherine said, her voice back to normal. "We need to get books for the week, John, they'll be closed in a little while."

"Oh, sure, we can do that." He didn't look mad at all.

Alice said, "But I don't have my card, though."

"That's all right. I have my card and you can check out on that. But don't forget to take them back, now!"

Alice laughed and they moved along, the strange man and the woman forgotten one they crossed the corner where the woman had first come up to them. Alice immediately found the next All-of-a-Kind Family book, and a new one, called Good Old Archibald that she could not exactly figure out but it appeared that there were some older kids with some poor kids and this one boy who was driven around in a limousine. It looked good. She and Marnie could read it together and make up the stuff they didn't understand. And she got a couple of picture books because all of a sudden she felt tired and they were pretty. She asked for the Five Chinese Brothers and got that, too. They got that one almost every time.

And standing in the line to check out, all at once she started to feel the noise and the commotion of the lights and again felt she had to get out of there fast or she would explode or something. She said, "Miss Catherine?" but both she and Father John turned around and Miss Catherine answered, "Yes?" Alice knew she could not explain it and said, "Oh, nothing," and put one foot around her leg, and waited.

"Oh, I nearly forgot," Father John smiled. "There is something for you at Marnie's house when we get back."

"Really?" Alice couldn't think what it could be. "Can you tell me?"

But the librarian said, "Shhhh!" and so she smiled and though she was excited and happy she still had to put a fingernail between her teeth and tried very hard not to chew it. She could not ask Father John to get out of there no matter what.

But all she could think about on the walk home was getting inside. The air was cold and the corduroy slacks and the sweater didn't help and although there were no real lights, the sounds of outside were loud and persistent, faded then loud and fading again in a pattern that seemed to get inside of her head and even into her body. She wanted to scream. She asked if she could run, and Miss Catherine said yes, but only to the corner. They repeated this four or five times, every time Alice jumping up and down while she waited, every time catching a snatch of conversation, "Well, I don't know why they have to..." and "Of course they used to, it's the history of mankind, for God's sake," and, "Well, that doesn't give me a very good idea of mankind, thank you very much."

And at last they were at the door, and Alice flew in, and ran to the kitchen, and promptly lost control of herself all over the linoleum and began to wail.

"Oh, my," Miss Catherine said when she caught up to her. "Marnie, stay out there," she called, and for the second time that day took Alice up to the bathroom and helped her out of her clothes. She looked at her legs.

"That wasn't there before," she said, and when Alice looked down there were big blue and purple bruises on her legs. She cried some more but could not speak, and Miss Catherine fixed her up without saying anything else.

She opened the door and they saw Father John standing by the landing. Alice quickly stepped behind Miss Catherine.

"You know what, honey, why don't you take a bath?" she said to Alice. "You're cold, why don't I run you a bath after all? We're fine, John, go on downstairs and read with Marnie a while."

Alice gingerly got into the tub when it was filled, Miss Catherine holding on to her arm and helping her sit down. It hurt her bottom a lot in the hot water and the bruised skin stung her, but she had stopped crying and didn't want to cry anymore. She felt a little hungry. The light from the ceiling was loud and hurt her eyes. When she got up, her legs felt stiff and it hurt to bend them even a little bit, and when Miss Catherine dried her off, she winced. Miss Catherine's face seemed to have nothing on it, but her voice shook.

"What, did you fall down?" she asked.

"Um, yes, at Carroll Park," Alice said. She didn't know if Miss Catherine could tell that she was lying, but she also thought, she wasn't lying. She wasn't saying everything but she didn't know what was missing, or at least, she couldn't remember if there had been anything else.

"Oh, I see," Miss Catherine said, and helped her into some clothes. "Well, you'll be fine," she said, and Alice believed her based on not very much more than that she was Miss Catherine and she had looked that way at Father John and said, "Is it?" to him, and for Alice that seemed practically the whole world.

When they stepped out, Father John was standing on the landing.

"What do you want now?" Miss Catherine said as if he were a boy in her grade.

"Oh," he said, "nothing, I brought Marnie upstairs and put her in your room."

"Oh, well, all right, then. Well, go on downstairs. I'll be down in a minute. The girls have to take a nap before supper."

He moved down the stairs, and Miss Catherine led Alice by the hand into her room and tucked her in to the big bed next to Marnie, who somehow knew to be quiet for a change.

"Close your eyes and get a little rest," Miss Catherine said, and they closed their eyes.

But when she was safely downstairs, Marnie said, "What happened?"

And that was when Alice wished again that Marnie would shut up sometimes. But she said, "We went into church and there was this man who came in and yelled at everybody. Miss Catherine got mad at Father John for not kicking him out."

"At church?" Marnie was horrified. "He did not either! She did not either!"

"No, on the way back."

"What was the matter with the man?"

"I don't know. He was really mad, I guess, he was yelling. He was Luthern, though, I bet. He didn't know it was supposed to be inside the confessional." She waited for a second. "Marnie?"

"Huh?"

Alice looked past her at the newish wallpaper, a kind of beige background but every so often the pattern of a long green tree stem with a small little bird sitting on it repeated across the wall. It was very simple, and pretty. Alice thought she might like to try to draw it some time, maybe on a piece of folded paper, and give it to Miss Catherine for a thank-you card. She felt that somehow Miss Catherine had seen into what was happening to them and had not looked away but had done something about it and had not bitten her tongue. She wondered if she should say anything more to her about the park. She would never tell her mother.

Marnie said again, "What?" Maybe she better tell her just in case so she would know to not ever go near Paddy Dolan. Or maybe if she told her, they could put together a plot to kill him or hurt his other hand badly somehow.

"Marnie?" she said again.

Hmmm? she whispered this time, and Alice knew she was falling asleep.

You know Paddy Dolan?

Of course I know him. He's the one with the foul hand. Everything was "foul" to them.

I don't mean that, I mean, do you like him?

No, I don't.

Why not?

Mommy said not to.

She did?

Mm-hm.

How come?

Marnie stirred in the covers. *I mean, she said if I ever go anywhere and he's there, I should go away and come back to her. She said I should never talk to him, and if he starts talking to me I should just leave.*

But he's a grown-up. How do you do it?

I don't know. I guess I never had to. He never tries to talk to me.

You're lucky. He talks to me all the time.

I know. You told me. But how come?

Alice couldn't keep on. "I don't know. Let's go to sleep."

And she turned over away from Marnie, and closed her eyes for good. While they slept she dreamed she was in Carroll Park next to a toilet that wouldn't stop flushing.

When she woke up, it was dark and Marnie was no longer in bed, and she got up and went down the back stairs, and, finding no one in the kitchen, through the middle room where Marnie's sofa bed was still open and made up as a bed. They were all sitting in the living room with Marnie on the couch. Father John was gone, and they told her she had gotten permission to spend the night and that her mother had put together a change of clothes and sent them over with her toothbrush and pyjamas.

"What about Angie?" she asked.

"Never mind about Angie, she'll be just fine," Miss Catherine answered. "Have some popcorn."

Marnie had already been to her second confession in two days with Father John, who had left to see about church and was going to come back again to spend the evening with them. They were going to play Monopoly until nearly eleven o'clock, Marnie informed her, when Miss Catherine would say, *Enough*! and send them both off to bed upstairs in Marnie's room, where Marnie told Alice she had not slept in weeks.

"Mommy sleeps in the living room on the sofa and I sleep on the pull-out these days," she said.

"Well, don't you ever go to the bathroom?" Alice asked, and then wished she hadn't, but Marnie didn't seem to notice.

"No, not really that often. At night I take a bath and I go then, and then in the mornings. It smells nice up there! I'm glad you came over," she said.

"Me, too."

She had never spent the night over at Marnie's before. Miss Lida said they better not wait for John and have some dinner before it got too late, so they went in to dinner. Alice thought she had never seen so many vegetables in her whole life. It turned out Marnie liked vegetables, which Alice didn't except for spinach and onions cooked with liver, and tomatoes if they were in tomato gravy over pancakes. But Marnie and her mother and grandmother liked things Alice had never seen before that it turned out made her feel sick, and while tonight they had usual things like green beans and peas and beets out of cans, which Alice of course knew about but avoided if she could, when she asked if there was any creamed corn, they said, no, but something even better. That turned out to be this ugly white stuff called cauliflower with melted orange cheese all over it and a dish of shredded apples with cottage cheese that Miss Lida called Waldorf Something. It made her sick to smell it and after she would associate the smell of cauliflower with the scent of public restrooms, bright lights, and being breathless. But they all ate theirs down and even Father John asked for seconds when he got there and nobody seemed to mind any of it at all. She thought, I'm never eating that stuff again.

After dinner was over, though it was dark Miss Catherine said the ice cream man was going to come around a second time and they should go out on the front steps and wait for him while Marnie and Father John sat in the window.

"You can run after it," she said to Alice, and gave her two dimes.

Marnie told Alice she had not been out front since right after school was over. "But that's okay," she said. "I didn't really want to that much."

Alice said then but didn't know why, "I'm sorry I never came over at first."

"You couldn't. They wouldn't let me see nobody. It was quarrenteemed."

"That's what they said. What is it?"

"Well, it means you can't see nobody that you don't want to give the disease to."

"Oh." Alice thought a moment. "Well, I would have took it. Then we could have had it at the same time and got over it."

Marnie looked grave and then snapped at her, "It was not the picking cotton chicken pox. It's why my other grandma died, Father John's mommy," she finished in a loud whisper.

"No, she didn't," Father John said in the voice of someone who had repeated the same thing umpteen times.

"Are you going to die?" Alice persevered in a whisper.

"No."

"How do you know?"

"Because they thought I was, and now I'm not. Here comes the dingaling man." She hopped over to the window and bounced into one of the chairs.

The ice cream truck was coming slowly down the street, so that Alice did not have to run after it. She didn't think she would have been able to if she tried. From her own window next door, she heard Angie say, "Hi, Alice!" but at the sound she turned ice cold again and didn't turn around. She stepped up to the truck where it stopped and asked for a strawberry Good Humor for Marnie and a chocolate one for herself, and turned to go back in. The whole time Angie was yelling, and then she started to cry, and Alice heard her mother pulling her away from the window and say, "It's too cold, I wonder she lets them have it." She never leaned out or said anything like, "How are you girls getting along?" She didn't remind Alice to watch her manners or eat everything on her plate or go to bed when Marnie's mother said they had to go.

She heard her say to someone inside, "No, she just Jewed me down, like always," and Alice had heard this phrase when her parents would talk about money things, that they had been Jewed down over something or that a pretty penny had changed hands over a particular transaction, and Alice was convinced that her mother was talking about her, that she, Alice had somehow Jewed her mother down and about how Father John and Miss Catherine were Jews.

She thought of a shiny new penny, rare that you could find one in a handful or even a jarful of pennies, and how her father sometimes called her his Lucky Penny. Alice was not a shiny new penny and not a lucky one and if he knew what happened to her he would not call her that anymore. No, that was not it, she realized. He must already know, and that was why he was not here with them. That must have been how she had Jewed her mother down. Her own mother must have given her up to Marnie's mother who ate cheese on vegetables and didn't care if you asked for something you ought to know better than to bother an adult by asking for. Maybe that look was a way to Jew somebody down. Maybe Miss Catherine and Marnie were second-hand, old pennies.

"I want to go home," she said all at once out loud, holding her ice cream out to Miss Catherine, who still stood on the steps.

"Why, honey, what for? Don't you want to spend the night over? For a treat?"

Alice was furious to hear that word. She did not need a treat, she did not want one, she did not want to be called honey anymore. Treats were for babies and she wasn't Miss Catherine's honey.

"I don't know. I just don't feel like it. I mean, I don't feel good." She wasn't going to be rude, she didn't mean to be rude.

"What? No! I want you to!" Marnie started to cry from the window, and Father John started to shush her. "I want you to stay over!"

And Alice thought again that the way Marnie was going back and forth was shocking, and, well, she didn't know, she wanted to get out of there and be in her own room and put the pillow over her head and then just nothing for a while, just nothing but in a heartbeat Marnie was crying too hard to talk and Father John said something to Alice about being nice and not making her cry, but Alice wasn't making her cry and he didn't know anything and why did Marnie always get what she wanted but Alice never did and she said again, "I want to go home."

"What's the matter, Alice?" persisted Miss Catherine.

She wanted to tell Miss Catherine that she was not her mother, but said, "Nothing. I mean, I'm sorry but I feel kind of sick."

"Do you? Well, where does it hurt?" And she looked so worried that Alice started to like her again, a little, and she wanted to cry and almost told her that it was nothing, that only her legs hurt and her stomach almost didn't hurt at all any more, but she heard Angie crying too inside her house, and wanted it to be her own mother not somebody else's who was asking her where it hurt and what she could do to make it better.

She said, "I just don't feel good. I want to go home."

"Well, all right. You can come another time. I'll bring your things by as soon as I get Marnie to bed."

Marnie had stopped crying but looked so bleakly at Alice through the window that she felt like the worst person that could be, because she didn't like Marnie anymore. She wondered how you could not like somebody anymore that fast and wanted to take it back, to say that she'd stay, but Marnie's mother looked down at her in such a way that it was impossible to change her mind. She had to go home.

She walked the half dozen paces to her own stairs. She climbed them one at a time in their turn. She knew Miss Catherine was watching from the door, but found she could not work her legs so that they would alternate. She tried the screen and it was open. She tried the front door handle and it opened to her as well.

No one was in the living room, not even her grandfather who ought to be asleep on the couch. She walked back to the kitchen, calling out, "I'm home!"

Her mother was at the sink, but didn't turn around. "Your grandmother took Angie up for her bath. Granddaddy's asleep."

Alice sat down at the head of the table, looking straight through at the back door. Her mother kept washing and fixing things, not looking at Alice at all. No shadow appeared on the walk or at the door.

Finally she said, "Mr. Paddy can come over if he wants to."

Her mother turned slowly around, walked over to Alice, and stopped. And then she smacked her across the shoulder. "*That's* for humiliating me in the street."

And then after another few moments, her face changing in some way Alice had not seen before, she smacked her across the back of the head with the tips of her fingers.

"And *that's* because *'Mr. Paddy's'* never going to come here again. Thank you very much for nothing, you, you—you stupid little thing."

She had not hit Alice very hard, not enough to hurt, but it felt worse than anything she had ever felt, and she sat with the words hanging between them until her mother said, "Don't look at me like that."

Alice didn't cry, but she said because she could not stop herself from saying it, "But I didn't do anything."

And as if this were what her mother had been waiting for, she let into her then with the fury that had been coming so often since they moved up here that Alice had begun to think of it as nearly her regular way to talk.

"Didn't do anything? After he was so good to you and put you on the swings and helped you when you fell down? And after all those days he waited for you at the library to make sure nobody ever bothered you? After all the good he's done for me? I'm surprised you have the nerve to look me in the eye, young lady, you, you—"and she did not seem to be able to find a word to call Alice that was bad enough. "I'm surprised you are sitting here at my dinner table."

"But I didn't. I didn't do anything!" She shouldn't say it, she knew it, but she still could not keep herself from saying it.

"Oh, yes, you did, oh, yes you did!" Alice heard her grandmother call down the steps, "Agnes!" but that didn't stop her mother and her grandmother didn't come down to them. She took Alice by the shoulders and shook her hard.

"All your caterwauling and sniveling and complaining, when all I wanted you to do was be nice and polite. All you had to do was be nice a while, just for a few hours. But it's always the same.

No matter what I want, I never get it. No matter what I ask for, you have to up and go and do the exact opposite. No man likes a crybaby. Just you remember that one. And now what am I going to do? I'm going to be alone for the rest of my natural life, that's what, and it is all your fault."

She finally paused to take a breath. She did not seem to be horrified or even sorry for what she had said but glared at Alice, and when she didn't say anything it seemed to make her mother not more angry but something else, something that said her mother had gotten her own way after all.

"Go on. Get of here," she said. "I can barely stand to look at you." She was satisfied, Alice could tell, satisfied and done.

Alice turned and left the kitchen, walked back through the house and out the front door, and limped down her steps and over to Marnie's. She stood looking at their front door. She climbed the steps, turned around, and sat down. It was nearly a half hour later when Miss Catherine came out with Alice's things to find her there, shivering, not blinking and not a tear on her face.

Part IV: Sunday, April 5, 1964
Father John Martin

Sunday Afternoon. Wool-gathering.

On the shallow steps of St. Martin of Tours Catholic Church, the priest stood smoking. It was a cold spring so far, it had been a cold winter. He wore a coat, and a plain hat, and the white tab of his clerical collar jutted out at the end, the top button of his shirt open, slacks still looking pressed from yesterday, bright-colored fuzzy slippers still on his feet. They had been a gift from little Marnie on Ash Wednesday, "So you'll have something to keep you happy during Lent." She had learned that year that Lent was a particularly difficult time for priests, though he had no idea why anyone would tell a schoolchild such a thing. He wasn't aware he had them on now.

John had been a priest for twelve years. He had begun, new-ordained, at the church of his deceased grandmother, Fourteen Holy Martyrs, just up from Union Square, and from there he had moved not five years ago to St. Martin's. He had not asked to move. But Fourteen's was likely to close at some point, they had said, though no definite decision had been made, but in any event it was a small parish that didn't needed an assistant. He had asked, if they were going to close it, could he stay until the end, but they had said, no, he was to go to St. Martin's, it was close enough to Fourteen's, and he had gone, and here he was.

You want to come up?

He shook his head as if to shake the words out of it.

It was cold. At Catherine's house they waited for him to join them for supper. His aunt Lida and cousin Catherine and little Marnie lived there in his grandmother's house, three blocks from Fourteen's and half a block from the square.

We could do something.

No, not today.

John threw his mind back into the longer past, to the second year of seminary when he had been allowed to visit his grandmother at her home. She had taken a bad fall at one point off the VFW steps, on the way in to bingo, and though she had not broken anything the fall had affected her mind. At the end she did not remember that he was her grandson unless Miss Maurice reminded her, and when she was reminded, she was pleased and asked him all manner of questions about her life, most of which he could answer, or if he could not answer he could invent. She did not remember Catherine at all.

"And who are you, now?" she would say, pleased to have a new visitor. "And so who are you, again?"

Mama, we aten all the saltines.

It was no good.

It was Sunday, and Sunday was the day that the people you loved didn't get out of bed, or you didn't get out of bed, or not much of anything happened except that you were not master of your own mind and where it wanted to take you.

Wool-gathering, his grandmother had called it. Day-dreaming, as he excused it within himself. Story-telling, he had been known for it in school, in seminary, at the bar, at the altar.

On Sundays he seemed to do them all.

Sunday Afternoon. Remembering.

He breathed in the cigarette smoke, and blew it out. Yesterday had been a strange day. A strange Saturday in Eastertide that had ended with a story.

He had been thinking about so many things, and then that terrible man had invaded the quiet of the church, yelling and cursing, and as it had always been, he was—not too afraid to come out and ensure that his parish was safe, that wasn't it, but something within him held him back. He assumed that the old people there were not being harmed, that the children were not being harmed. Maybe he should not have assumed that. Catherine had given him what-for, as she nearly always did, and he had probably deserved it.

"But come on over," she had said, and he had gone, and had been there when Marnie's friend Alice had come over to spend the night, Alice, who to his shame had been in the church that afternoon and had heard Catherine give him a talking to, Alice who Catherine worried over, on top of her worries about Marnie and Marnie's health, Alice who apparently had gone out and sat on the front steps in the dark and none of them had known she was there for half an hour.

When Catherine had gathered her back inside, without explanation or even really a pause, the girls had settled down and normalcy had taken over as it so often seemed to do regardless of what had come before. They begged him to stay longer and longer the later and later it got, just as Marnie had begged the night before. Catherine's was home to him and he would stay as long as they let him, but it was more than that last night. Alice had looked, he didn't know, troubled in some way, and it seemed important to both the girls that he remain, and so he had stayed. They dragged the Monopoly game out longer and longer until somebody finally had to win, and then as if she knew he would get ready to leave, Marnie had shouted out, "Tell us again about the Age of Reason!" and he had burst out laughing.

"Oh, I'll tell you that one, all right. But wait a minute, though," he had said, remembering what he had promised Marnie on Friday and Alice yesterday afternoon, "I can't believe we nearly forgot something!"

"What?" they had whispered together, their faces nearly bursting with light.

He reached into his pocket and pulled out two small paper boxes with clear lids, each holding a stainless steel medal upon a chain, each medal resting on a small, velvet-covered cardboard within the box. The girls cried out as he held them out to them, and Aunt Lida called from the front room, "Be quiet in there, you two!" John said, "Shhhh!" and they clapped their hands over their mouths, and giggled, and looked at him as he thought in wonder.

And in that moment he heard the voice say again, *We could do something.*

He had pulled himself together and smiled again, and said, "I told Sister Immaculata Marie that Marnie had forgotten her Medal on the way to the hospital, and then I told her I also needed one extra."

"And she *gave* it to ya?" Marnie gasped. Alice put her box in front of her as if she thought he would have to take it back now that he admitted he had gotten it from the Sister.

"Yes, she did. I even tried to pay her for them, but she wouldn't let me. She didn't like it much, though!" he said, and he winked at them.

They squealed with laughter and he said, "Shhhh!" again.

And then they had sat straight up, and waited, and he told them to first hold out their right hands, and he had picked up the boxes again and put a box into each of their palms.

They had, seemingly, been silenced into a solemn, austere, and complete silence he had not known a little girl could achieve. They seemed immobilized by a feeling of holiness, he would have said if he'd had to give a name to the feeling, and he was very moved by this, and said, solemnly and kindly, "All right, now what?"

Alice looked at Marnie, and Marnie sat up straighter and gave it some thought.

"You say something in Latin," she said to him, and Alice looked back to him and nodded.

"A prayer, kind of," she said.

He said, "All right, that sounds good. Now, here we go. Ahem. Bow your heads and pray for God's blessing."

Their beauty, Marnie's gamine sturdiness despite her illness and Alice's more translucent fragility, shone under the reflection of the bedside lamp. He had had to pause as their heads remained bowed, and finally he had begun, "Dear Lord, bless these Miraculous Medals *in nomine Patris, et Filii, et Spiritus Sancti, Amen.*"

"Amen," they had responded together, crossing themselves.

And then for reasons he did not understand, he began the prayer, "*Suscipe, Domine, universam meam libertatem,*" and then stopped as he heard Marnie begin to say along with him, "*accipe memoriam*, um, intelligam, omnam..."

She lifted her head and whispered, "I don't know it all the way yet."

He smiled and raised his eyebrows, but said only, "That's okay, that's okay. Can you both say the Gloria?" They nodded, and they said it together, and the girls waited.

He searched for the right blessing.

"All right," he had said at last, "By the power vested in me, these now-blessed medals are thine to wear in perpetuity, from this day forward, Catherine Mary Signorelli and Alice—

"Elizabeth Smaling," they said.

"—Elizabeth Smaling. Keep them, and guard them, and be blessed and protected by the blessings within them. Amen."

"Amen," they repeated.

"And now you may put them on."

They had taken them tenderly out of the boxes and lifted them over their heads, and looked at the medals on each other's chest, and Marnie sighed as deeply as it was possible to sigh, and Alice touched her medal as if it was slightly hot.

"Oh, wait up," she had said. "It's backwards." She readjusted with some help from John, and touched it again, perhaps, he thought to be sure it would stay there. He felt he had done something important, and then chastised himself for thinking this, as if it were pride or a possessiveness to which he was not entitled.

"All right," he said after a moment, "Bedtime."

"Noo! The story! The Age of Reason!"

"It's nearly midnight!"

"Tell them, John," Lida said from her room. "I'll never get a wink of sleep if you don't."

He smiled crookedly and said, "Yes, ma'am," and settled back, and began.

Sunday, After Midnight. Storytelling.

It was an understood thing in our home that from Monday morning through Saturday night, my mother was the absolute head of the house. Not overbearing, not unreasonable, not by any means unkind or cold, but the head. My father was the head of the boiler room at the synagogue, but even so, my mother's place was not only fair but right, and everybody thought so, and everybody loved my mother.

("Yes, they did," said Aunt Lida from her room.)

Like many another little boy, I thought of her as the woman I would marry when I grew up, as she was all that in my view you could want in a woman: funny, kind, plump, beautiful, with brown eyes and black hair that pierced you like Samson before Delilah and her gang got ahold of him. She was the head: it was an understood thing.

("Who's Delilah?" Alice said, and Marnie said, "She cut off his hair." Alice looked a bit nervous, but they both settled back down on the mattress, cross-legged and elbows on their knees. John had to look away as they mouthed words they either didn't understand or wanted to save for later so as not to laugh at them. He leaned back again and looked up at the ceiling for a moment, and they waited.)

But it was also an understood thing, he continued, that on Sundays, my mother didn't get out of bed, not for breakfast, not for supper, not for Ed Sullivan.

("And then she died," Marnie said. "Yes, sweetheart, and then she died, but not then.")

And from when I turned seven and entered the age of reason, it turned out that she had not been getting out of bed every Sunday morning for a very long time, and that this Sunday morning I had to make breakfast. Shabbas was over, so that was no problem, but there's not much a seven-year-old boy can make, even for breakfast, that his father will consider eating before throwing it back in his son's face, and I definitely had the kind of father who would do that.

("He did, too," said Aunt Lida.)

He wasn't mean by any stretch, my father, but he took my mother's weekly defection as a personal insult, a kind of Roman Catholic vengeance on him, though she had converted to marry him, made a beautiful Shabbas each week, and put up with his mother, and though strictly speaking I was an Irish Catholic, or so he said when he was most irritated.

"*Everything* comes down through the mother no matter what, young man," he would say as if this were something I ought to have burned into my soul.

Still, before I was seven and entered the age of reason, I don't remember my mother not getting out of bed, but after I realized that my parents' bedroom door had been shut and stayed shut with my mother on the other side of it every Sunday for as long as I could remember, I was scared.

Before I turned seven my Aunt Lida Marie, my mother's sister ("Grandma!" Marnie whispered) was living with us anyway, and she cooked and did for my father before he went up Edmonson Avenue to see what the matter with the boiler was or whatever it might have been at B'nai Israel. His job in those days was bundling the morning edition of the Baltimore *News-Post* for the carriers and the newsstands. He ought to have been in the first war but had had some kind of lung problem that kept him away, but I think he was the only one who had been unhappy about that.

At any rate, Friday and Sunday he bundled newspapers in the varied darkness of early morning, then spent the days recuperating over the kitchen table when he didn't have to go up to the synagogue. At the breakfast table he would read the headlines to me as my mother made my pancakes and got me ready for school or to go out and play. He didn't bundle on Saturdays, when he'd take me up to shul where his work consisted of very little beyond sweeping off the front stoop, which he often had me do for him, and carrying out the garbage cans, which if they were not too full, likewise, but he was helpful if the pipes backed up or the oil for the furnace was running low, and on Friday evenings he had also established himself as the doorman for the older ladies encrusted in rhinestones from the Hecht Company or Hutzler's who let their husbands drive them up to the curb and drop them off for service before finding a place to park their big, black cars that looked like the ones from the movies.

You can bet we didn't have a car, but it wasn't because my father couldn't afford one, it was because nobody had cars back then, only the very, very rich. Besides that, my mother could not ride in a car or in anything other than a streetcar or a nearly empty bus. Taxis she could go in okay if they smelled deeply of cigar smoke, but if the taxi was too new or the smell of gasoline too strong, she would sigh, gain about fifteen pounds and ten years right before our eyes, stand upright, and, placing the strap of her pocketbook firmly in the crook of her elbow, turn without a word and walk three blocks up Eastern Avenue to catch a streetcar. Not even a bus would work if she had caught a whiff of new leather or fresh gasoline.

She had married my father young, and nobody was particularly happy about it, but they fell in love and they married. It was all right with my grandmother, because my father's last name was Martin and she sometimes attended St. Martin's Church. None of us knew why my father's last name was Martin. His grandfather's first name, he had told us, for his grandfather had died years ago in the influenza epidemic, was Isaac, and so that should have been my name, but my mother insisted on naming me John after her father, and so I was named John Isaac. But my father's people had been Milovisces, from Czechoslovakia, I believe, and, though you might assume it was a change that had happened at the immigration gate, that was not so: Milovisc was found written out correctly on his grandfather's entry papers, and it had been his father's last name. Still, Martin was the official entry on my father's birth certificate, and so Martin we were. I suppose this may have saved me from some of the—*Jew-baiting* John had been going to say, but he looked over at the girls and amended it to *bullying*—I might have been in for sometimes, but I was never particularly aware of being Jewish or Catholic one over the other, they both seemed the same to me.

My mother and Aunt Lida both worked out, cleaning houses with my grandmother, Catherine Rafferty, on West Lombard Street close to here and Miss Maurice, who herself cleaned for my grandmother. (*That's our house*, Marnie whispered, and *I know*, Alice whispered back.) I knew about the age of reason from my grandmother and Miss Maurice, who was also her best friend and who sometimes took me to Mass at St. Peter Claver, which I'm pretty sure would have given my father an attack if he had known about it.

The entire year I was six, she and my grandmother would hint darkly whenever I did anything they felt was on the edge of damnation.

"Wait and see, young man. Wait and see, Mister Smarty Pants. The Age of Reason is coming. Then you'll see, Mr. Winston Churchill."

As they did not elaborate and I did not attend Catholic school in the first grade, I honestly had no idea what they meant, but it turned out they were right: right after my seventh birthday, I all of a sudden realized I could see and feel things I had never been able to before, paramount among them that my mother never got out of bed on Sundays.

This particular Sunday was the one after Aunt Lida had gotten married to a very nice Jewish boy whose name was Bernie Bernstein ("Is that Grandpa?" Marnie asked, and "Yes, that's your Grandpa," John said) who always made my mother shudder when he came around the house. I later found out it was because his mother thought my mother was a complete disaster, and Bernie only ate at our house when his own mother was in Atlantic City or visiting her eldest daughter in Timonium. "How you can eat with those Ketlicks," she would chide, but the answer was obvious: anybody who had ever gotten half a peek at my mother's little sister would have had a Catholic for breakfast to get her ("Darn right they would," Aunt Lida said), and why she chose Bernie over all the handsome well-off guys from her high school, I couldn't tell you, except that trust with few exceptions any member of our family not to marry money. Not just money: most of those other guys were lookers, even from my point of view, and Bernie had an Adam's apple that went on for two weeks, like the actor who played Gershwin in the movie. His legs were so skinny I had to punch out a guy or two about it over the years, but he was no dope, though. He got baptized just so they could have a church wedding—

("I said, I wasn't going to convert to anything having to do with his mother—")

("Aunt Lida, who's telling this story?")

("All right, all right.")

Anyway, that wedding was small, only my grandmother and my mother and father and I attending. As a matter of fact, for the benefit of his own family they had been married at the court-house earlier in the week, and then had the church service, and after that they threw them a big party and he stomped on the glass and everything. My grandmother cried a little bit, but she went to the reception.

"It don't mean nothing," Bernie said as we stood against the wall of the reception hall and ate slices of cake, and that made sense to me.

At any rate, Aunt Lida married Bernie and the next morning I arrived at the realization that my mother never got out of bed on Sundays.

It started out like this: My father yanked the covers off my bed around 8:30 that morning and said something like, "Where's the coffee?"

"Huh?" I said, one eye open and my face still plastered into the side of the pillow.

He cuffed me on my backside where it was launched like a flag-post over my knees, themselves practically molded into my stomach.

"The coffee, buddy. The coffee? Your aunt Lida said you would make the coffee." He looked around as if I might have it brewing on top of my dresser drawers.

"Huh?" I repeated.

"Jesus Christ, I *said*, where is the damn coffee? It is 9:30 in the damn morning."

My father only swore like that when we were alone. But by now I was more awake and hazily remembering Aunt Lida's parting whisper to me as she and Bernie linked arms at the door of the wedding hall: "Johnny, remember, tomorrow you need to make the coffee."

And it all came back to me, how she had showed me earlier in the week how to make it, how to put one egg into the grounds without the shell, how much water to fill the pot with, and how we had practiced and practiced until Bernie said he thought pretty well anybody could stand to drink it.

("It was good, too," said Lida from the darkness.)

I bolted straight upright and smiled my best cowboy Western movie smile at him.

"Okay, right, Daddy, Aunt Lida told me. You just sit down with the *News* and I'll get it made right away. And toast, she said," I added, and scrambled down from the bed.

He reached out and ruffled my hair. "That's my good boy. And cut me a piece of cheese while you're at it, and make the toast from a little bit of that bakery bread. And a roll, you should find a sweet roll in the bag on top the icebox."

All this I could do. I flew downstairs to the kitchen and opened the icebox door.

No eggs.

Who had forgotten to buy the eggs? I panicked for a second, but then I figured it would still be coffee without and maybe it wouldn't be noticed. I'd give my father a lot of Pet milk to put in it.

I got out all the stuff I needed, set the percolator on the stove right, lit the match with one hand, turned on the gas with the other, and stood back and threw the match under the pot like Lida had showed me so I wouldn't blow up myself or the kitchen, turned down the gas to where she said was the right sized flame, and then cut the bread and cheese, got out the sweet roll, and placed everything in what I hoped was a masculine yet pleasing arrangement on the good but not best china dish.

When the little glass dome on top of the coffee pot lid stopped bubbling, I turned off the stove, poured out a cup, slopping a little bit of it into the saucer, debated a moment to determine whether this increased or detracted from the overall bachelor effect, decided that it was good, chugged in the milk, and then called out to my father exactly as my mother would do tomorrow morning, "Daddy, it's ready, come eat!"

He trotted in from the living room, newspaper in hand, his natural good humor restored, and slid into his seat and tucked his napkin into his shirtfront. He sipped the coffee and I held my breath. His eyebrows went up and he beamed at me.

"This is a good cup of coffee!" he said. "But you know, I like a little bit of sugar. We got some?"

I had no idea but I was not about to say so.

"Sure thing, Daddy," I promised, then as he turned back to the paper I raced through to the front of the house and up the stairs to my parents' bedroom door.

"Mommy?" I whispered. There was silence, and I repeated her name.

"No," she said through the door, loud. "Get away from me."

"Mommy, it's me. I just need to know where the sugar is."

"What? Oh, Johnny. *Shoot*. Okay. Daggone it." Except she said all the worse words instead.

("She would have, too," said Aunt Lida and the girls giggled a little but John could see they were nearly asleep.)

I heard her roll over on the mattress, he continued, but nearly as if to himself, as if it were himself to whom he was telling the story and not two little girls.

"Okay, Johnny," she said, "it's in the sugar bowl, downstairs in the right cupboard."

I hesitated, then said, "What's the right?"

Her voice seemed to explode through the door.

"Oh, for pity's sake, it's on the *right*. My gracious, don't you know your right from your left? It's on the right, the *right*. Okay? The *right*. Now, go on and leave me the hell alone."

Her voice caught then, and I heard her say, lower, "Ah, Lord help me. Bastards."

And she didn't say, *My gracious*, but something a lot worse. I had never heard her swear before, not once in my life. She had never spoken to me in that tone of voice before, she sounded like somebody I had never met. The tears started to come, but then I thought, *I just made breakfast all by myself*, and so I wiped my hand quickly across my eyes. I still didn't know which one was my right, though, and so I stood there. But after a moment I heard her again, sobbing, softly but with sadness that—well, anyway, the sound of it stopped me as I lifted my fist to pound on the door again, to call out to my father that my mother was in trouble, to beg her to let me come in and help her feel good again, to remind her that she loved me best of everything.

"Ah, Johnny," Lida said from her room.

He paused. The girls were asleep and he said so.

"Tell me the rest, Johnny," Lida said. "Can you?"

"All right. Yes. But if I hear you snoring," he rallied, "I'm going to quit."

She chuckled at him. "Go on, you," and he told the rest.

Well, at that moment, it came to me that perhaps this was it, this is what I had yet to find out about the age of reason, that this must be what all Catholics wound up doing on Sundays, that they suffered as if someone had nailed them to something, for Miss Maurice probably the kneeler that hurt her legs so bad and made her rise up from the pew all stiff, and my mother apparently had been tied to the bedpost and couldn't get away. And in that realization, I knew that my grandmother and Miss Maurice had been right: the age of reason had arrived and it had gotten me. Still, I was only seven, not as grown-up as eight yet.

"What'd *I* do?" I muttered as I turned and ran back down the stairs, but not before hearing my mother cry out again, as if someone had swung a hammer down for the next blow.

I made it back to the kitchen in time for my father to ask, "So, where's the spoon?"

After he was done and I set the dishes in the sink for him, I went back upstairs, tiptoeing past their room and diving under the bed when I reached mine. I spent the rest of the morning there, reading the funny papers I had grabbed off the table, trying not to recall the sound of my mother weeping and calling me a bastard. Maybe I was a bastard. I realized I didn't know what a bastard was, though the way anybody said it, I knew it was bad, and I wondered if finding out you were also a bastard, or at least that you had bastard-like qualities, was also some accoutrement of the age of reason.

Then I heard the front door open to admit my grandmother, who had come over to make us lunch, as I had known but had forgotten she was going to do, and at once the earth turned back into the place I recognized and was at home in. And then I realized that this, too, the arrival of my grandmother on Sunday at noon, was something that had been happening for a long while, and I added this knowledge to the store I had accumulated so far that morning. When she came into my room and found me under the bed I pretended I had been playing submarines.

"Sure, sweetheart," she said, like what I had said was reasonable, you know, submarines.

She had had me baptized when I was four days old, also on a Sunday afternoon. Though I have no real memory of this, the day had been described to me in such detail so many times by so many ladies it felt to me by the time I was seven that I did remember everything about it. In attendance had been herself and Miss Maurice, who acted as my godmother, and about a half dozen other ladies among their friends, and I knew without being told that I was never to talk about that day at home. After I was taken care of at the church, we went back to my grandmother's house where they rounded up the rest of the ladies who came for the weekly poker game (they had no objections to playing cards, even on a Sunday—"It's after church," my grandmother explained when I was old enough, "and it's very restful") and knowing I would soon have my *bris*, everybody took a last admiring peek at my—well, never mind that part.

Anyway, Grandmother was bent over and peering under the bed, and she said to me, "You want to come with me after you get done eating, Johnny? Let's go see Miss Maurice a while and play some cards." I was more than ready to go. I scrambled out and changed out of my pajamas while she went downstairs to fix lunch, and then plugged my ears with my index fingers on the way past my mother's bedroom.

Everybody knows about Miss Maurice, especially that her parents had thought Maurice was a beautiful name for a girl. When her husband died she moved in with her best friend, Carmella, and they were both best friends with Grandmother.

Miss Maurice always let me help her cook whatever she had on the stove, and she always had something going. Every Saturday she just about cleaned out one of the little bakeries on Baltimore Street, and Sundays her coffee table seemed to sag a little bit under all the food and drink set out for the card players as if it were doing its own regular job.

The game started around noon and went well after eight o'clock at night, and the food on the table and the beer bottles never ran out no matter how long everybody stayed. Their house there on Lemmon was the most exotic place I, or anyone, I felt, could imagine. When I married my mother, I planned to take her to live at Miss Maurice's.

But on the streetcar over there, I was still worried.

"Grandma?" I said.

"Yes, Mr. Winston Churchill, what can I do for you?"

I stared out the window and didn't answer for a minute, and she waited. At last I said, "Grandma, I think I am in the age of reason."

She looked down at me. "How old are you again?"

"I turned seven on the 16th."

She squinted for a second in thought, and then said, "Oh, my goodness, that's right. That's right. We went and lit a candle for you at Fourteen's, didn't we, and then we got that submarine from Woolworth's, didn't we, and a bag of those red candy pennies, and then we had that party with the terrible-tasting cakes at your mother's house. I must have forgot to talk about it in all the hubbub. Well, my goodness, that's something."

She paused a second, but I didn't know what else to say, so I stayed quiet.

"So," she said after a moment, "was there something you wanted to know? Do you need to go to confession, or anything? I don't know how we'll do that, but I can ask Monsignor right away and I'm sure he can fix up something."

"Oh, no, ma'am, I don't need to, I don't think, not right away. It's just—Mama stays in bed on Sundays, Grandma, don't she? Or something like that?"

She looked down at me without much expression on her face but her old eyes turned a little pinker around the edges. And then she leaned over and gave me a hug with an extra squeeze, and kissed me on top of the head. I didn't mind. She wasn't the kind of person that a hug in public would bother you. Besides which, she understood everything. You never had to tell her something twice, you never had to fill in the things you'd left out by mistake or because they were too difficult to say out loud.

She said, "It's just one day, sugar. Don't worry about it." And with that, I was fine again.

On the rest of the ride we didn't say much. When we got to Miss Maurice's, there were about a dozen women there of several ages, most of them in their 60s like my grandmother and Miss Maurice. Several "Heyo, Maurices!" were exchanged because by that time, half the colored ladies and girls around the block had Maurice as their first name, middle name, or, in the case of my grandmother's numerous god-children, their confirmation name. They all beamed down on me, all except one white girl I'd never seen before, who was not much older than me, maybe eleven or twelve. The ladies stroked my curly black hair and talked about my Jewish future while I stuffed my face with crullers or onion rolls or whatever was sitting there.

"Miss Nancy, he going to be a high priest someday, he going to be a prophet to the nations," one of them would say, and the rest would all say "Amen!" loud, in a way I never heard that word said anywhere else in my life. And then the ladies would fetch me to get some more beers for them from the big wooden box filled with ice that stood in the kitchen next to Miss Maurice's old tin sink. My grandmother, who turned colored faster than she turned Jewish, started calling me "sweet britches" and told Miss Olene she didn't have all day to sit up there and wait on her.

"Deal them cards, Olene," she said across the table. "I got to get my money back from last week."

I shied away from the table as soon as I could, meaning to make myself scarce out in the kitchen so I could think some more, forgetting their orders of beer almost as soon as I left the room. But when I found an open bottle sitting on the kitchen table, about half-full, right away I thought that day would be a good one to try some.

I looked over my shoulder and then picked up the bottle in both hands and took a pull. The beer tasted odd, foamy and sharp, but good. I liked it. I took another drink and then set the bottle carefully back down on the rough wood table top.

"Oh, that's where you are," I heard a voice say, and I whipped around.

It was the white girl. I didn't answer.

"That's all right," she said as if I had, "I don't care if you have some. Take another drink if you want." She smiled at me, not friendly but not unfriendly, either. "Who are you?" she asked me.

Without taking my eyes off her I reached for the bottle, took another drink, set it back down on the table, and put my hands behind my back. "I'm John. I'm Miss Catherine's grandson. I know Miss Maurice," I said, trying to be helpful and comprehensive and knowing I had to belch. This I did.

She laughed at me. "I'm Carmen. I know Miss Maurice and I know Miss Carrie, Miss Maurice's girl. She's going to get married soon, Carrie."

"Are you colored?" I asked, and then immediately regretted it as she let out a whoop of laughter.

"Yes. Are you?" she said.

"No," I answered. "I'm Jewish."

"You're kidding," she said. "I hate Jews usually. You must be a good Jew."

"I'm a pretty good one," I said. "Why do you hate them?"

"Oh, I don't know. Everybody hates them, don't they?"

She sat for a minute, and I waited. And here is what's funny, Catherine met her when she was a kid, right after I came to Fourteen's, and Carmen said the exact same thing to her, and when we talked about it, we felt the same thing about her.

He took a breath and listened for Lida, who was silent.

I liked the way she looked, he went on. Her hair was short, and dark, and curled all over her head like mine, and her arms were like a small man's, and her eyebrows were the thinnest little things I ever saw. I remember she wore a lot of bright red hair bows, which in those days a girl that age would have worn pink or white.

"Can I have some more beer?" I asked her. "Do you like it?"

"I don't know. Don't everybody like it? I like whiskey better, but I don't guess they got any whiskey in the house." I believed her then. She looked around, as if she might find some sitting on a shelf there. "Besides, I can't drink any beer right now. I have a date later. With a man. Mr. Morris." She was quiet for a moment and I sat and digested all this. I wasn't sure whether to believe her or not. "Hey. You want to see something?"

"Sure," I said. I always wanted to see something.

"Okay, c'mere."

I walked around the table over to her side, and she unbuttoned the two top buttons of her blouse, and then opened it up and leaned over. "Look at that," she said.

Under her collar bone next to the strap of her undershirt there was a raised sort of mark, part of it red, part of it black, making the shape of a tiny lizard, with a long tail and four legs.

"What is it?" I asked her.

"It's the mark of the devil. The devil's in there," she said, and put her mouth into an O! and laughed.

"That was exactly the same thing she said to your mother, Marnie, when she met her," he said, as if the girls were still awake.

I stepped back, he went on, and said to her, "It is not. The devil does not live in that."

"Oh, yes he does," she said again, lowering her arms again and buttoning up. "It itches sometimes, but that's about it."

And I didn't know what to say to her after that, but she stood up then, ran her hand over my hair like one of the old ladies, and said in a calm, pretty voice, "Goodbye, little boy. Nice to meet you," and then walked out of the room like I had never been there and we had never said a word.

After another few minutes, Grandma came in with Miss Maurice. Still burping a little from the beer, I felt I better assume an expression of innocence, though I wasn't sure if I was doing it right.

"No," she was saying, "I got to take him back and make him supper. I got to pick up some things at the Jewish market to make dinner for him."

They stopped talking when they saw me, and Miss Maurice looked down. "Where's them beers, boy? Didn't you hear everybody tell you?"

She glanced over at the table and saw the open bottle. "You been drinking, boy?" she asked, her eyebrows almost on the ceiling. "Don't lie, now. Miss Catherine done told me, you reached the age of reason last week, which I know because I already went and lit the candle on it. So you know what." Meaning, *Lie now and it's straight to hell and I won't even see you in the funny papers.*

John stopped and listened to the girls breathing in their sleep. A thin strip of light, moonlight, maybe, shone across them. Lida had not interrupted in a while and didn't say anything now. Still, he wanted to tell the rest.

"Yes, ma'am, I had three sips," I admitted immediately, like it was confession, but *Telling the truth makes you suffer,* I thought. *I'll tell the truth.* Still, I was surprised it came out so quickly, without any of the shivering or terrible feeling to the stomach I always got when I admitted to wrong. And then I thought, *Ah, this is how you do when you are a grown boy in the age of reason.*

And I thought for sure one of them would pull me up by the elbow and swat my behind and give me a good talking to, but my grandmother didn't do anything, and Miss Maurice only said, "Oh! Well, that's all right, I guess, honey. That's not much, and you didn't lie on it. But don't you go having any more, you hear me, young man?"

"No, Miss Maurice, I won't," I said. Something was happening to me then, but neither of them seemed to notice. Didn't they see I was trying to tell the truth? Didn't they see that I needed to suffer?

"All right, then," Miss Maurice was saying. "Now, baby, you tell me what you want to be when you get grown."

"He wants to be a rabbi," my grandmother said immediately.

"No, I don't," I said right back. I looked them full in the face, those faces that were the same as they had been before. "I want to be a priest."

Sunday, Before Dawn. Wool gathering.

And in that moment, ending the story, John had had the kind of large thought that comes to one in an instant, known comprehensively and without words, about that change within him that he had thought of so many times since. He couldn't understand any of it, all of it more confusing than at that first meeting with Carmen and all her devil talk.

He had finished the story. He heard a noise on the landing, and looked over to find Lida watching him.

"You can stay up in the back room if you want," she had said, "Catherine's downstairs."

"No, thank you," he said. "It'll be an early morning anyway, and I need the walk."

"You know there are not two other children on the face of this earth who would have wanted to hear that damn story."

"I know. And they fell asleep."

She laughed softly. "Well, that's all right. I like hearing about Mom and your folks. Ah, I miss them."

"I do, too."

He had gotten up quietly and followed her downstairs to the front door. At the screen, he turned, and said, "I know I'm a coward. I don't need you to tell me."

She pulled her mouth at him. "You are no such thing. Don't stand there talking nonsense to me," exactly the way his grandmother would have. He smiled at her.

"Goodnight, John," she said, and leaned down and kissed him on the cheek.

On the walk back to the rectory in the absolute dark and quiet, he had thought some more on that afternoon at Miss Maurice's and what it might have meant to him.

I wish I hadn't had a pair of old ladies who were ready to sweet-talk me out of anything once it was too hard. He remembered when he had realized that he was not going to have to suffer, thinking, *What a gyp!*

He laughed at himself. When he entered the rectory he'd felt cold, cold as the beer bottles in the crate, cold the way some sunless days are cold, cold the way water coming out of a spigot in December is cold.

He found a stale piece of pie on the counter, ate it, and got ready for bed for a few hours of sleep. He thought of Camille, and pushed the thought away again. She had become a kind of talisman against Carmen's little girl, but in truth, thinking about Camille never worked very well or made much difference for very long.

We could do something had been the last words he heard before sleep found him.

Sunday Morning: Visions

He had slept, dressed, prayed the Rosary, and gone outside for his first smoke of the day. He'd passed some small talk with Jeb Heath out front before the first Mass. The routine was fixed, comfortable, assured. But at every single Mass of the day, when he had held up the chalice, he had seen the lizard on Carmen's neck, and heard her saying, "Here, let me show you something!"

After the last of the Masses, having turned down a half-dozen invitations to dinner, and as nearly every priest he had ever met said he also would be, nearly swooning on a stomach empty of all but altar wine and wafers, he sat down to an enormous luncheon produced by Mrs. Galchriest, the woman who made his dinners and his weekend meals.

"Here, let me show you something!" she said, all smiles, but it was only a snapshot of her latest grandchild or great-grandchild or someone that she wanted him to see. He wondered if he might need an exorcism. He wasn't the type who believed in them.

He'd remembered that to the announcement back in Miss Maurice's kitchen that he would be a priest, his grandmother had merely remarked, "That's not an oath." But Miss Maurice had said, "It sure sounded like one to me."

He had spent the rest of his childhood reading comic books and following his father around here and there, playing with the kids on his street, going to school, all the rest of it. Aunt Lida resumed her Sunday morning duties at the house, Uncle Bernie happily in tow, and in some way he had been allowed to forget again that his mother did not leave her room on Sundays. At thirteen, he celebrated his Bar Mitzvah, which everybody knew about, and was confirmed, which nobody but his parents and his grandmother and Miss Maurice and the priest did. By that point he figured he was related to half of Southwest Baltimore by confirmation. The war came, but he was not quite old enough to go, and nobody he was close to was young enough.

His grandmother had insisted on his attending St. Martin's High School. He had not planned on going to Catholic school at all, but he also hadn't particularly cared one way or the other. There had been some kind of quarrel about it behind closed doors, but in the end he had been allowed to go. At St. Martin's and at home, he had been sheltered from most of the worst news that had come out of the war. It had not really touched him. He had even almost gotten married to a girl who decided on someone else before they'd had a chance to get engaged. Of all people who should not have, he had had a normal life, at least on the surface of things.

He shook his head again as if to shake out every memory, every vision, if visions were what they were, to bring himself back to the day, the rectory, the dining room table. He had to get out of there.

"I'm going out," he called. The housekeeper didn't answered. Perhaps she had gone home.

"I'm going down the bar," he said. She didn't know he did any such thing. Still she did not answer. She must be gone.

"I need to think," he had said to no one in particular.

There was a tavern he went to, where, if anybody knew he was a priest they never said so, and he could drink beer and smoke through the afternoon, and he decided to get his things and go. In reflex he lit a cigarette as soon as he stepped out, and as suddenly as it always seemed to happen, no matter what, that night came back to him.

A dozen years ago. He is new ordained, a junior pastor.

It is twilight, it is early April. A cab pulls up, two people get out of it. He knows them both, has known one of them well since he was a boy. Paddy Dolan and Carmen.

Whatever it was they had come to since, wherever else they had ever gone, in his mind they arrive home every day at the same time, always in a taxi, always stopping in the middle of the block on Lombard Street just up from Union Square, and he is standing on a set of steps, smoking a cigarette, seeing them emerge from the taxi. He is shocked at them because Paddy Dolan's father has just died and he is making a fool of himself on the street with a woman who wears a birthmark in which she believes lives the devil.

It is twelve years ago. He throws his cigarette away. Carmen falls into him, he walks her home, the heads of the little girls hang out the window. Carmen and the girls invite him to go up, and the moment presents itself and pauses and lets itself pass without him.

The moment when he could have gone up those stairs, to who-knew-what.

The two faces in an upper window, little girls, ghostly as he had thought then, the night a dozen years ago when their mother had staggered with him all the way down a city block, grabbing at him and pushing herself against him, he trying to imagine that to anyone who might be watching, all it was, was young Father Martin was helping that drunk Carmen home and either they thought nothing worse or they thought, *Well, you know what that means*. And he somehow had not known she had children. He had never seen her children even sitting outside on their steps.

He shivered and threw his cigarette into the street. He looked down Fulton Avenue and remained standing on the step, shoulders hunched, teeth chattering a little. The street was flat and level, the darkness gathering. You couldn't look very far down. Not like Lombard Street where you could look to the end of time.

He was ashamed of it, he had remained ashamed, and he determined again now, as he did nearly every night at twilight, looking and watching and smoking until the dark had its way with the street, that not a scrap of St. Martin's parish would be unknown to him, down to the storefront church goers who lived in the alleys. *Even they,* he thought, *the least among you,* and swelled with what he didn't was the worst pride he could fall prey to, didn't recognize as the very thing that nearly always kept him from seeing what was right in front of his face.

It was cold. He would do better tomorrow. He stepped down to go up the block for that beer before dinner, realized he was still in his slippers, and went back inside to change his shoes.

As he walked past the church steps, he thought of old St. Martin, who was, he had read years ago and again many times since, "a man who could not be described, who neither feared to die nor refused to live."

God, it's raw out, he thought.

He feared death less now than he used to, but he feared it, the same way he feared the refusal to live that had taken hold of him a dozen years ago and would not now let him go. All he had wanted was to do the business of a parish priest, and for that business to be singular, and meaningful, and then, after the night when neither of those were any longer going to be, all he had wanted was simply to stop remembering.

He had suffered enough, he thought, but there was nothing to be done.

St. Martin's was a good place, his congregation beginning to overflow, beginning to be a parish that needed a younger man to handle.

He felt hope and immediately he felt the flimsy candle flame, the burning-out lit cigarette tip that his hope was. And, by the by, he would have said to anyone at all, he was not singular, he could already name a dozen other priests who had reached the other end of their lives refusing to live and fearing to die, and so he would be one of them. And, so what? There was, he thought, no way to arm yourself against it, not in the end. What made him so special that he could get around it?

Hey, you want to come up? she had said.

That moment upon which he had elaborated so many different endings over nearly every evening for a dozen years remained static. Lucille, of the light, had not said another thing, nor had she gone back inside the window, but sighed a little as if she knew he was going to refuse, but that she had to ask him anyway and that when he said no, as she knew he was going to, she had to keep looking down and after at him, not waiting for him to change his mind and return, but as a sentry would.

He had felt her watching him walk up the side of the park, and well after she could have seen him any more at all.

And he could not even now pretend to himself that he had ever planned to go back, that something had gotten in his way but that he had meant to help those girls, find out about them, do something. And now it was now, and he stood in another rectory doorway evening after every evening, smoking cigarette after cigarette, still trying to make something noble of that.

Then he thought of the girl he had been going to marry, but who had chosen the other boy. He could not remember her very well, and then there had been Camille, whom he put out of mind as soon as thought formed her name. He thought of Carmen, how he had first met her when he was a little boy. He shivered.

He was cold. It was time to get that beer and then go down to Catherine's for supper.

Sunday Afternoon: Storytelling

John was set up at the bar, a beer and an ashtray in front of him. The bartender was a very young fellow, John didn't know his family, he didn't think.

He felt like telling a story. Funeral stories were always good, he thought. He thought of his grandmother, his grandmother. The news of her death had come while he was working for a couple of months in the South Seas as a part of his diaconate. He was young, twenty-two or three. He had thought he would go to be a missionary but wasn't yet sure and they had needed someone quickly in the Philippines, and as often happened, it seemed, at one moment he was deep inside one world, and the next had been transported to another.

He had been rubbing his calves with some ointment against the unbearable itching of the carpet of mosquito bites that covered the backs of both when one of the Brothers had come to the door with the telegram. A day later he was driving out, and five days after he boarded an airplane from Manila. He'd spent one night in San Francisco, and the next three at the seminary on Roland Avenue. On the Saturday morning, he was walking down Fulton Avenue where he had not been for easily two years. He wore the simple black suit of the deacon, with the small crucifix pin on the lapel and the white collar, but no cassock out there on the street. His mother and father, who lived on the east side, were not expecting him right away and he'd wanted to come first to her neighborhood, his grandmother's neighborhood. He had asked permission to drive right down and spend the night at St. Martin's rectory, and that had been given.

She was dead and that was all that he could take in. She had been alone in the house for some reason, Lida and the infant Catherine away to who knew where, his mother's, maybe. Miss Maurice had stopped by but decided not to stay for dinner. And his grandmother had blown out the gas on the range but forgotten to turn the handle, it must have been, and she had fallen unconscious over her dinner, and died. The back door had been closed and the windows shut, and the swinging door between the kitchen and the dining room would have been enough to hold the gas in and let it build up. It was also why, when Lida let herself in later that night, the place hadn't been blown to Kingdom Come. She'd smelled the gas right away and gone next door with the baby to get help.

So he had come home for her funeral, which would be held early Saturday afternoon. They had held off with it until he could get home. It would be a closed casket.

He hadn't been able to sleep well, had wakened a little after four, and finally had risen, shaved himself and dressed, stood in the front parlor and said his morning office in the dark. He wasn't hungry and didn't eat. He'd heard the pastor rousing at five-thirty and went outside to smoke, and then walked down Fulton Avenue in the cool of the morning. The shade on this side of the street was cold, but the sun on the opposite side promised a warm day. He noted the marble steps of the row houses here, the neatness of them, how clean the streets were. Milk bottles were lined up on top steps, a few trucks and carts ambled by, a streetcar hissed its way past him.

He didn't know where he wanted to go. He hadn't been to the house yet, somehow he didn't want to go there. He reached Lombard and noted the mix of well-kept and deteriorating house fronts, went another half block, turned down Lemmon. It was too early to knock on Miss Maurice's door to pay his respects to her and Miss Carrie. He didn't know how much company they had or how late they had been up. He would go by later that afternoon.

He had kept walking until he reached Calhoun, turned north and went up to Hollins. These streets were more obviously less well-kept, looked a bit less prosperous, less clean. He checked his watch, saw it was after 6:30. He saw the Schlitz sign lit up in the window of Mike's Tavern, pushed the door and went in.

That barman, Eddie, a square fellow with thinning hair in his late 30s, had looked up, smiled, walked out from behind the bar and up to John, held out his hand. "It's good to see you, Father," he said.

"Good to see you. Not Father quite yet, though," he had smiled.

"Oh, yeah? I didn't know. What, do you still have to take a test or something?"

"Something like that." They paused. John had felt a bit uncomfortable suddenly, and looked down to the floor.

"My respects about your grandmother," Eddie said. "She was a fine lady."

John looked up at him again, grateful. "Thank you, thank you very much. We all loved her."

"Sure. And it was a good way to go. She went in peace, thank God."

"Yes, it was a good way."

"You doing the funeral?"

"No, but I'll be there. I'll serve."

"Oh! Sure. That will be nice. I'll be there; we're closing for it."

"Thank you," John said again. He felt old.

"What can I get you?"

"Oh! Well, a beer, I guess. If it's not too early for one."

"Sure. Why don't you come sit down here at the end where nobody will bother you, collect your thoughts and everything. I could get you some eggs and bacon if you want."

He said that he did and asked if there were coffee. He got up on the stool, didn't particularly look around. The bar was as familiar to him as his mother's house. He only wondered that Old Levy hadn't taken his place on his stool yet, but as he'd had the thought, the elderly man had come in, paused in silhouette at the door, seemed to recognize John, nodded as if this were satisfactory, and had taken his place squarely in the middle of the barstools. He paused only to say, "My sympathies," and turned away.

Old Levy, John thought, pulling himself back into the present. Old Levy must be dead twelve times over by now. Nobody knew where he had gone, because nobody had ever known anything else about him than that he spent his working days, as he called them, sitting on a bar stool and calling whoever tended bar, "Eddie," though the original Eddie had long been retired and Levy had been perfectly aware of that fact.

And the original Eddie was long gone, and the bar, and his grandmother. John was still cold but beginning to warm up sitting on his stool. He nodded his head for a second beer. He felt for another cigarette and lit it. There was a little too much to think about, Union Square, Catherine's house that had been the home of Aunt Lida and Uncle Bernie, the home of his grandmother and grandfather before that, where his memories outstripped Catherine's by more than a decade, where first his grandfather and then his uncle had been laid out, and Miss Maurice had wept over both of them and had held his grandmother in her bony arms. He had made sure that Catherine, and Marnie in her turn, had known who they had been.

Sunday Afternoon. Story-telling

Oh, Miss Maurice, John thought and took a sip of his beer. On the wall in front of him were the autographed photographs of baseball players and lounge singers and local politicians hanging in small frames, and there was one of the renowned boxer Red Fitz in his silks. He looked over to the boy wiping glasses near the tap pulls.

"I met him once," John said, nodding over to the photo of Fitz.

"Oh, yeah?" the boy, said, interested, and leaned both arms straight out on his side of the bar, smiling and ready to listen.

John looked at him, and then said, "Yeah." He looked away, and the boy sighed and went back to his glass-wiping.

John had met the Fitz the day of his grandmother's funeral, as a matter of fact. After breakfasting, he hadn't been quite sure what he would do or what he wanted to do. He had boxed some in high school and still used boxing from time to time. After walking around the neighborhood and stopping into Fourteen's to say a decade of the Rosary, he had decided to go over to the Boxing Club and work off a little steam before getting ready for the funeral. Everyone had seemed to know who we was, nobody appeared surprised to see him, nobody said anything to him apart from a murmured "Sympathies" or a quiet, "Dear lady." He had felt at home.

He recognized O'Dougal at once, a coach who had taken him up for a while in high school, when his father had unusually persisted in allowing him to fight over the protests of his mother.

"But if he loses a tooth! If they beat his face up! He has a lovely face!" his mother had expostulated, but his father had been firm. Since John's confirmation his father had taken him much more seriously as a person and had paid close attention to all of his masculine enterprises.

"This is a man," he would say. "This man has had a bar mitzvah and a confirmation. You think the Lord isn't paying attention to this man?" His mother would smile tremulously and his father would kiss her on the cheek and pat her shoulder, and she would frown and look proud and say nothing more.

The tenderness of his parents and their psychological acuity was something a lot of people would give a lot for and he had not taken it for granted. On the day he entered the boxing club after this exchange he felt nervous and yet protected on all sides. He would later recognize this as innocence, innocence lost at the threshold of adulthood and the rest of life spent working to regain.

The bar-boy set something down with a clatter and brought John out of his reverie. He took a sip of beer and thought, *Well, yes. That is where I am now. Still.*

On the day of his grandmother's funeral, he remembered how he had felt that protection still, still benefitted from its innocence. He had breathed in the scent of the boxing club, changed into a pair of shorts and an undershirt, put on a pair of gloves, and went up to the desk for a time slot. There was half an hour before he was set to go. He saw a slightly younger man whose name he knew, Paddy Dolan, come in after him. He nodded to him, but John had graduated ahead of him and hadn't come much in his way. Dolan nodded back to him in a friendly way, not at all arrogant, he thought, not like what you often heard about the boy.

John went down the still-familiar narrow hallway, dark and smelling of cigars and who knew what else, to the door he pushed open into the enormous meeting room that had been made over as a kind of gymnasium, with one large boxing ring in the center, and three smaller rings positioned variously around it. These were full, but the eyes of all who were not practicing were on the center ring, where a tall white man with still-red hair was boxing with a slightly shorter Negro man of similar build and similar age. They were boxing hard, but, John could tell, not in a way that meant it was a match where there had to be a winner.

A whistle blew after a few minutes, and the men stopped and went to their corners and had their gloves and helmets taken off them. They shook hands over the ropes as they exited the ring, and after they climbed down the white man stayed and began talking to Mr. O'Dougal, and the black man nodded and left.

After a small while, O'Dougal saw John watching them and beckoned him to come over.

"Red, I don't know if you know this young fellow, Father John Martin. He's going to practice today. Father John, this is Red Fitzhugh."

John couldn't believe he had not recognized him. He shook his hand, mumbled *How do you do*, and forever after was thankful that he did not make the mistake of trying to say something else except the usual, "Not quite Father yet, sir."

Red smiled at him. "Ah, I see. So, you're here to practice, are you? I hope you're not setting him up with Dolan, Bill."

"Oh, for Christ's sake, no. Dolan would have him for tea. He's not up to his weight, for one thing. No, I thought I'd put Dolan with Smithie again. Work the bugs out of him." And then as an afterthought, he had said, "John here is home to bury his grandmother, rest her dear soul."

And Fitz had murmured and looked grave.

"I'd like to practice with Dolan once," John found himself saying aloud. "That'd be all right, I think."

The two men forbore to laugh at him, but Red said, "No, Father, I think I know what you're feeling, but that wouldn't do. It wouldn't do at all." He was kind but insistent. "With every respect, I would just say, remember that you don't never fight a man, in the ring or out of it, that you're not up to the weight of."

John found himself getting angry, but said merely, "Even just to work yourself out?"

"Well, I don't know. Maybe then. I would still say be careful, though, and still, Dolan is too far off."

He considered the point for a moment more, and then said, "Did you see that boy I was in the ring with now? All I do with him is practice. We never fight. He's shorter than I am, for one thing, and I'm just that much heavier. Not a lot, but enough. The thing is, though, we understand each other. We know what the other one is looking for, what he needs. That's why he's good for me. But I'd never get into the ring with him any other way. You see, it's just not a good fight then. Don't ever get into a fight in the ring if it's not going to be a good fight. You understand what I'm saying to you?"

"Yes, sir, of course I do. But, still, then, why not practice with Dolan, though?"

Again, neither of them seemed to want to say anything, and when the Fitz finally answered, John knew that he was dead serious.

"Because he doesn't practice. He only fights. And he's a damned devil when he does. So, whoever he's with has to be a devil right back."

"Oh."

That was all that John had been able to think of to say, and he wondered, did that make him a coward? He had felt the anger continuing to pool within him, so much that the feeling was completely foreign to him. He found himself thinking that somebody should teach this Dolan shit a lesson if that were the case. Someone should teach him a lesson. Somebody should take him down a notch. Someone needed to stand up to the devil, he thought.

And, thinking this, John realized that whoever it might be, it would not be him. He hoped this was not what these two men were also thinking about him, though, and he looked away from them as if he were interested in something else.

"Come on, Father, I'm going to put you in with Bobby, here," O'Dougal was saying.

John forbore to correct him again, saw that Red Fitz had moved away, and found himself in front of a skinny man with iron arms and a soft bit of pot belly on him. As he stooped under the ropes, he saw Dolan come in and go right up to Red, speaking gravely to him, Fitz turning Dolan's hands over and examining them with a professional eye, O'Dougal now next to them at Fitz's elbow, speaking quietly as a kind of shadow. Dolan did not look like a shit or act like someone who had the devil in him.

Twenty minutes later John was winded and despising the sight of freckles on the human face. He was hot, sweating hard, and not feeling he had acquitted himself well, realizing that three years in seminary had made him soft. It was thinking about Dolan the whole time that had taken it out of him, though, he knew this, and he thought that where always before in the ring he had felt free, dispassionate in a way, this time he had been trying way too hard with the skinny kid, proving something that didn't exist to prove while in the back of his mind wondering if Dolan were watching them. He was angry with himself, felt younger than he was, felt stupid and clumsy and leaden.

He heard a whistle and one of the other coaches motioned them down off the ring. When their gloves had been taken off, they shook hands and the man ambled off without giving him a second glance.

Paddy Dolan walked by then and gave John a nod and friendly smile, and headed toward the ring he had vacated. He watched him get helmeted and laced up, and saw his opponent, an older and ugly-looking fellow whose rearranged face spoke to many years in the ring. John went over to O'Dougal.

"Would it be all right if I watched for a while?" he said.

"Sure, Father, sure. You can stay as long as you want."

John found a folding chair along the wall, pulled it up but not too close, and watched the fight begin.

The other man held back, feinting away from Dolan, not precisely as if he feared him but as though he might be trying to forestall the inevitable for a little. But Dolan went in blazing, every bit of him as if he were afire or electrified, arms up, head down but eyes forward, and then John understood: Paddy Dolan looked as if this were the thing he had been invented to do. John did not think he had ever seen a boxer who looked so completely at one with the action he was performing, even Red Fitz did not look like that. He tried to think of what it was, and then it came to him, something Father Cannello had said in a lecture once about the difference between an artist and a professional. He had said, a rare man could be both, but you had to work to be at least one or the other, and you had to discover which it was going to be pretty early on. To John, the Fitz looked like both, he had that gift, but there was no doubt about Dolan: he was an artist and an artist alone. There was not a moment of time for him in the ring in which anything else was happening. He was the ring, he was the fight, and, clearly, John saw, the fight was not just dead serious to him, it was death itself. Not life-and-death, not even life or death, but death. He had death on him, he was death's delivery man. He was not, like John, the man who held onto the delivery address.

When they finished Dolan's partner had taken a bad beating, bleeding from his nose and many fresh bruises already starting to come up, sitting on the corner stool to catch his breath. An attendant poured water onto him and rubbed him down and someone in white was checking his limbs and torso and teeth. Paddy came out of the ring with his chest heaving, but didn't look as if he had done much more than run around the room a couple of times.

John found himself transfixed by the sight of him, as if Paddy Dolan were not a three-dimensional person there in the room but more that he was a projected image on a screen, or a view on a slide under a microscope. He might even be a saint—no that was stretching it, that was fanciful. He must have been staring hard, for as he walked in his direction, Paddy stopped and stared back at him, but strangely, nearly equally transfixed it seemed, but so far from displeased as to appear delighted. In another moment his face was suffused with joy.

"Niamh?" Paddy had said to John, as if he were saying a word that expressed disbelief, and wonder, and even salvation.

John had been sitting in a patch of light that hit the top of his head, and as he stood it was difficult to see beyond it. When he could see him clearly again, Paddy seemed to have caught his mistake.

"I'm sorry, sir. I mistook you for a friend of mine. Beg your pardon," he said, and smiled, and looked a bit bereft, and then laughed. "Silly, isn't it, what you think sometimes?"

"Sure," John said. "But I hope it was all right. I was just watching your match."

"Oh, sure, you can watch any time, you're very welcome." Paddy looked back over to the ring where the other man was slowly pulling himself together, and grinned, and looked down at the chair where John had been sitting. "But I've not seen you here before, I don't think?"

"No. I'm visiting. I used to come by when I was younger, high school. I went to St. Martin's, and Mr. O'Dougal let me come by today. But I don't come regular. I mean, I don't box regular, I don't live near here anymore." John had not known why he needed to explain himself.

But Paddy had seemed to understand him.

"Ah. Well. It's how I started, from St. Martin's, of course. Well, if you come by again, say you know me, and they'll treat you right."

"Oh, thanks. Thanks. Everyone has been very kind. I met Red Fitz today." Again he felt himself blushing as if Paddy were senior to him and somehow he needed to please him.

"Yeah," Paddy had said, and something on his face changed. "That's a lad, now. Yeah, that is. Hell of a lad. Well, take care of yourself, boy. And, you won't mind me saying this, but maybe boxing's not for you, I mean in the long run if you see what I mean. It's a great exercise, of course, and I can see you're just here exercising, but as to boxing regular, if you see what I mean—maybe not."

And John had thanked him again as if he had been the boy, and he had waited a modest amount of time before following him into the changing room. And he remembered his grandmother, and wondered what she would have thought, and left to get ready for her funeral.

And there in the church, hearing all the words and seeing all the faces of those who had loved her, and his reunion with his father and mother and all the relatives including the schoolgirl Catherine, somehow all of this affected him and was married to what he had seen and felt about Paddy Dolan, and it instilled in him a happiness and a fervor he had not so far felt in all his training for the ordination ahead. "First fervor," they called it in the seminary, and he was glad to be visited by it and overjoyed to know that it was real.

And still attended by this fervor which showed not one sign of abating, he had returned to the missions for a few more months, come back to Baltimore, and completed his remaining two years of preparation for ordination. His parents had not precisely washed his hands of him when he had entered the seminary, but as he had worried they would, they had never been able to understand it, and had never reconciled themselves to an old age without grandchildren. But they had also not seen him ordained. Not too long after his grandmother died, his mother had not woken up one morning and his father had followed her in grief within the six-month. They had not known him as a priest, and in some way he was grateful for that.

By February of 1952, he was assistant pastor of Fourteen Holy Martyrs Church. He had sailed through the artistry of his first Lent as a priest. He loved the parish and the people loved him. He was ardent for their happiness and their well-being, and also not incidentally their salvation.

And then had come the Psalm Sunday evening when Paddy Dolan had called him "Father" and rushed past him, and he had steered Carmen home, and in his complacence had betrayed her daughter nearly without a second thought.

John now thought about all this for the hundredth or thousandth time, walking or standing or sleeping or sitting at a bar. He said none of it to this unknown bar-boy. What of it could he say aloud? It was not a story for children. He wanted to get up but instead asked for another glass of beer and lit another cigarette. The bar-boy served him with a smile that had become comprehensive in its indifference.

But John still felt that it had been given to him to watch something privileged that afternoon at the club, before his grandmother's funeral, something that he'd learned from, something that had made the pair of them, him and Paddy, equals in a completely unanticipated way. He had stepped out to it, searched for where it might be showing itself to him, planned for its fulfillment, and had begun to weave dreams and visions around it.

And, again, like a horse you don't particularly like the look of on a merry-go-round, he did not much care to revisit the memory of himself two years after first speaking to Paddy, himself freshly ordained and assigned to Fourteen's, standing on the steps of the church and smoking, thinking of not much except that one thing: there he was a priest, and there he was becoming a priest who was also going to be an artist.

And that evening, Paddy and Carmen had spilled themselves out of that taxi.

Sunday, Later Afternoon: Visions

Certainly over the years he had reflected that Paddy Dolan had satisfied his brief and never very strong desire for retribution in finding that Paddy had turned himself into a catastrophe, a useless man with, as little Marnie always put it, a foul hand. John had only thought of Paddy in the interim between his grandmother's death and his return to this place as an idea, an icon, a banner of what he wanted to achieve. He had taken on the idea of the priest as artist like a sacramental, an aid to faith and hope and charity, and he believed in it. In every other respect, however, he had not even followed the news of Paddy's rising celebrity in the neighborhood, had not thought of him particularly as a person except that he came to Mass on Sundays and the stations on Fridays and was probably engaged with some of the girls his age in a way he probably shouldn't be, and that was all.

So that when he heard on that first Palm Sunday morning he had celebrated as a priest that Paddy had broken his hand and that he was not going to fight Red Fitz after all, the news had not taken away from the elation that had carried him out of the church. He had felt only pity and the certain distaste you feel when something unpleasant happens to someone to whom you are not particularly close.

Yes, God, what a shame it was, John had thought as he stood on the steps of Fourteen's that evening, smoking and again considering from a most superior distance all the ways a person could go wrong. It was a damn shame, the more so because everyone nearly literally worshipped Paddy and had fervently anticipated his victory and were crushed to seem him destroyed. Nobody had wanted that for him, and nobody had understood what it had been about, at least as far as John could tell, so that even the pleasure of gossip and rehashing the whole thing was nothing anybody could indulge in for very long. Worse still, and he was ashamed to realize he had not thought about it all day, Paddy's father had died that early morning on Friday. John had wondered if it had been from shame. He hoped not, that would have been terrible.

And continuing to consider the whole mess in that detached way, John hadn't thought he'd ever encountered anyone so comprehensively taken down by sheer appetite, sheer inclination, sheer inability to park his feelings to the side until he had gotten what he wanted. Not fate, not accident, as John saw it, but that he had chosen it. As he had heard it told that morning, Paddy had simply gone and ruined his hand beating up a kid the very night before he was supposed to fight, a fight that regardless of the outcome would have set him up for the rest of his life. And for some reason, who knew what it had been, he could not wait, and had ruined himself.

How do you choose to break yourself like that? John had thought, and tutted a little.

And when Paddy and Carmen had driven up in the taxi and spilled themselves out into the street, Paddy with his ruined hand still wound up in a rag, as he had hustled past, John's first thought had been, *Your father's not even in the ground.*

But then he thought, *He's thrown it away,* and then, *No, I've not found it yet.*

And in that moment the entire world seemed to move away from him, its center and its edges. And in the next moment, Carmen had fallen into him and had dragged him down to her front door, and the voice had sounded above his head.

Is he coming up with you?

We could do something.

We could do something, Lucille had called down to him.

He had thought he would be all right, and he had gone on, although—and this was not by will or decision—no further thoughts of artistry beckoned to him or lifted him up. He realized that there had been before, himself, John, moving forward into the great composition of his life, and there had been him walking away from Lucille's face looking down from the third-story window, and there had been the rest of everything after those two things.

In the years that had passed, sometimes he would see Carmen, a little grittier and grimier and older than the time before. From time to time he saw her daughters and the little son who had come along walking up and down the streets, seemingly doing the shopping for the household, fighting and hitting each other and sometimes just standing there. After a couple of years it was only Lucille and not her sister dragging the boy along such that John had had the sense she was raising him. And after a while he never saw Carmen anymore, and when Miss Maurice passed away at last, she had not been at the funeral.

But Lucille had been there, standing in the back.

She would have to have been what, sixteen? Seventeen? She was thin, and her skin was brown and her eyes small, and even from where he stood he could count the bones in her hands and nearly the bones on the back of her neck, the way her head was bowed, as if she believed she did not deserve to hold it up, or perhaps even did not know how. And throughout the funeral at St. Peter Claver, surrounded by godsisters and godbrothers named or unnamed Maurice, as John assisted at the Mass he almost felt he could see Lucille mouth the words, *Hey, you want to come up*?

And the next day he had not been able to get out of bed.

Sunday Evening, Walking. Visions.

He stirred on the bar stool. He deliberated whether to have another beer, decided against it. He nodded to the boy, put out his cigarette, stood, put his money on the bar, and went out.

He headed north again. He needed a few extra blocks. *I better walk off these beers before I get to Catherine's*. He lit another cigarette, squinted over the smoke into the deep grey air.

And then, in the next instant he was back there, on that mattress, unable to move his legs.

He laughed, and snapped his mouth shut, and tried to think. Maybe he was a little drunk.

The strangest thing about it had been that he was not surprised. *Oh*, he had thought, *This is what she meant*, meaning, of course, his mother.

He had prayed, unable to leave the bed, unable even to sit upright, for hours. Everyone else in the rectory must have presumed him to be out. He prayed the rosary five times in a row. He prayed silently, he read his office, he said the Mass out loud and responded to himself as the altar boy would have done. Finally, the housekeeper had opened the door to make his bed and clean his room, and clutched her chest when she found him lying there. When he tried to explain, she appeared to understand him, kindly, but without saying much.

The pastor had finally come up to his room, and he had been able to speak to him but when asked couldn't he come downstairs for dinner, he could not answer and still could not move. The housekeeper, again, seemingly without any judgement about the matter, brought him a plate of dinner, and afterward a pot and a jug and made sure he had a glass of water at night, and emptied his ashtrays a couple of times during the day, and remembered to bring replenishments of cigarettes along with his meals.

But he could not get up out of the bed.

At last someone from the Chancery had come and spoken to him for a while. John had babbled about "visions" and "daydreams" and "Mr. Winston Churchill" and "voices." He didn't know if he was making any sense at all, but the other priest stepped out and came back with a glass of whiskey and they had talked some more and John had been able to pull himself together a little more rationally. Then he was so tired, and closed his eyes, and after a pause the priest said they had had some luck with this kind of thing down in D.C., and he'd recommend that John maybe could go down there and talk to someone. John had merely been surprised that there were enough priests not getting out of bed that somebody had seen enough of them to have had some luck with them.

And they had lifted him into the car that took him down to the seminary residence and out of it into a wheel chair, and left him to rest, and prayed with him, and wheeled him into the gallery that was connected to the dormitory where he could hear Mass being said in the chapel below, and something about all of this at the very least had allowed him to sit in a chair, and then stand, and then get about on his own in the wheelchair on his own after the first few days.

He had been grateful. He worried that so young as he was they would recommend he leave altogether. Still speaking and acting as if what was happening to John was well within the normal reaction, they had explained that they wanted to send him to a kind of doctor, not a psychoanalyst, he didn't precisely know what she was. Not a medical doctor, he didn't believe, but she might have been. He had not recognized her name, but knew that she herself was a nun, a nun who for all the various reasons that they came to see her treated nuns and priests and helped them through the difficulties they presented, that were, as his seemed to be, beyond the reach of common spiritual remedy.

On the morning that he was able to walk on his own using a cane, had had been accompanied by another priest to the place where this treatment was to take place, the other priest leading him in by the elbow as he assisted himself with the cane. An impossibly officious middle-aged priest had greeted them in the outer office, a Fr. Seddon. He barely looked up, but said, "Please be seated and wait your turn." In a few minutes, a buzzer sounded, and he stood and said, "Follow me, please."

John thanked the other priest and said goodbye, and then followed Fr. Seddon as quickly as he was able through a door, and from there down a longish corridor, and then turned before another very handsome door with a sign that said, "Welcome." Fr. Seddon pushed through it, and when John finally caught up to him, waved him down into another chair in yet another anteroom. He knocked briskly on what John hoped was the last door, and was called to open it by the person inside.

"Your visitor, Sister, Fr. Martin," he announced, and then, "Please enter," to John.

Her name was Sister St. Camillus, but he learned that she always called herself Camille, that it had been her own grandmother's name, and he thought that nice. She was young, he thought, for the job she did, but then discovered she was near to his own age, perhaps thirty or a little more. She was not very pretty but attractive enough, obviously intelligent and perceptive, and something else John could not name, a strange kind of combination of opposites. She seemed warm and impersonal, kind and distant, eager and—not diffident or shy, but whatever you would call those qualities in someone who appeared to be without a stake in the world outside her own sphere. Later he would say to himself that she was completely free of ego, but that was not accurate, either.

They shook hands, and she thanked Fr. Seddon, who ushered himself out, "If there were not anything else." John noted that her eyes were not precisely bloodshot, but tired, and there were grooves starting on both sides of her mouth, but she was smiling and he saw that she found Fr. Seddon amusing, and he laughed a little in return. Her smile, her entire face was pleasant and calm, he thought. In fact, everything about her demeanor suggested calmness and self-possession. Nothing, in fact, indicated anxiety or worry except that certain fragility about the eyes, which, of everything about her, he would remember afterward most clearly. She invited him to sit.

"Please call me John," he said.

She thanked him and sat again, clasping her hands in front of her on the desk blotter, and, he saw, appraising him. He was not embarrassed or confused, but discomposed somehow just the same. This passed very quickly, however, and all at once he felt as if they had been stopped in mid-conversation some day before, had met again, and were comfortably waiting to pick up the threads of what they had been discussing. He watched her and waited much as he would have done had she come to see him as a parishioner or a teacher at the school.

She had pressed her lips together and then breathed in rather heavily. She seemed to making a decision of some kind and it seemed not to come easily.

"I imagine you know better than I why you've been asked to see me," she said at last. "If you don't mind, though, it might be best to begin by your telling me about that, and we can go on from there if that's comfortable for you."

He smiled at her then. "Comfortable. What a nice word."

And then he didn't speak. They sat looking at each other for a couple of minutes.

She waited as if she were accustomed to waiting, looking every now and then at the small clock that faced her on the desk, that ticked the minutes faithfully back to them. There was a kind of a pottery vase next to the clock that held a lovely sprig of willow that he finally reached over and touched, and then pulled his hand back.

"I'm so sorry," he said. "I don't know why I did that, I didn't mean to touch your things."

"Not at all," she said and did not smile, for which he was grateful.

He got up from the chair using his cane, passed his free hand over his face, and looked down at her, showing had he known it the first trace of disease but also resolution.

"I don't know what the matter is with me," he said. "I'm not insane."

She said, "You don't appear to be."

He sat down again with some difficulty and leaned forward.

"But I feel I might be," he said. "Not because of the daydreams — I don't know how to explain except that they are too clear. They should not be this clear. You know, I never forget who I am, or where, or anything of the kind, though, it's just — they are beginning to feel more real than I do."

She nodded. "I see. That's good to know."

"Is it? It doesn't seem as if it would be," he said, but nodded back. "I don't know. That's been since I was a kid, I think. My family is sort of larger-than-life, if you know what I mean. I mean, they are wonderful, and I love them. It's not that. It's just that everything has to mean so damn much every single moment. And it doesn't. It doesn't to me, anyway, not anymore. Not for a while.

"And it's since then, what has happened since I was a kid. At first it seemed so clear to me, that God was speaking to me, but I couldn't make it out, you see, what it meant, do you see what I mean?"

He didn't look up but kept talking, more quickly and less lucidly but still he felt as if the words had been rehearsed or were false in some other way, not because he had invented them but more that he just needed to say something.

"I don't drink often, not every day. Well, not every day. I'm not lonely. My prayer was full for a long time, but you know, it doesn't stay that way. I have a sound relationship with my confessor, I mean, for the most part I do. He's the pastor, he's the first one I spoke with the day I couldn't get out of bed.

"But I hadn't told anyone that I had started having these visions—or day-dreams, or whatever you want to call them. My grandmother would have called them day-dreams." He laughed shortly. "Miss Maurice said I did more wool-gathering than anybody she ever met, which I thought was a strange thing to say."

He paused and then took up the thread again, his thoughts going faster than he could say them, one thing not much connected to the other.

"Oh, and I should tell you, since the first one followed a period of prayer, I assumed it was the normal kind of intrusion that can happen, I'm sure you're familiar with what I mean, I mean, you know what that means, right?"

She nodded. He nodded back.

"Perfectly normal, perfectly understandable," he said.

He stopped again then, shrugged, and leaned back and closed his eyes. He could feel her waiting, he didn't know if she watched him or not, and barely cared. He began to speak again without opening his eyes.

"So, just once each time, every day that I could not move myself in that bed, I had the same vision, the next day, and the day after that. I felt myself before each one, and after, though I was shaken, I didn't have any unusual emotional reaction and I did not feel I'd had a break with reality." He paused again and opened his eyes.

"I had had this vision almost every day for twelve years. I could always put it aside, I never had any difficulty such as this. Never. I barely even thought about it except when I could not stop myself from thinking about it."

"I see," she said again. "In that case, what did you think had happened?"

"I began to believe, and my confessor thought it might be true also, that I was having an ecstatic vision."

"I see."

He was ashamed. "I'm sorry, I know you know all this."

"Yes. I read the dossier. It might be helpful for you to know that I don't particularly believe in such visions—if they do exist, I feel they are very rare. And I know you know as well as I do that if this were the only worry, you would not be sitting here speaking to me." She paused for a moment, and looked out the window, then back at him. "You'd be in Rome or somewhere."

They both laughed.

"And in any event," she said, "that's not quite what I meant. I was wondering what had happened that seemed to add the physical deficiency."

But John had not been able to answer her.

She waited for a moment, and then said, "I can see it's costing you something to talk about this, and I understand, but it would be helpful for me to know why that's so."

He thought she was trying to keep her face neutral. He sighed, blew out his cheeks, raised his eyebrows, and finally barked a laugh of self-disgust.

He said, "All right, but you'll think I'm crazy. So what it is, is, well, it's that I have come to believe that someone is going to die, and that I may be asked to die in his place."

He did not look up at her. What he had said was most certainly not what he had intended to tell her.

"So," he said, again blowing out his cheeks, "neurotic? Attention seeker? Hysterical?" He barked another laugh and looked away.

"Well, I think they reserve 'hysterical' for women."

He looked back to her, and she winked at him, and he laughed. He felt good all at once then, good and sane.

But he felt also a line of perspiration on his forehead below the hairline, felt his ears red and his face slightly flushed, and then was embarrassed again. He clasped his hands together over his knees so tightly the joints of his fingers felt swollen.

"Well, all right," she said in a matter-of-fact claustral tone that said *That is enough of that for now.* "Nothing I see here indicates that you are enjoying any of this, so that's a good start, if you are interested to know. If you wouldn't mind, though, before you leave at this point I would like to hear about your family, if you would? They sound very interesting."

He said, "Sure. But, I'm sorry, you know all about me, and I don't know anything about you."

She smiled again. "No, that's right, you don't. Sadly, that's the way it is." She appeared to be amused but he was not offended. "You're shall we say a little too much in the business of listening to others, and that's not exactly what you're here for, and it's not at all what I am here for."

He raised his eyebrows and nodded. "Oh. Yes. I see. I hadn't thought of it like that, actually. I see what you mean. Okay."

And after a very short moment, he began to speak. He told her about his mother, although not that she could not get out of bed on Sundays, and about his father, and Aunt Lida and Uncle Bernie and being two things at once, and the war, and the people they had lost, and being nearly engaged and the girl marrying someone else, and the seminary, and the Philippines, and his grandmother and Miss Maurice, and there he stopped.

"I guess that's all," he said.

"It's quite a lot," she said. "Thank you. Your family sound wonderful." She smiled, and then drew her brows together. "I can tell you that you have some of what I am seeing a lot right now, and it might be driving your conviction a little that you have to fulfill some degree of substitutionary atonement."

"Really?"

"Yes. I'm seeing it in chaplains, and in teachers who have lost former students. I have to admit that you're the first person who to my certain knowledge has Jewish relatives, or was raised Jewish, but I'm sure they are out there in numbers."

"I see." And he did see. "So, you think that's it?"

"Well, possibly. Such a feeling can often produce an acute reaction such as yours. We should meet a few more times. Nobody is expecting you back for a while, so shall we try to give it a month? I'd like to see you again this week, and then a couple of times after that. Would that be all right?"

"Yes, sure, absolutely." He was stunned by the feeling of relief. *So, what, it was the war? This was all because of the war?* He said only, "Yes, all right, then what should I do?"

"Let me look in my book," she said, and they fixed on a few more appointments. She rose, and leaned over the desk to shake his hand. "I'll see you next time, then."

"Thank you, Sister. Do I—?" He turned toward the door behind them.

"Oh, no, sorry," she said, and grasping the edge of the desk with one hand, seemed to step down. "It's out this way."

He then saw that one of her legs was a good bit shorter than the other and when she moved away from the desk that she walked by making nearly a full circle of movement as her step switched between the long and the short leg, which he later learned rested on a small block of wood when she sat at her desk. She kept talking as they walked, as he thought to keep one or the other of them from embarrassment. He was mortified to feel revulsion, but also that she had betrayed him somehow, that she was going to turn out to be a person who kept things from him, and this made him as angry as he had been at the boxing club when Red had told him not to try to fight Paddy Dolan.

She was saying, "I think after next time, I'll know better—." She had been looking down at the steps and holding on to the railing, but there in mid-sentence smiled up at him.

Whatever it was that she saw on his face, she barely paused in her thought, "—then what might be the best route to go," but the warmth and friendliness left her face in that instant. She turned and resumed her slow way to the bottom.

He pushed past her to open the door, slightly pushing her aside. Her eyebrows raised and her head tilted back a little. He didn't move, his hand on the door, and he thought he could see an equal degree of anger in her as he felt within himself.

"Was there anything else, Father?" she said, smiling but as a doctor or nurse would smile at the end of an examination.

He was ashamed.

"I beg your pardon, Sister. No one told me. I hope your leg doesn't pain you too much."

Her brows slung together, but she smiled again, the same clinical smile. "No, Father, not at all. I'm quite used to it. You must forgive me for forgetting that not everyone else is."

She held out her hand again. "Thank you for coming, Father. Until next time, then."

He smiled, thanked her, and said goodbye.

"Jesus," he said as the door closed behind him. He looked over the lawn and saw the priest who had brought him standing next to the car, smoking, and slowly walked over to him, and he was astonished at how good it felt to move.

And the next time he saw Camille, he told her of his studies, his travels, his encounter with Red Fitz and Paddy Dolan at the boxing club, of his solitary Sunday afternoons drinking beer and smoking cigarettes at the tavern that was not in his neighborhood. He told her what it was like to be the godbrother of dozens of Negro persons in Baltimore, what it felt like to be the pastor of one of his godbrothers whose job it was to sweep the steps of his church. He told her of the impossibility of taking Saturday confessions seriously, and the necessity of doing so. By the third week, there was no longer any talk of visions or day-dreams. Their conversation, he believed, had become necessary to them both. They discussed the Council proceedings, he told her about some priest or other who had come back from Rome still flabbergasted at what he'd experienced there, she speculated on the future of enclosure and the role of active nuns. *There you are,* he found himself thinking again and again, *Where have you been*?

"And *that's* why there are no women priests!" he laughed one afternoon, finishing up a joke he'd been told by another Vatican expatriate. She laughed, throwing her head back. Making her laugh out loud had also become necessary to him, as he believed telling him her stories had become to her. She told him about her art training, about the work she did at the seminary, and about the sisters in her community who could be such a trial to her.

"Sis-tuuuur, would you please lead prayer tonight and pray in a *very* special way for a *very* special intention?" she imitated in a half-whisper. "Sr. Camille is a *very* gifted healer," she lisped, and they laughed.

"Oh, yes," he said. "I've met that one. She must have been in seminary with some of our men."

He winked at her and she smiled, and they sat that way for another moment, and then they were no longer laughing nor smiling, as he felt, but Sr. Camille looked down at the notebook that was in front of her, the shadow of a pleasant smile still on her face.

John felt then the taste of his fiancée's mouth. He had enjoyed but not hungered for her the few times she had let him kiss her, and immediately imagined the taste and the feeling of Sister Camille's thin, humorous lips, how different they must feel, how hungry he was to taste them.

And then he thought in that instantaneous fashion that had become second nature to him when sitting with her, that in the few weeks since they'd first seen each other he recognized in her a thing he had never had, that he should have had, ought to have had. He ought to have recognized part of what had fallen away from himself ten years before, standing on a sidewalk below the face of an impossibly wounded little girl, down the street from an impossibly old and insulated church, was this—he didn't have the word for it, this vitality that he had been suffused with one moment and had been taken from him the next.

Is he coming up?

We could do something.

And then he looked at Camille as if at a stranger. He wanted nothing from her after all, he thought, and, God, he was angry again. He didn't know why he was angry, no, furious, he would not be able to contain it for much longer, and, transported to that place and again flung back, he knew he had to leave at once.

He looked at her, and believed he saw in her face the same, a woman transported, and again returned. He felt he had gone from being "John," a man who loved persons, to, for the first time, a nameless and nearly faceless entity who wanted to have this taste from this set of lips, and all that he had felt for her to this moment, affection, intimacy, trust, as quickly as they had been given to him at first seemed to have altered instantly into hunger, and that perhaps for the first time in his life he was aware that a woman carried the answer to such hunger in her body, in her mouth.

He had not felt this for Carmen, in that stairwell.

And then all sensation was gone, again all at once, even the rage leaving him and making room for the emptiness that had brought him there and that had taken possession of his body's ability to move when the last of those old ladies who had brought him into the age of reason had gone.

And in the next instant, he knew for certain that this exchange, this nearly bodily transportation of ecstatic feeling to senseless, lifeless desertion would continue through the rest of the course of his life, that it would not cease, that any feeling or desire or loss would present itself and then snatch itself away, over and over, regardless of where, or what, or with whom he was. And everything afterward in those moments seeming to have been either strange, distant, slightly far off, or too close, too necessary, too much.

And he realized he pitied himself, that was all. He felt pathetic.

"I'm sorry," he said. "I was getting a little bit off-track."

"No, that's quite all right," she said in the same implacable, slightly warm voice she had always used and he ought to have known he had always heard come from her and nothing more. "I understand. Sometimes it's good to let your hair down. Although in my case you'd never know." She smiled again.

He didn't return the smile, he could not look at her, and then again felt in some primitive way betrayed by her, that she ought to have told him somehow that this was who she was, as she ought to have told him about her leg. He could not tell if she understood him at all.

He stood up, and she rose but did not step away from the desk.

She said, "John, you know, I've had the feeling that there is something you did not tell me at our first visit. Would that be right? I'm sorry, but is there something?"

And he was enraged again. How quickly he could feel it with her from moment to moment. He didn't want to answer her. He thought it would be somehow unwise to try to explain.

"Of course, I told you," he said. "I told you everything you wanted to know."

"But—I'm sorry, I truly don't wish to pry. Still—was there something else? I mean, perhaps something more you wanted to tell me?"

And as he had foreseen, he was then transported by her kindness, eager again, stepping forward, his hand out to touch her arm, ready to embrace her, looking full into her face and eyes.

And, as he had predicted, he stopped and was emptied and she was snatched away from him again. He dropped his arm to his side.

"John," she said. "I'm sorry, but no. That's not going to help either of us."

No, she didn't understand. He smiled crookedly and said, "How do you know?" And then said, inventing the embarrassment he thought he ought to feel, "No. I know. I'm so sorry. I didn't mean to—"

"It's quite all right. Please don't worry about it. It a kind of thing that can happen sometimes."

She said this but it seemed meaningless to him. *She doesn't know what she's talking about*, though he certainly had been aware of the dozens of women who had felt something for him over the years, that he had been able to disregard or push aside. It didn't matter.

"I'll come back next week, at the same time, if I may," he said at last, as if it were their first meeting.

"Surely," she replied, and smiled. "You know your way out by now."

He turned and left.

The week following had moments of light and he wondered at last if these might be part of some other thing expelling itself from him, or whether it was simply more temptation to believe in what would not last, what was not true, or stable, after all. He had no sense one way or the other and he could not stop thinking about Camille. And when he returned, she spoke to him not as they had before, but crisply and at length, clearly in summation, saying she felt their sessions had been helpful, that she was glad he had come and that they had been able to talk things through, but that she did not believe his concerns were on-going, that he had been overcome and overwhelmed by them for a while, and that from what she had seen he was now recovered and that there was no cause for concern. He assumed that she was as embarrassed as he.

But she said only, "I am going to recommend that you return to active ministry. Do you want to go back where you were, or would you rather be somewhere else?"

"Camille," he said.

She looked at him. "You know, I think better Sr. Camille, don't you?"

"Oh, yes, sure. It doesn't matter. Fine." He stopped.

She waited, and then asked, "What is it, Father John?" and he could hear something of warmth in her voice, but as with his grandmother and Miss Maurice, rather than being comforted, he felt cheated.

"Please! Don't."

"I'm sorry, I don't know what not to do. I don't know what it is that I am doing to upset you."

"Don't you? I think you do."

"No, truly. What you imagine is not what is happening. I promise you."

He looked at her then, and into her eyes, and what he saw there was indeed no reflection of what he expected to see, not the face of a lover or of a woman who held a beautiful secret. He slumped in the chair.

"I'm sorry."

"There is truly, truly no need, John. I promise you."

"I don't know," he said.

"You don't know what? What is it?"

"How do you know?" he answered. "How do you ever know what is happening? What is truly happening?"

"I see," she said. "Can you say a little more?"

For God's sake, she said it for everything, why did she have to say that for everything?

"You see. You *see*. Can I say a little *more*? *Why*? You don't see anything! What else is there to say? I told you, *I don't know*."

And immediately he thought of his mother and how she would say somebody had been spitting bullets, and he smiled. He turned away from Camille, but she said, "What's so funny, then?"

And he looked at her, and he was just himself, and she was just herself. Again.

"I really don't know," he said. "I'm very sorry. I don't know what got into me."

"No, no, that's all right. Please don't worry."

"Thank you," he said, and looked down at his hands. If this were the last time they would speak, he could go and live with what he lived with unanswered, or he could try one more time. The thought of either was unbearable, but then he heard his mother's voice, on the other side of her Sunday bedroom door. And he thought, well, he could suffer a little while still.

He leaned forward to touch the willow in the vase again, and sat back, and looked at her.

"You were right," he said, "there is one more thing to tell you, and I need you to listen to me. You were right, I didn't say it all before. Can you listen to it now?"

"I shall do my best, John. I mean it, I'll do my best."

"All right. But you have to listen," he said as if he were binding her with a penance.

And he told her about Carmen in Miss Maurice's kitchen, and laughed a little at himself when she laughed, and then about entering the seminary and that it likely had killed both his parents, but that first his grandmother had died and he had found Paddy in the ring and had decided to be an artist, and being ordained, and celebrating his first Paschal Week Mass and how happy he had been and yet how alone he had felt.

"It is very difficult," she said. "You loved them very much."

The comfort in her voice only made him feel cheated again, just as cheated as when his grandmother and Miss Maurice had not let him suffer for stealing the beer, but this time he was able to laugh at himself about it. He waited for the feeling to change, but it seemed to wish to rest with him.

"You don't know," he said merely. "They were magnificent. My mother and father were magnificent. You would have loved them."

"It sounds as if anybody would. I'm sure I would have."

He didn't know if he could go on, but when she said again, "And what is it, John?" he knew that he could.

"I have to tell you the last thing," he said.

"Sure. Please tell me."

"There was a girl."

"A relationship? You mean with the girl who married the other boy?"

"No, no, not that kind of thing." He swallowed and clenched his hands. "She was Carmen's daughter, she was a little girl."

And then he felt her stiffen across the desk, and when he looked at her saw that her face had become closed and terrible, and the thing within it indispensable to him was not only gone but as if it had never been.

"What is it?" he said. "Why do you look that way?"

She pressed her lips and folded her hands, but did not speak. She looked at him as if she did not know him and he felt cold and the room begin to shift a little, the sensation he hated more than nearly anything. He had to get rid of the sensation, the idea that she did not know him, and spoke her name.

"Camille, what is it?"

She said, but as if the words were dragged from her, "Father John, I have to ask you this. I'm very sorry. I have an obligation to ask you."

"What do you mean?"

She made an almost spitting sound, and looked to the window, and then said very quickly, "Did you do something? I am sorry, I mean did you do something of a sexual nature."

"What?" he said, and then, "No, I didn't have a relationship with Carmen, I mean, yes, I kissed her when she jumped me in the vestibule, but that wasn't it."

"I see. Then what was it?" Her voice was still cold and he did not know if he could push past it.

"I'm trying to tell you," he said. "It was the little girl."

And he told her about looking up, and seeing Lucille, and what she said to him, and about not going in to check, and that he had heard those phrases over and over again ever since, and on nearly the first day of his life as a parish priest, his life had seemed to have been ended by them.

"I haven't been having any visions," he said. "I don't even know what to call them. Intrusions. Thoughts I can't get rid of. Anywhere, any time. I go to sleep with them, I wake up with them, I hear them at the altar and at the bar and when I am hearing confessions. But I wasn't exactly lying to you, either, because they were happening almost always when I was praying or at the end of prayer. And I know I have been trying to day-dream myself out of hearing those words for eight years, because day-dreaming is what I know how to do, it's what have always done, and the day-dreams are, they really are different—I can command them, I can keep track of them.

"And then, I don't know, I came out of the confessional one afternoon or something, thinking how dead my advice and my absolution seemed to be, and then Miss Maurice passed and I served at her funeral, and then the next morning I could not get out of bed. And so now I'm here. I'm sorry, I didn't mean to distress you. I don't know how I could have."

She looked at him until he had to look away, and at last said. "Wait for a moment, Father." She stood and sat down again, picked up her pen, seeming to see something within its glazed surface.

"This is—" she began at last. "I see. You are going to have to forgive me. I am hearing things in this office that you might not be surprised by, but that I hope would horrify you."

He did not reply but what she saw in his face seemed to satisfy her, and she said, "Good. It is still difficult for me to understand that they do not horrify everyone, but seemingly they don't. I am deeply sorry that I suspected anything like them in connection with you."

She leaned her arms over to him across the desk, not to touch him but he thought to reassure him and to obtain his forgiveness. He only wanted to embrace her, and he was silent. She moved back and continued.

"John, I am listening to what you are saying to me. I can see how terrible it was to walk away from that girl. I can see how guilty you have felt about it afterward.

"But, forgive me, because this will sound glib—but—I never know how to say this. We are taught, not only we religious, that our duty is to save the world. Yet we cannot save the world. We can't even save the part of it that is right in front of us, and you of anyone have had to find this out in a very difficult way.

"And I don't want to hurt you, but I agree with how you feel. You did betray that girl—out of tiredness or diffidence or even cowardice, whatever it was. That's not for me to say, and it's probably not important to anyone except yourself. But, this is the important thing that I want you to believe—I don't believe you could have saved that girl.

"Having said that much, this I will tell you—if you come upon the chance to make up for that night, you should take it. My guess is that it will cost you something terrible. But take it."

And she paused, and then said, "I believe there would be real artistry to that."

He thought he would remember the look of compassion with which she said these things for the rest of his life, and he waited for the back-and-forth, the filling-and-emptying, but it did not come. This was the release he had not known to expect. He sat back softly in the chair, happy as he didn't think he would ever be again. His mind felt cleared of everything but himself, John, returned to life. There was nothing he could or wanted to say now.

"Thank you, Sister," he said to her. "I'll try."

And then they smiled at each other as ever they had before.

"How's that for substitutionary atonement, then?" she said.

He laughed. "Well, like they say, I guess I go out where I came in."

"I guess you do."

It was interesting that he knew the hunger he felt for her would remain with him, that there was nothing to do about it or with it, but also that it was not likely to hurt him in the way he had feared it would. It would not empty him out, rather it would help to keep him full, and in that, he was as satisfied as he needed to be. He was cured, he knew it. He was cured.

They ended the time with a few commonplaces about how difficult the world had become. He did say he would like to return to St. Martin's and she said that was what she would recommend.

"I don't suppose I'll see you again," he said.

"No. After treatment, we don't see each other again."

He stood up. "I love you, you know."

She did blush then, but faced him. "Yes, I know. But it will be all right."

"Well. Thank you for everything."

"Thank you for letting me help you. I know you'll be fine, John."

She held out her hand, and he took it.

"Goodbye."

And he had come home, and been a priest, and watched his little cousin come into the age of reason herself, and confessed her and given her communion from his own hand. Carmen and her family drifted away from his notice after all. He had never discovered, but equally had never sought, a moment in which he could have redeemed himself to Lucille, and after some time passed he forgot about it, and became if not himself, John, a satisfactory version of himself, Father John Martin, a man who was not completely afraid to live and not completely prepared to die.

And this Sunday night in Easter Season he arrived at Catherine's for dinner and stayed to play Monopoly just as he had the night before, and little Alice was there for supper, and she was going to spend the night again. She pulled out her medal from under her top shirt button and showed it to him, proud, but he also thought as if she was making sure she had the right to be there, if her medal made it so.

He wanted to find, or know, a similar gesture that he could call his own.

At bed time, he asked if they would like a story, and Marnie said, yes, there was a picture book he could read to them if he wanted, and could he sit with them again until they fell asleep?

Of course he could do both those things.

They lay together on the fold-out couch that was big enough to hold them side-by-side. He read and finished the book and closed it, and saw their eyes closed but that they were not asleep. Marnie was holding Alice again under her shoulder, and Alice appeared so small and thin he worried that she might not live through the night, a foolish thought, but he stooped over them, and pulled the blanket up and tucked it in tight around them.

"Goodnight, Father John," Marnie said.

"Goodnight, Marnie," he said. "Goodnight, Alice," he added, but she said nothing. Marnie was patting her shoulder with a skeletal hand and her medal was floating out behind her throat and caught up in her hair.

And then he heard her say, *I didn't want to,* low but not in a whisper, *I didn't want to.* She said it in the voice of approaching sleep, to be tucked away and not remembered in the morning.

Marnie continued patting her the way a mother does, an unconscious solace John knew he had never intentionally extended to another person in his life, and he immediately thought if only he could find Camille he would touch her that way. He wanted to find Lucille and tell her that it was all right, to not worry, that he loved her. He wanted to tell Paddy Dolan that he understood. He wanted to tell his grandmother and Miss Maurice that he had loved being their little boy and that they had cheated him of nothing. He could do none of those things.

He thought this was how he would always see them, Marnie and Alice, together and for each other.

He thought, *Someone needs to do something. Why doesn't someone do something?* And immediately he heard the voice floating down from an upstairs window.

"We could do something."

And then he heard and saw Camille as a vision, as it seemed, within him, sensing where she was, feeling what she was doing. He wanted more than anything to talk to her. It might be too late, but maybe it wasn't.

The girls now were breathing lightly in sleep, and he took a step back from them.

They're all right, he thought. *They'll dream now.*

And he turned from them, and walked through the empty living room, and let himself out the door.

Acknowledgements

This book is a work of fiction. Any resemblance to actual persons or events is entirely coincidental.

Many thanks to director Kevin Atticks and the editorial team at Apprentice House Press, for believing in these books and for their professionalism, patience, and kindness.

A portion of Part III appeared in an earlier form as, "The Skin of an Onion," published by New Libri Press as a Coffee Break Shorts e-book. My thanks to the editors of New Libri for taking the piece.

I am sincerely grateful to Kristina Marie Darling for her expertise and hard work and support. My thanks and obligation to Charise Alexander Adams for her editorial contribution to the book, and to Michael Anatole for his perceptive and helpful comments.

My thanks again to colleagues at the University of Nebraska-Lincoln, Pacific Lutheran University, and Creighton University, especially Jonis Agee and Mary Helen Stefaniak, for their generous comments on early sections of the novel. To Jim Madison, a continuing debt of gratitude.

To my husband Mark and my daughter Clare, all my love forever. Thank you for your endless patience and encouraging words.

This book was written for Nicky, Archy, and Cece, wherever they may be.

Acknowledgments

About the Author

Poet, novelist, and nonfiction writer Adrian Gibbons Koesters spent much of her childhood in and around the Union Square neighborhood of southwest Baltimore. She holds an MFA in poetry from the Rainier Writing Workshop at Pacific Lutheran University, and a Ph.D. in fiction and poetry from the University of Nebraska-Lincoln, where she has taught creative writing. She lives in Omaha, Nebraska.

Apprentice House is the country's only campus-based, student-staffed book publishing company. Directed by professors and industry professionals, it is a nonprofit activity of the Communication Department at Loyola University Maryland.

Using state-of-the-art technology and an experiential learning model of education, Apprentice House publishes books in untraditional ways. This dual responsibility as publishers and educators creates an unprecedented collaborative environment among faculty and students, while teaching tomorrow's editors, designers, and marketers.

Outside of class, progress on book projects is carried forth by the AH Book Publishing Club, a co-curricular campus organization supported by Loyola University Maryland's Office of Student Activities.

Eclectic and provocative, Apprentice House titles intend to entertain as well as spark dialogue on a variety of topics. Financial contributions to sustain the press's work are welcomed. Contributions are tax deductible to the fullest extent allowed by the IRS.

To learn more about Apprentice House books or to obtain submission guidelines, please visit www.apprenticehouse.com.

Apprentice House
Communication Department
Loyola University Maryland
4501 N. Charles Street
Baltimore, MD 21210
Ph: 410-617-5265 • Fax: 410-617-2198
info@apprenticehouse.com • www.apprenticehouse.com

CPSIA information can be obtained
at www.ICGtesting.com
Printed in the USA
BVHW042259210420
578043BV00009B/369